THE MINDBENDING MINECRAFT
GRAPHIC NOVEL ADVENTURE!

GOING VIRAL

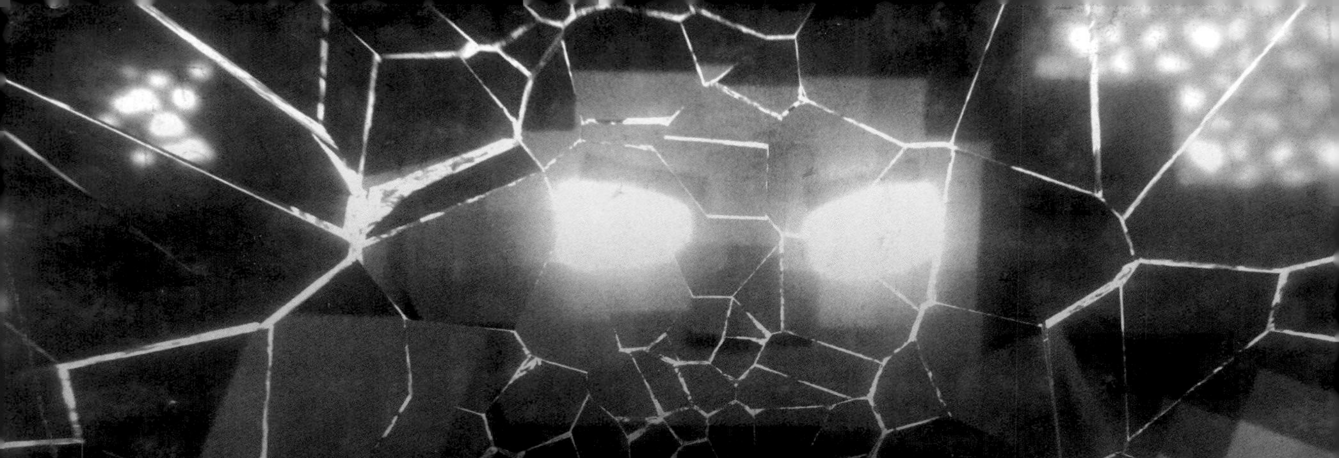

THIS IS A CARLTON BOOK

Published in 2019 by Carlton Books Limited
20 Mortimer Street, London W1T 3JW

A catalogue record for this book is available from the British Library.

ISBN 978 1 78312 495 4
Printed in China

10 9 8 7 6 5 4 3 2 1

Creator: David Zoellner
Script: Eddie Robson
Special Consultant: Beau Chance
Design: Darren Jordan/Rockjaw Creative
Design Manager: Matt Drew
Editorial Manager: Joff Brown
Production: Nicola Davey

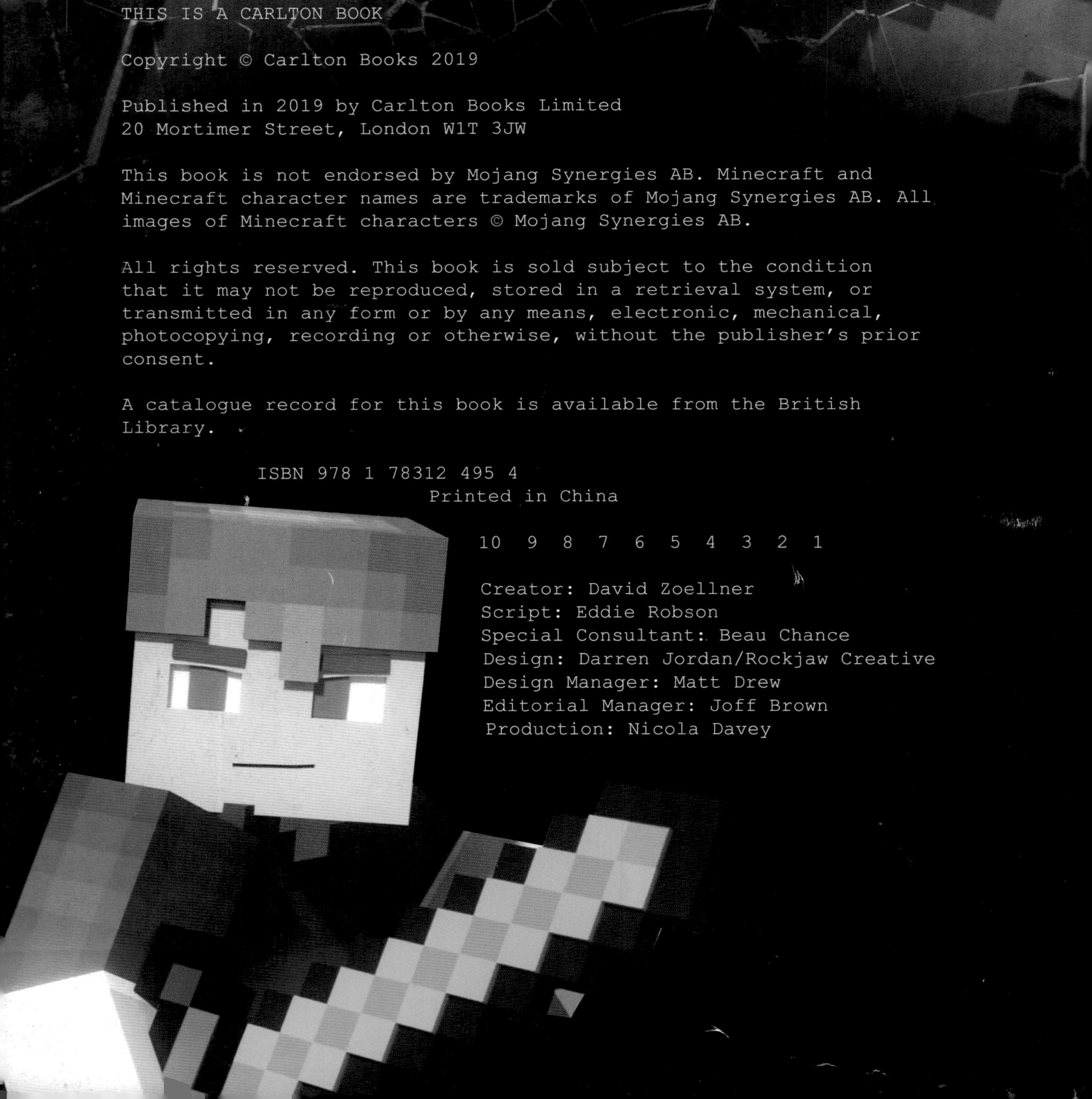

INDEPENDENT AND UNOFFICIAL

THE MINDBENDING MINECRAFT GRAPHIC NOVEL ADVENTURE!

GOING VIRAL

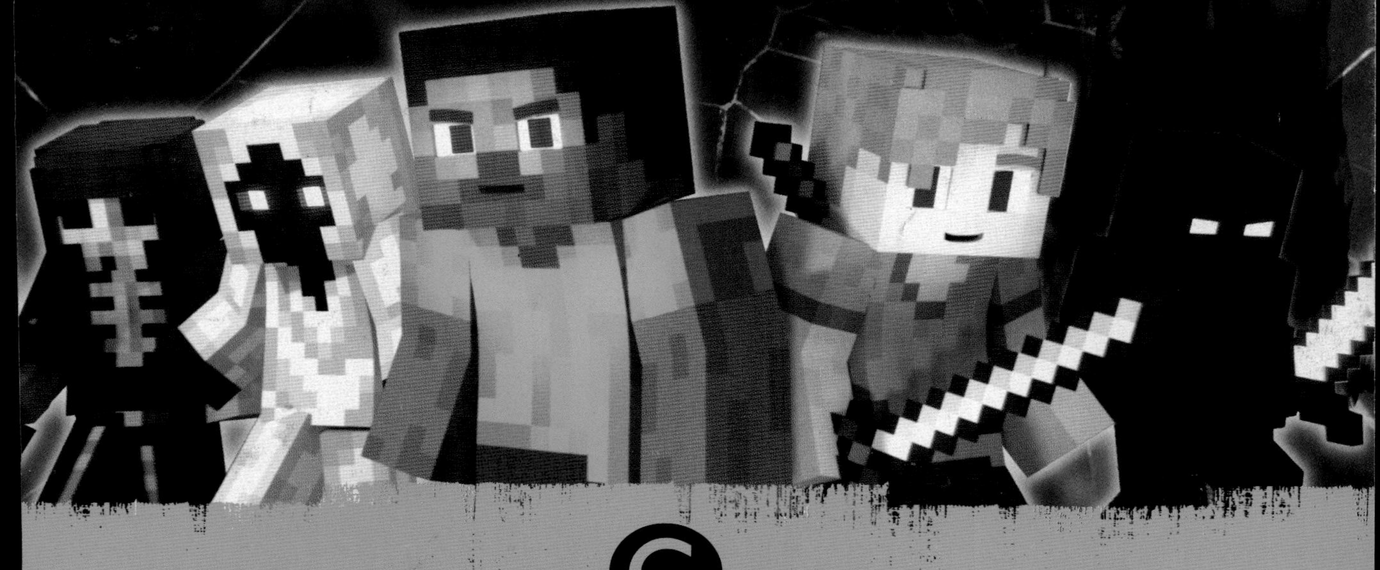

CARLTON BOOKS

ABOUT THE CREATOR

DAVID ZOELLNER, BETTER KNOWN AS ARBITER 617, IS THE DRIVING FORCE BEHIND BLACK PLASMA STUDIOS, THE BLOCKBUSTER INTERNET ANIMATION POWERHOUSE WHICH HAS CREATED VIDEOS WITH OVER 32 MILLION VIEWS. HE LIVES IN THE USA.

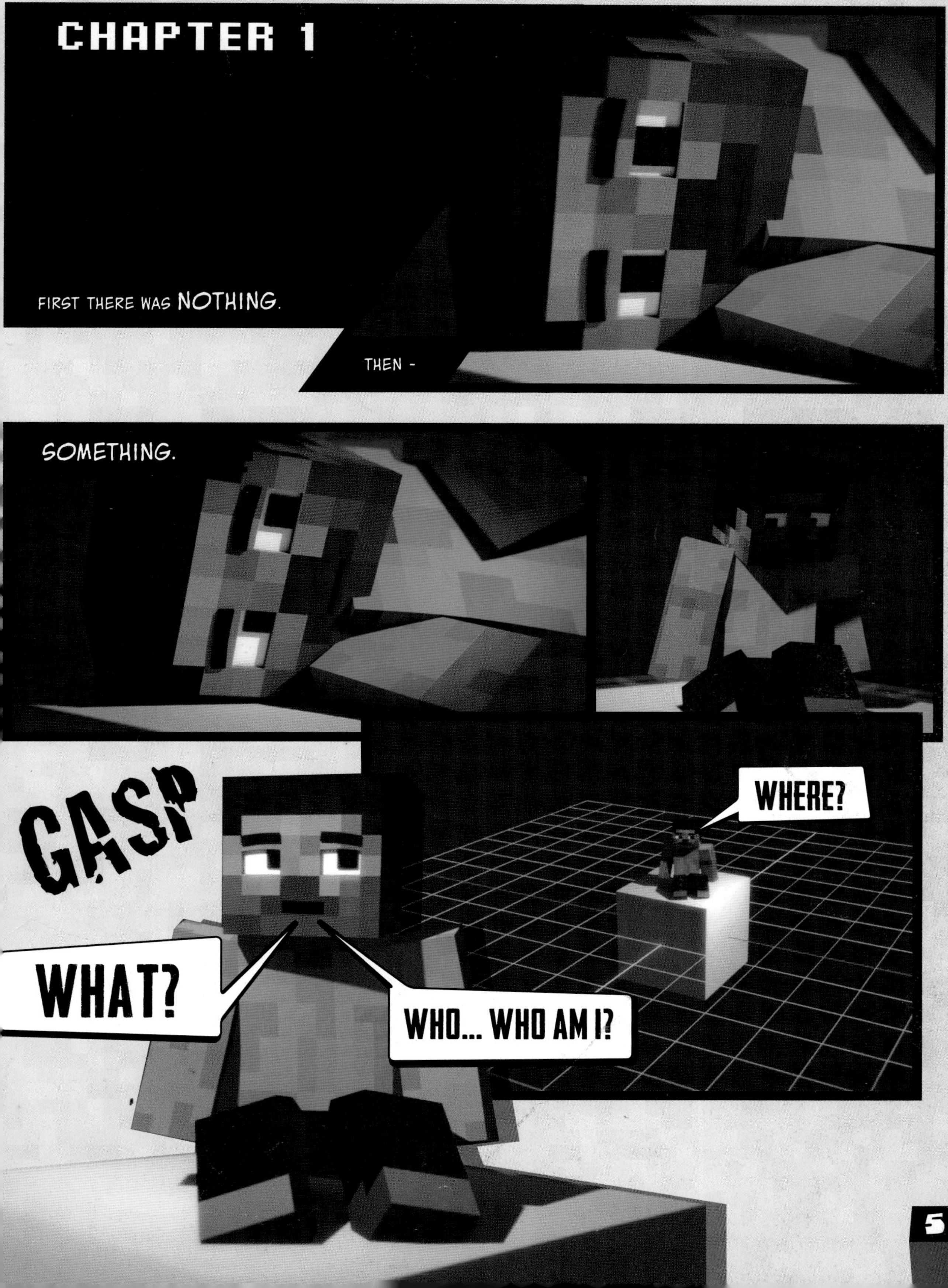
CHAPTER 1
FIRST THERE WAS NOTHING.
THEN -
SOMETHING.
GASP
WHAT?
WHO... WHO AM I?
WHERE?

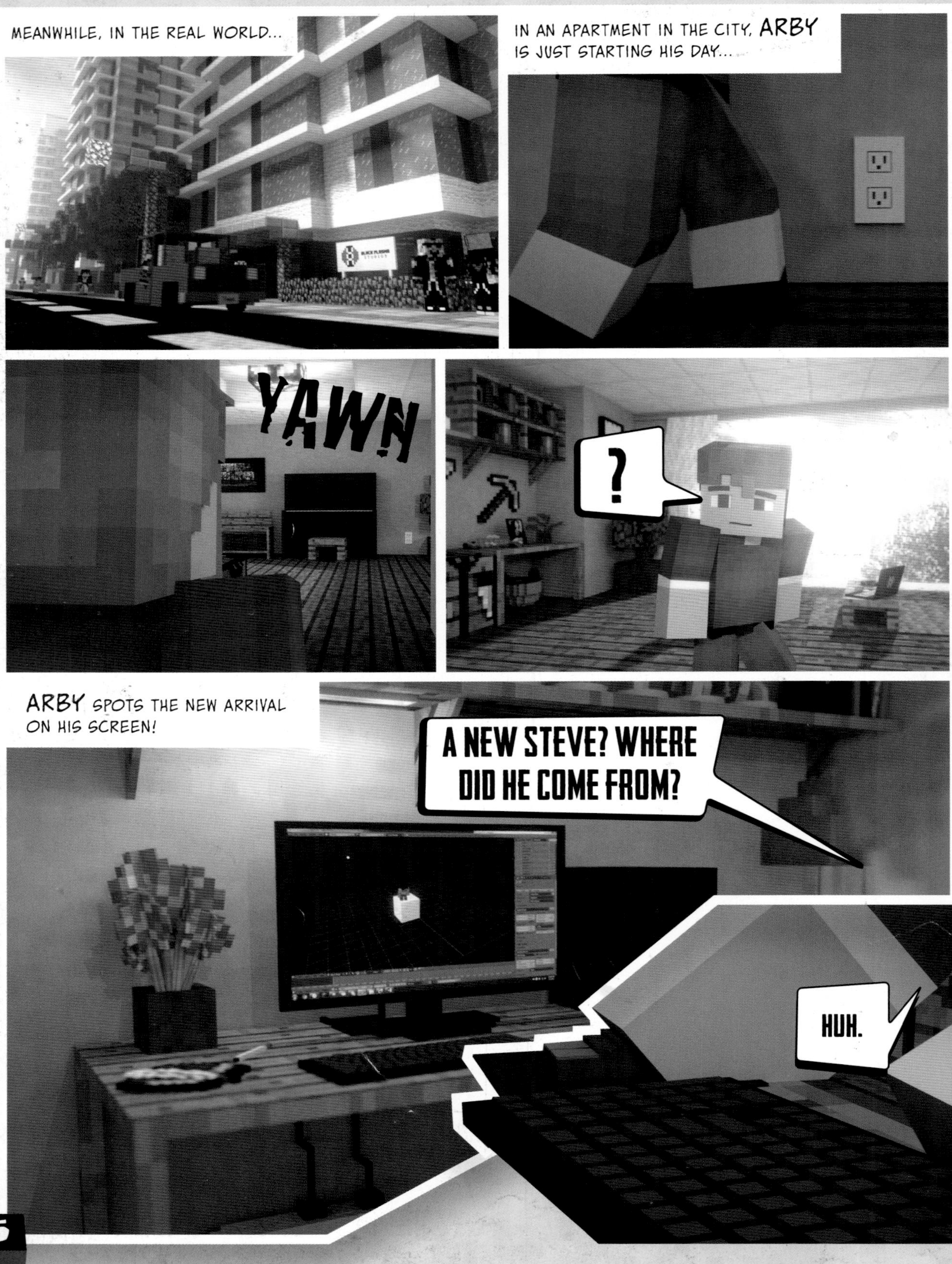
MEANWHILE, IN THE REAL WORLD...
IN AN APARTMENT IN THE CITY, ARBY IS JUST STARTING HIS DAY...
YAWN
?
ARBY SPOTS THE NEW ARRIVAL ON HIS SCREEN!
A NEW STEVE? WHERE DID HE COME FROM?
HUH.

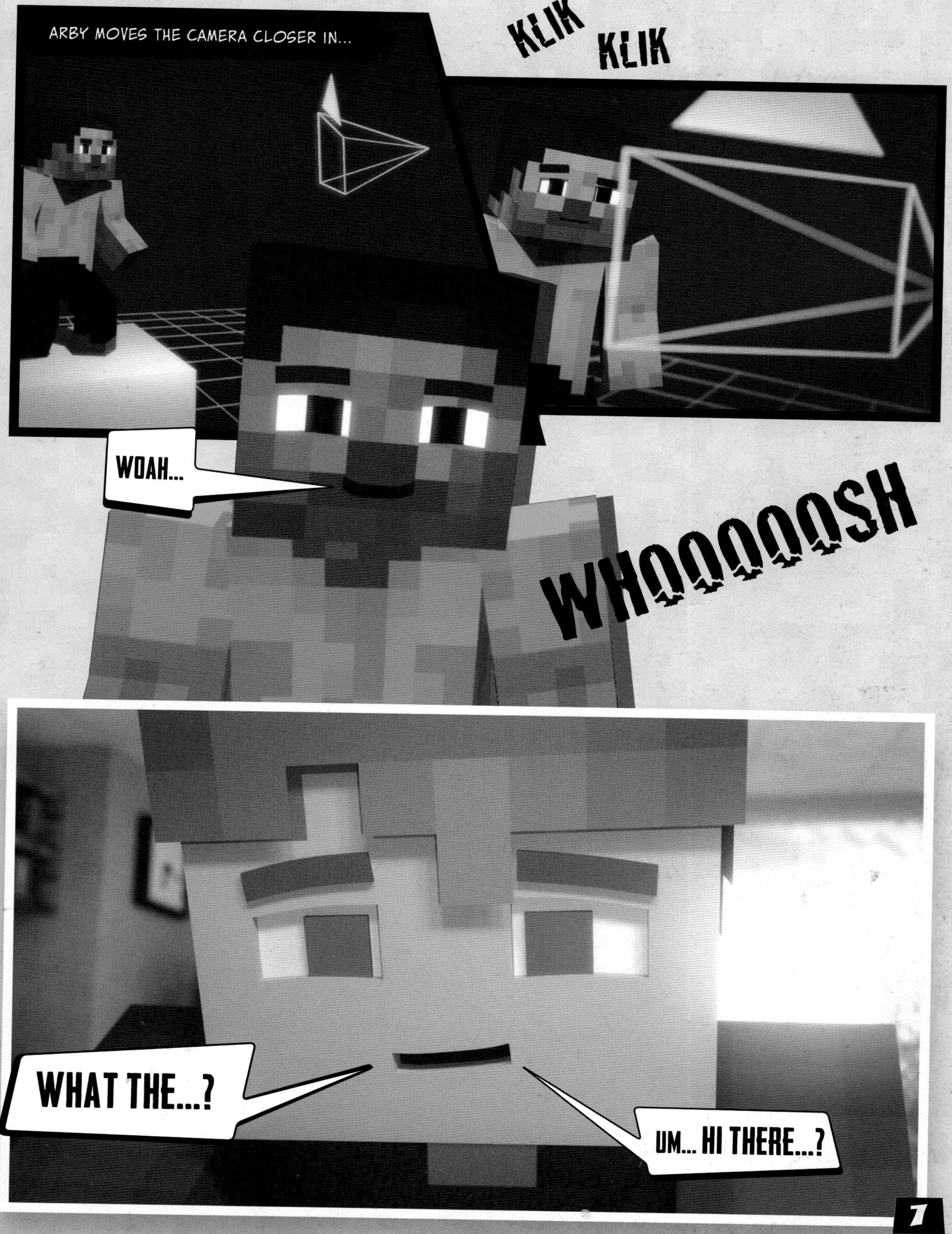

ARBY MOVES THE CAMERA CLOSER IN...
KLIK
KLIK
WOAH...
WHOOOOOOSH
WHAT THE...?
UM... HI THERE...?

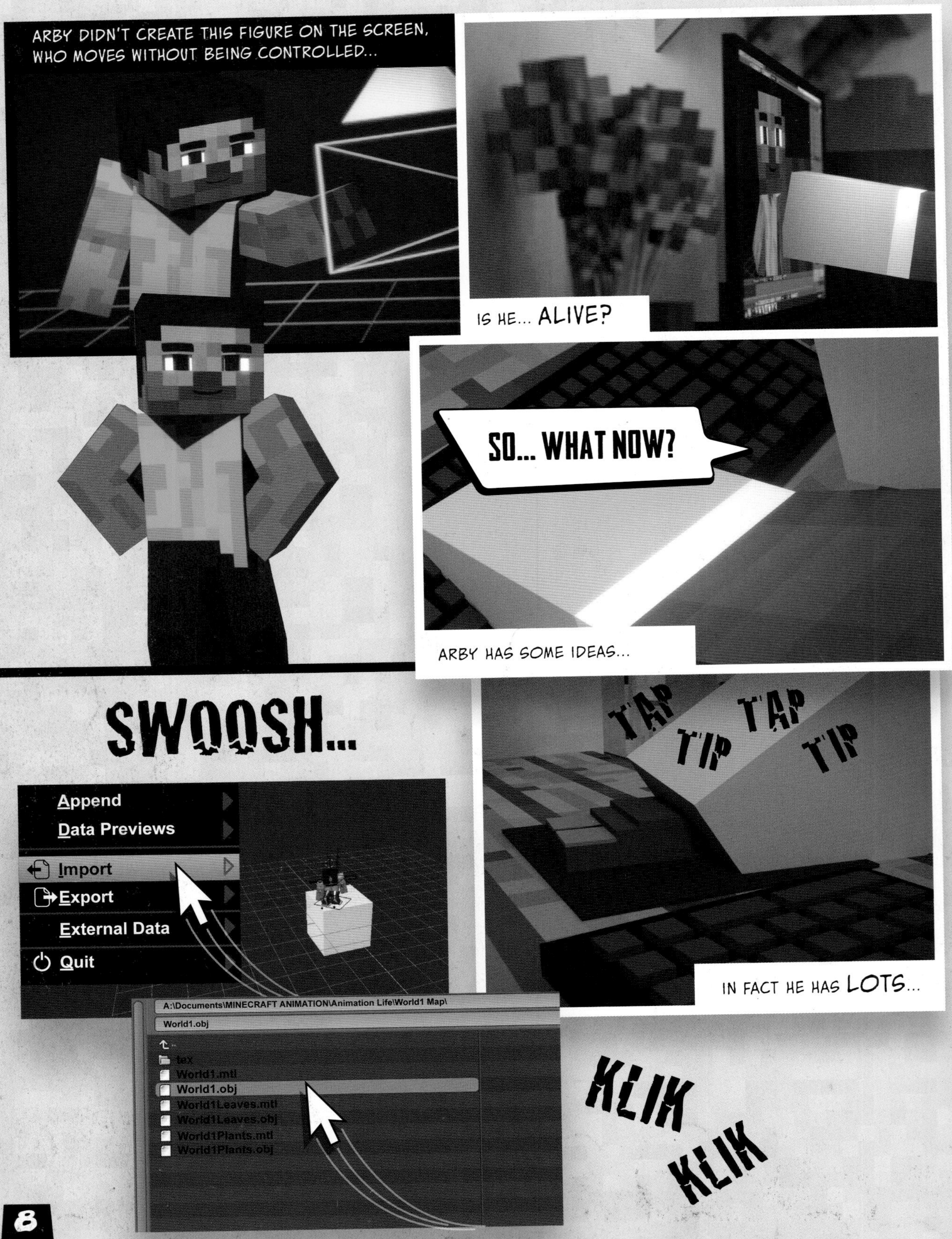
ARBY DIDN'T CREATE THIS FIGURE ON THE SCREEN, WHO MOVES WITHOUT BEING CONTROLLED...
IS HE... ALIVE?
SO... WHAT NOW?
ARBY HAS SOME IDEAS...
SWOOSH...
TAP TAP
TIP TIP
Append
Data Previews
Import
Export
External Data
Quit
A:\Documents\MINECRAFT ANIMATION\Animation Life\World1 Map\
World1.obj
tex
World1.mtl
World1.obj
World1Leaves.mtl
World1Leaves.obj
World1Plants.mtl
World1Plants.obj
IN FACT HE HAS LOTS...
KLIK
KLIK

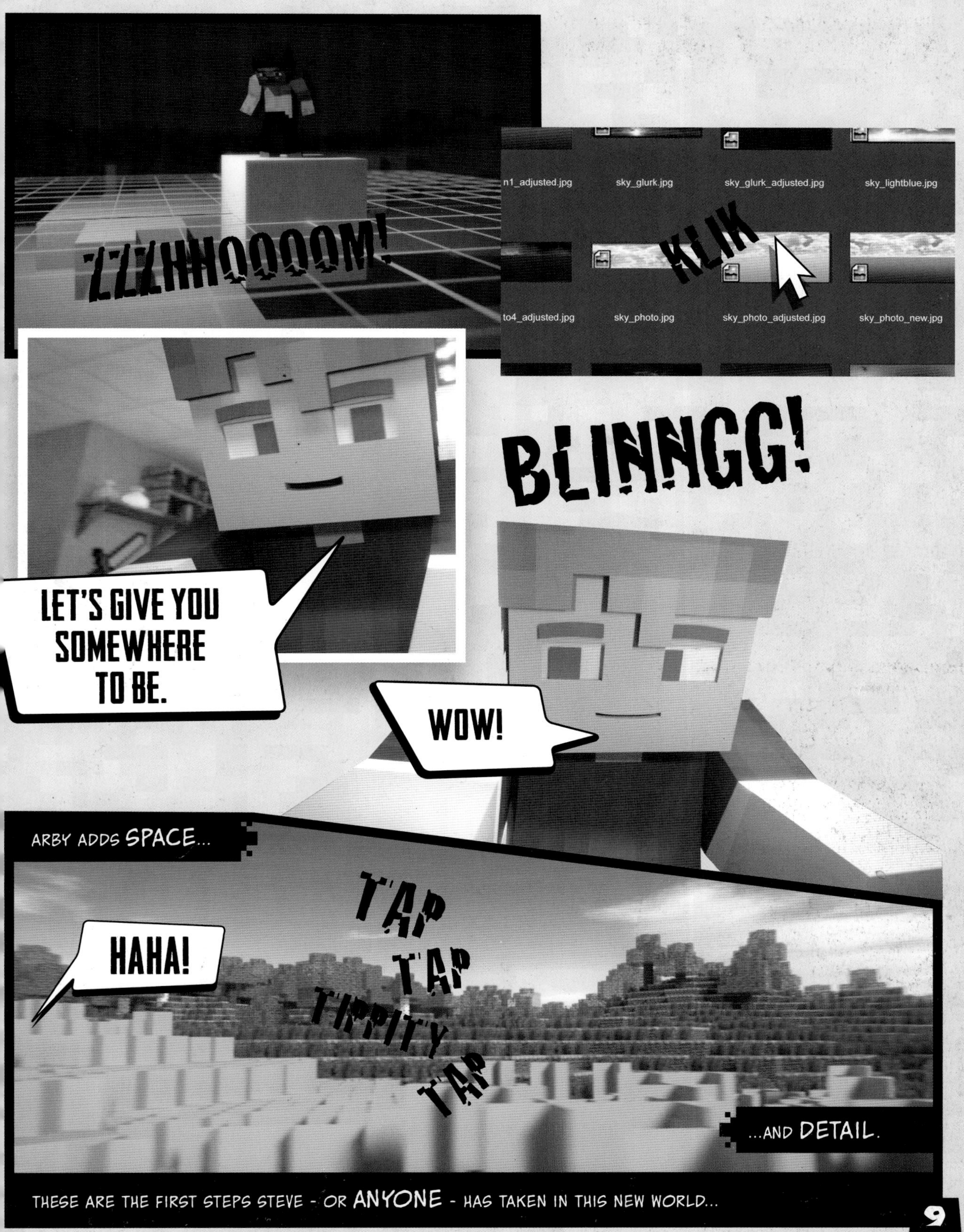
ZZZHHOOOOOM!
n1_adjusted.jpg
sky_glurk.jpg
sky_glurk_adjusted.jpg
sky_lightblue.jpg
KLIK
to4_adjusted.jpg
sky_photo.jpg
sky_photo_adjusted.jpg
sky_photo_new.jpg
LET'S GIVE YOU SOMEWHERE TO BE.
BLINNGG!
WOW!
ARBY ADDS SPACE...
HAHA!
TAP
TAP
TIPPITY
TAP
...AND DETAIL.
THESE ARE THE FIRST STEPS STEVE - OR ANYONE - HAS TAKEN IN THIS NEW WORLD...

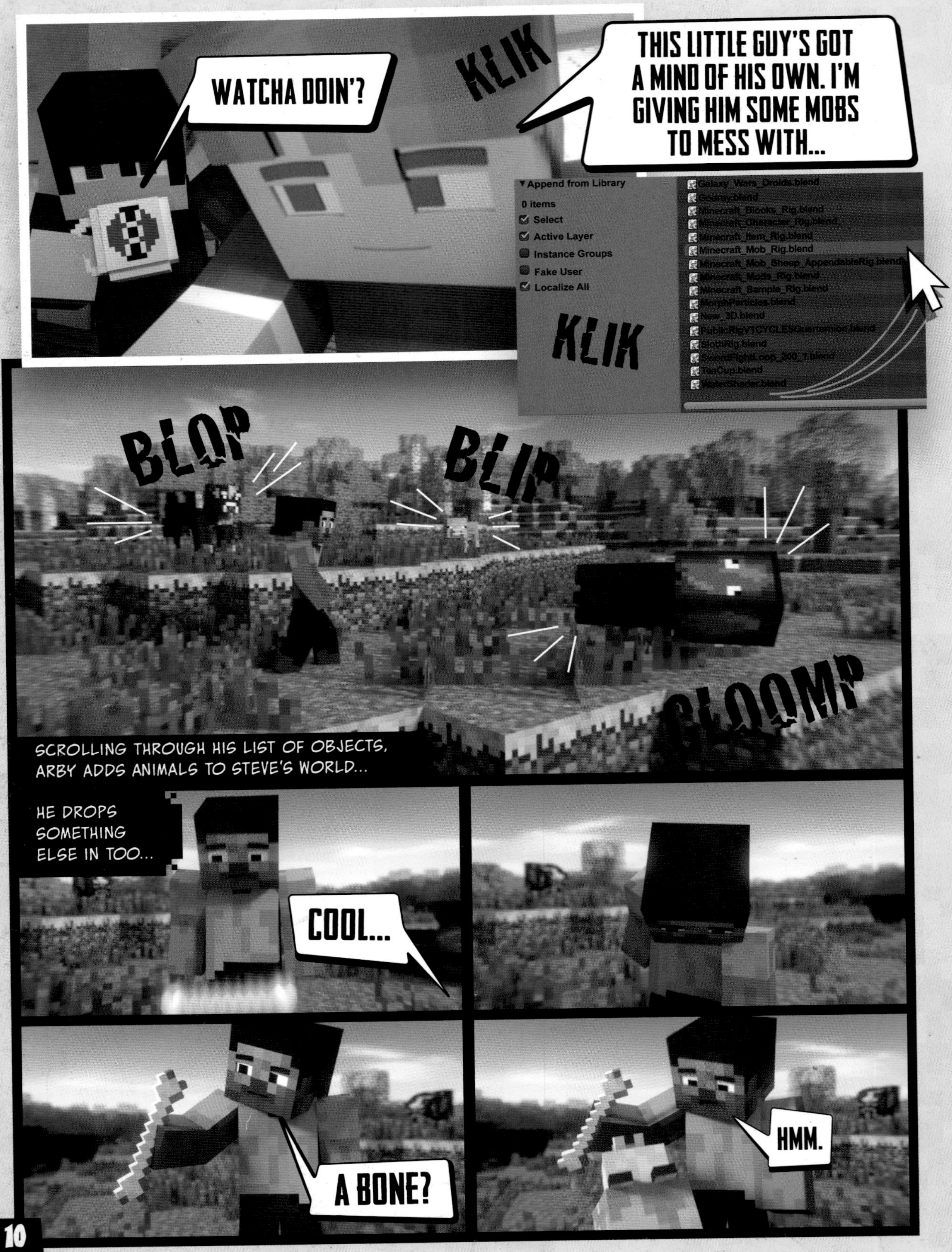
WATCHA DOIN'?
KLIK
THIS LITTLE GUY'S GOT A MIND OF HIS OWN. I'M GIVING HIM SOME MOBS TO MESS WITH...
Append from Library
0 items
Select
Active Layer
Instance Groups
Fake User
Localize All
Galaxy_Wars_Droids.blend
Godray.blend
Minecraft_Blocks_Rig.blend
Minecraft_Character_Rig.blend
Minecraft_Item_Rig.blend
Minecraft_Mob_Rig.blend
Minecraft_Mob_Sheep_AppendableRig.blend
Minecraft_Mods_Rig.blend
Minecraft_Sample_Rig.blend
MorphParticles.blend
New_3D.blend
PublicRigV1CYCLESQuarternion.blend
SlothRig.blend
SwordFightLoop_200_1.blend
TeaCup.blend
WaterShader.blend
KLIK
BLOP
BLIP
GLOOMP
SCROLLING THROUGH HIS LIST OF OBJECTS, ARBY ADDS ANIMALS TO STEVE'S WORLD...
HE DROPS SOMETHING ELSE IN TOO...
COOL...
A BONE?
HMM.

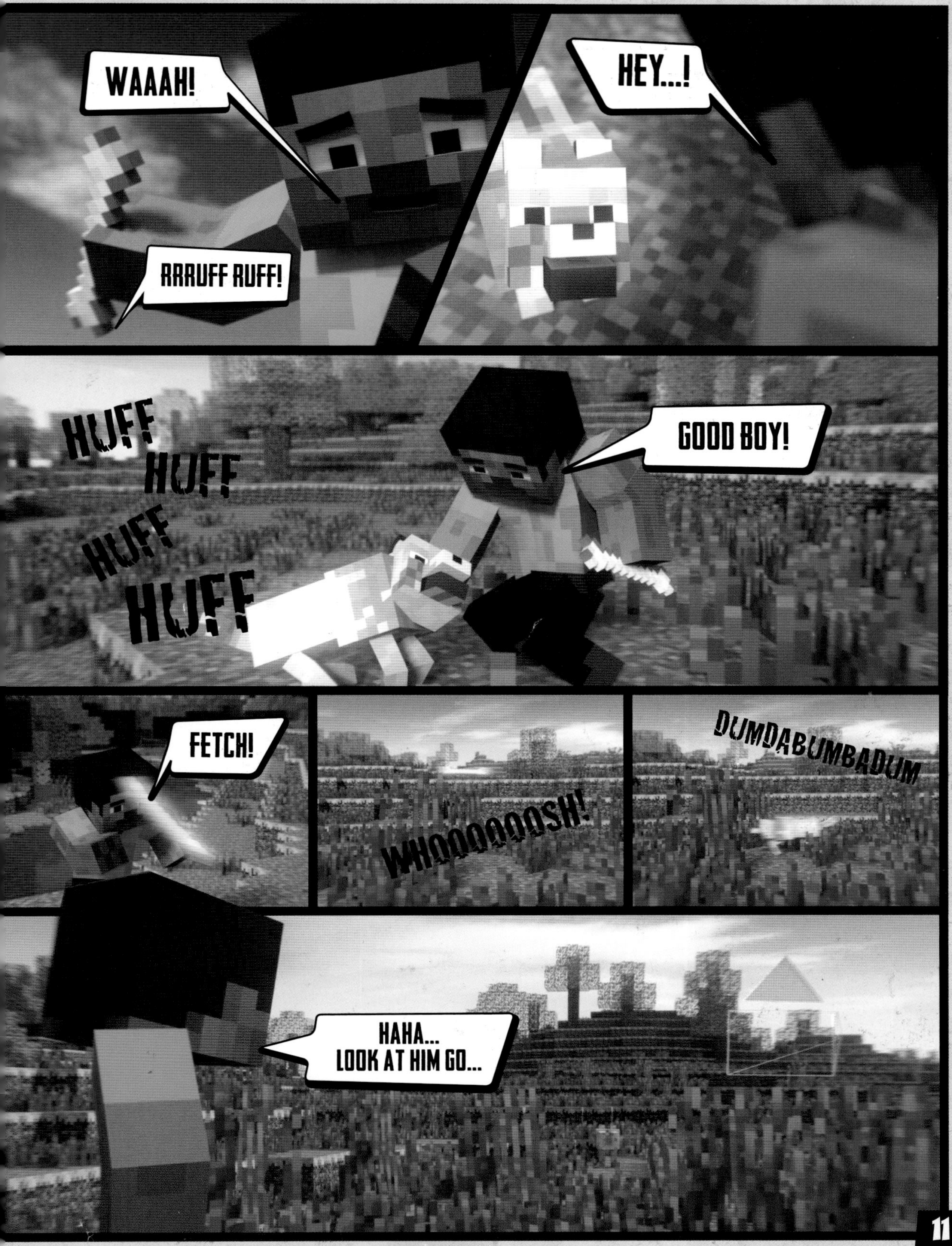
WAAAH!
RRRUFF RUFF!
HEY...!
HUFF
HUFF
HUFF
HUFF
GOOD BOY!
FETCH!
WHOOOOOOOSH!
DUMDABUMBADUM
HAHA...
LOOK AT HIM GO...

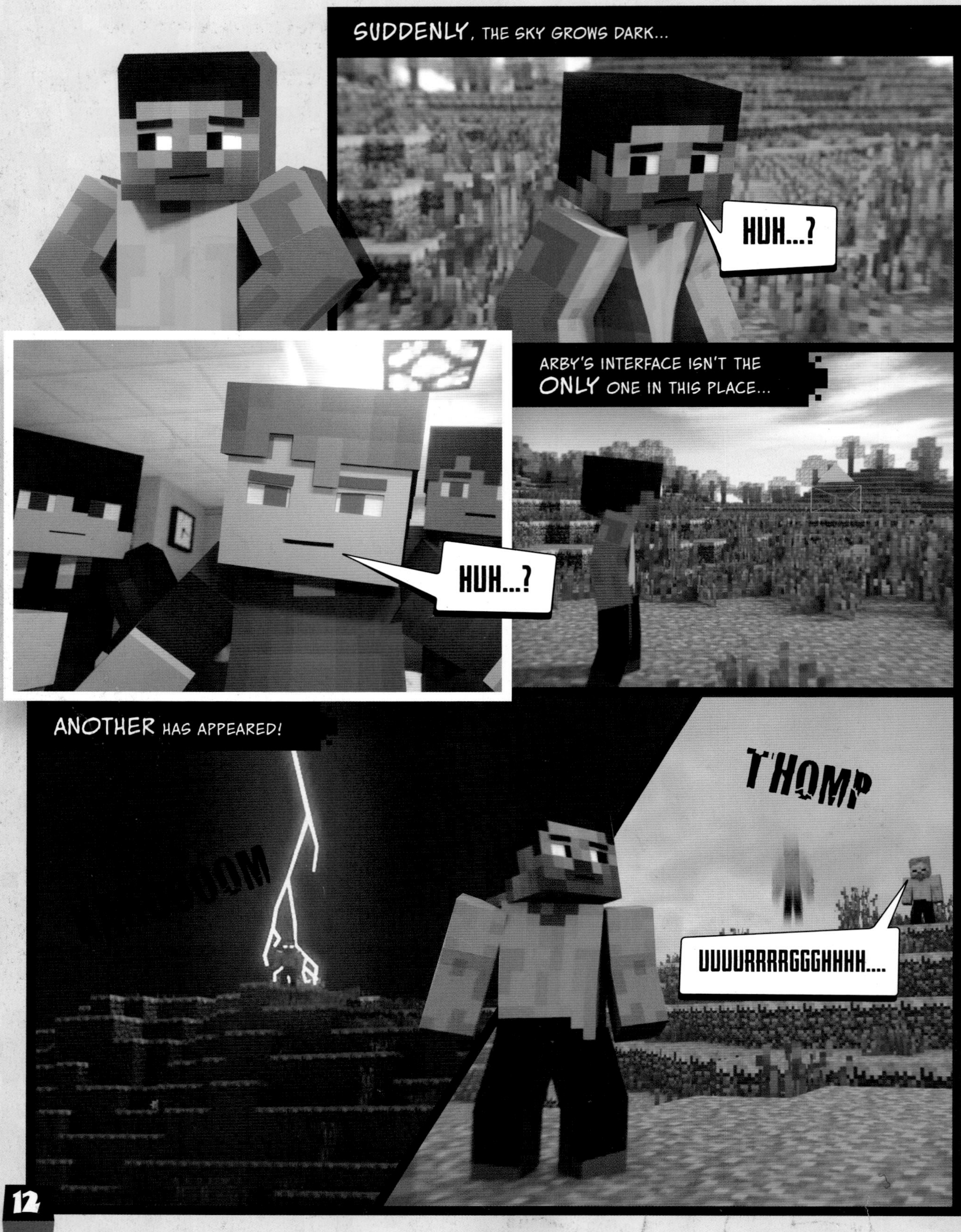
SUDDENLY, THE SKY GROWS DARK...
HUH...?
HUH...?
ARBY'S INTERFACE ISN'T THE ONLY ONE IN THIS PLACE...
ANOTHER HAS APPEARED!
THOMP
UUUURRRRGGGHHHH....

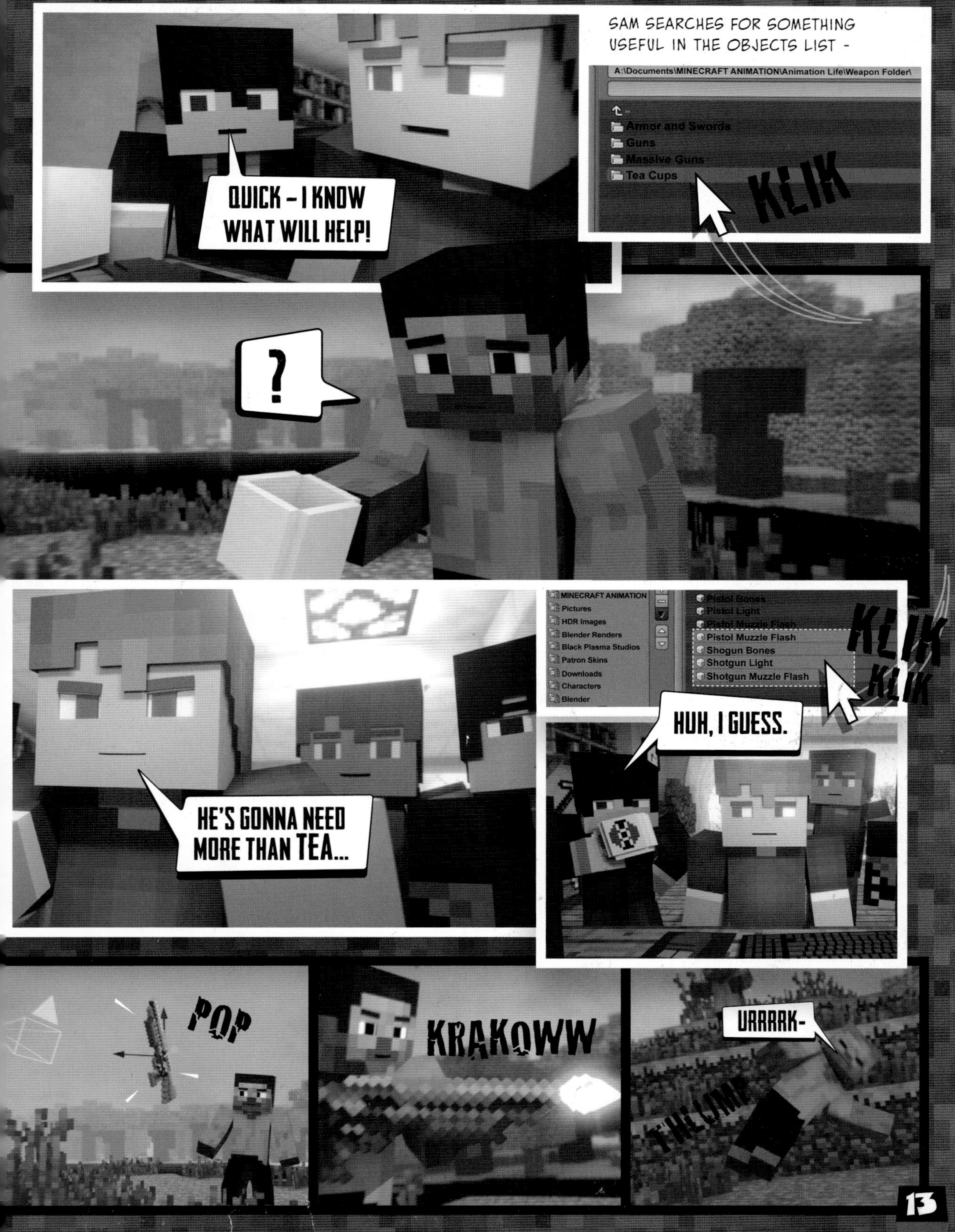
QUICK – I KNOW WHAT WILL HELP!
SAM SEARCHES FOR SOMETHING USEFUL IN THE OBJECTS LIST -
A:\Documents\MINECRAFT ANIMATION\Animation Life\Weapon Folder\
Armor and Swords
Guns
Massive Guns
Tea Cups
KLIK
?
HE'S GONNA NEED MORE THAN TEA...
MINECRAFT ANIMATION
Pictures
HDR Images
Blender Renders
Black Plasma Studios
Patron Skins
Downloads
Characters
Blender
Pistol Bones
Pistol Light
Pistol Muzzle Flash
Pistol Muzzle Flash
Shogun Bones
Shotgun Light
Shotgun Muzzle Flash
KLIK
KLIK
HUH, I GUESS.
POP
KRAKOWW
URRRRK-
THUMP

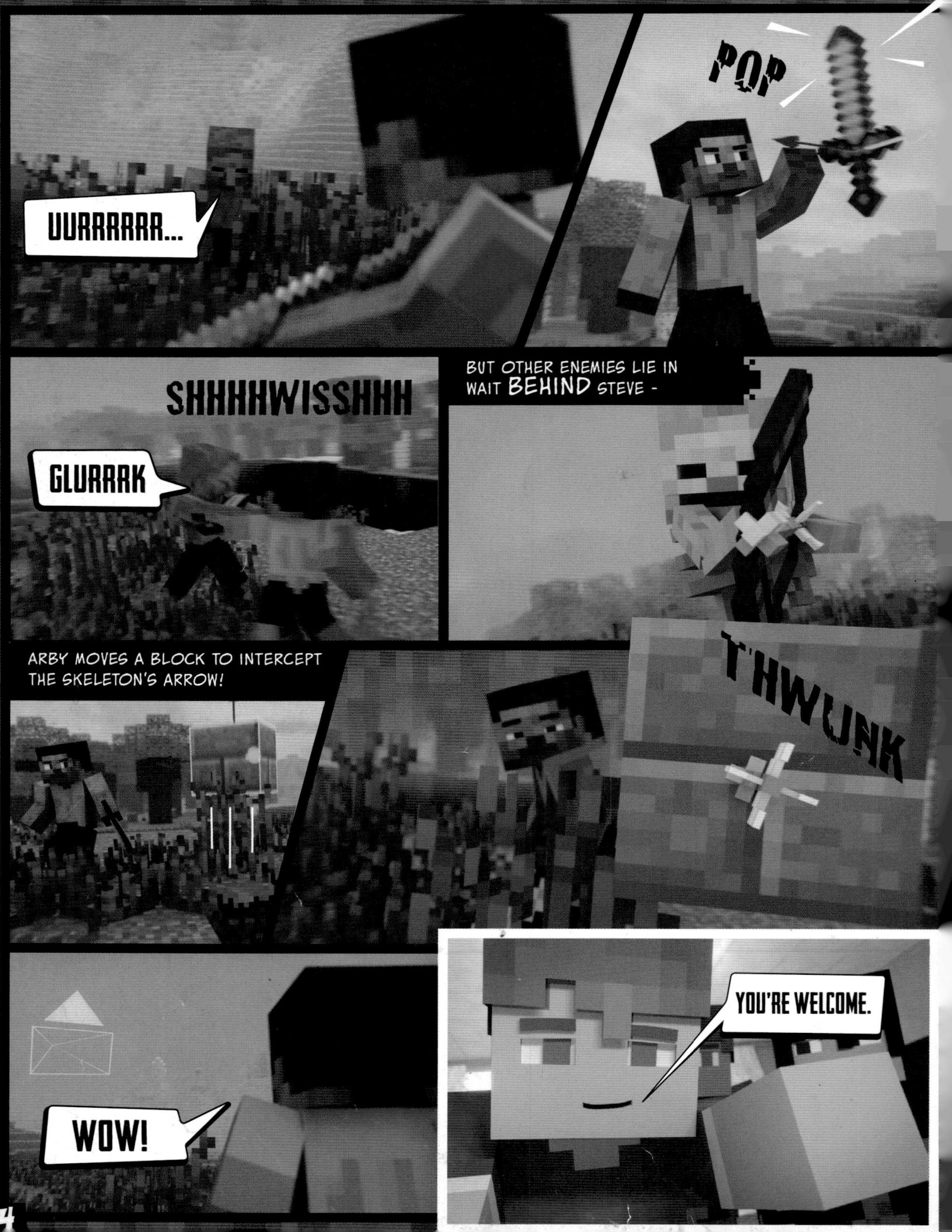
UURRRRRR...
POP
SHHHHWISSHHH
GLURRRK
BUT OTHER ENEMIES LIE IN WAIT BEHIND STEVE -
ARBY MOVES A BLOCK TO INTERCEPT THE SKELETON'S ARROW!
T'HWUNK
WOW!
YOU'RE WELCOME.

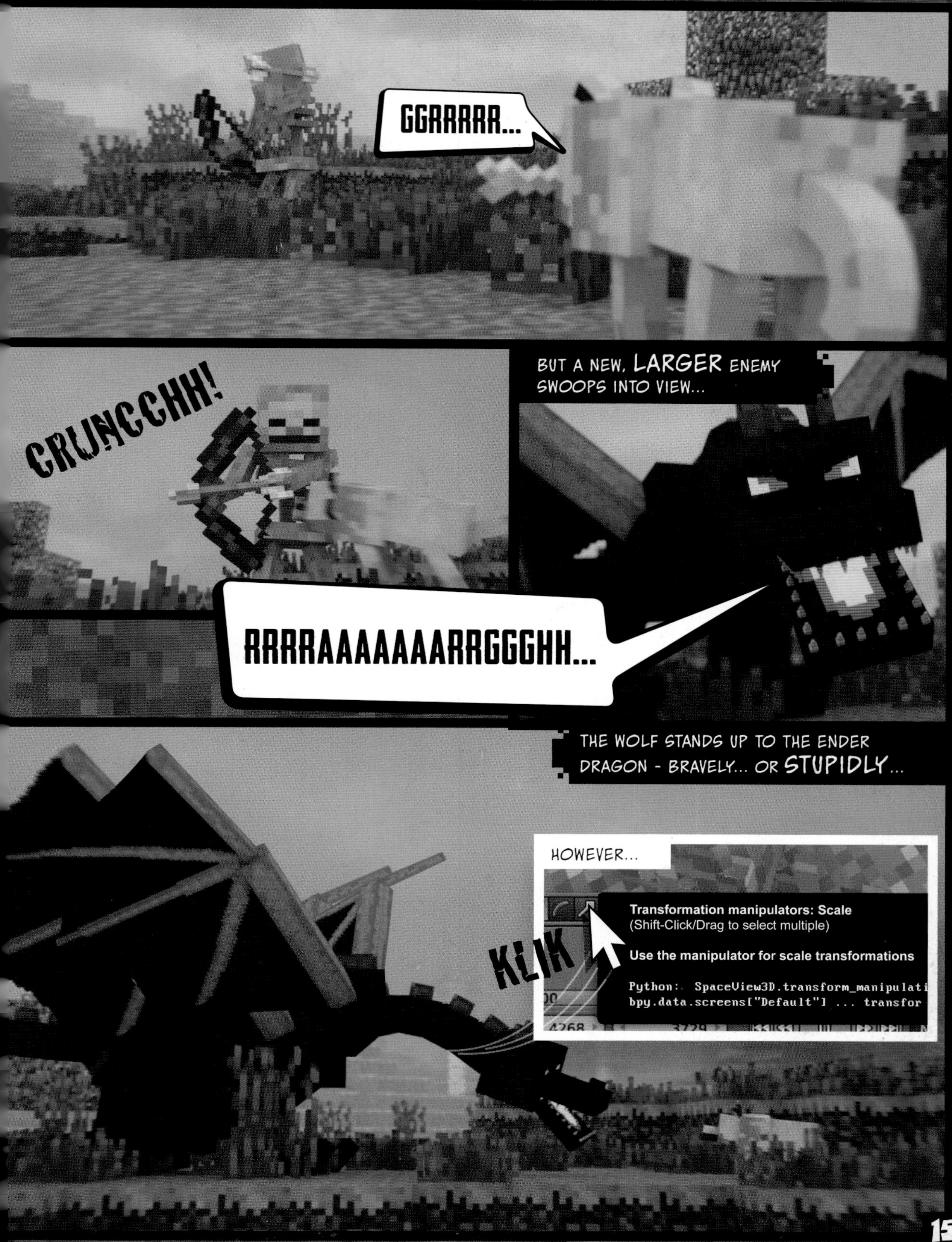
GGRRRRR...
CRUNCCHH!
BUT A NEW, LARGER ENEMY SWOOPS INTO VIEW...
RRRRAAAAAAARRGGGHH...
THE WOLF STANDS UP TO THE ENDER DRAGON - BRAVELY... OR STUPIDLY...
HOWEVER...
Transformation manipulators: Scale
(Shift-Click/Drag to select multiple)
Use the manipulator for scale transformations
Python: SpaceView3D.transform_manipulati
bpy.data.screens["Default"] ... transfor
KLIK

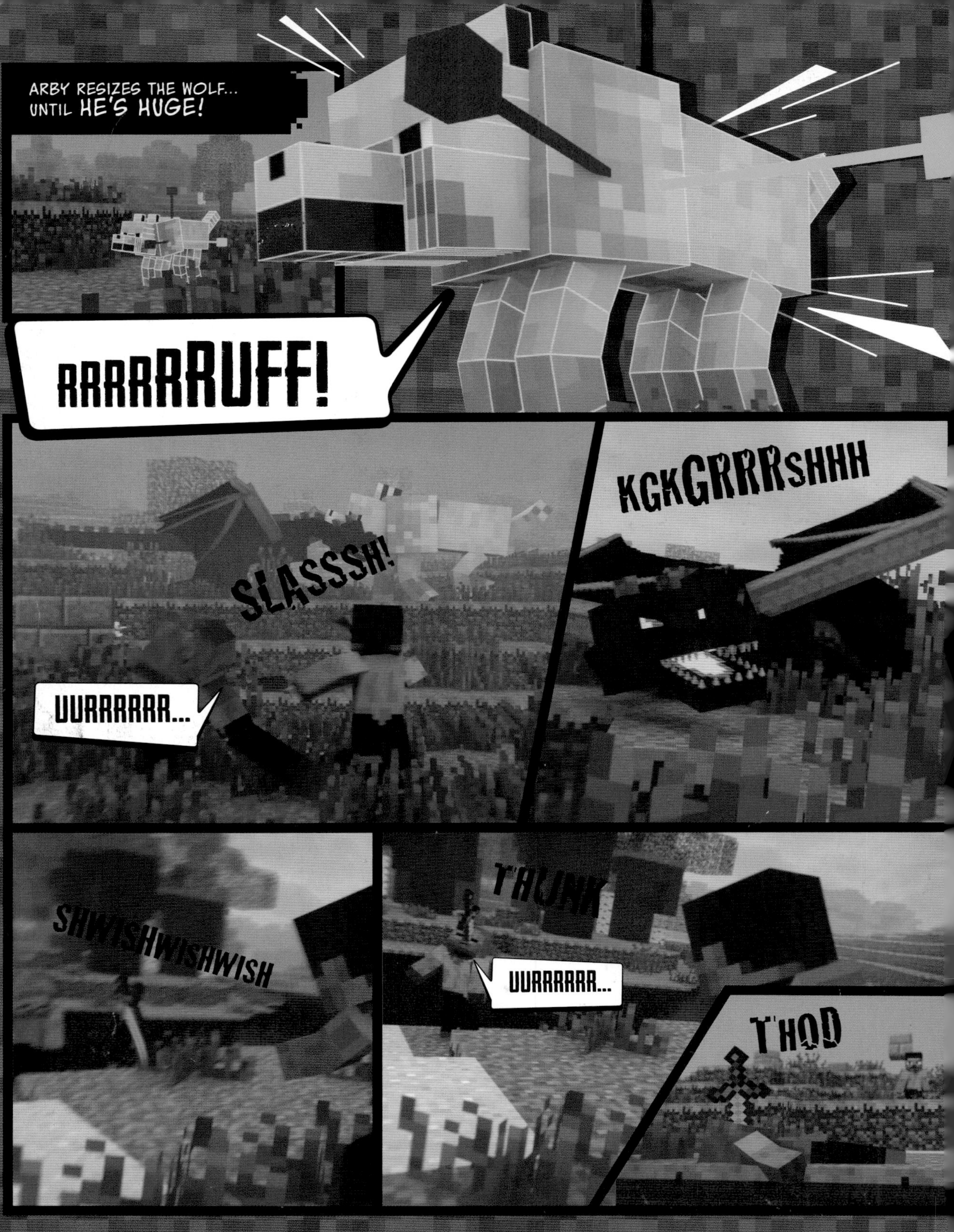
ARBY RESIZES THE WOLF...
UNTIL HE'S HUGE!
RRRRRRUFF!
SLASSSH!
UURRRRRR...
KGKGRRRSHHH
SHWISHWISHWISH
THUNK
UURRRRRR...
THOD

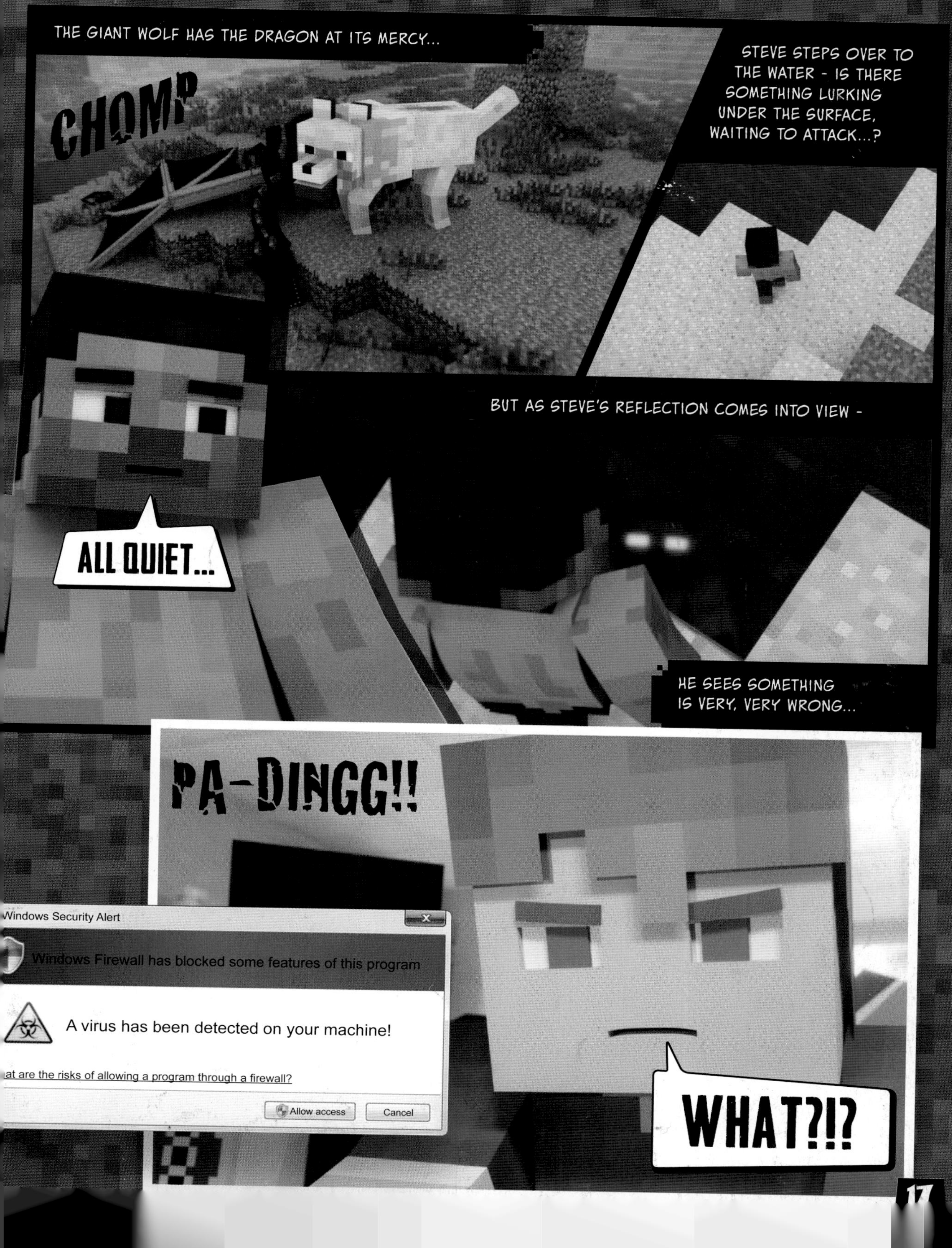
THE GIANT WOLF HAS THE DRAGON AT ITS MERCY...
CHOMP
STEVE STEPS OVER TO THE WATER - IS THERE SOMETHING LURKING UNDER THE SURFACE, WAITING TO ATTACK...?
ALL QUIET...
BUT AS STEVE'S REFLECTION COMES INTO VIEW -
HE SEES SOMETHING IS VERY, VERY WRONG...
PA-DINGG!!
Windows Security Alert
Windows Firewall has blocked some features of this program
A virus has been detected on your machine!
Allow access
Cancel
WHAT?!!?

KRAKOOOOM

THE WOLF IS RETURNED TO ITS NORMAL SIZE –

THE PROGRAM REFUSES TO SHUT DOWN!

Load Factory Settings	▶
Link	▶
Append	▶
Data Previews	▶
⬅ **Import**	▶
➡ **Export**	▶
External Data	▶
⏻ **Quit**	▶

BUT... I DIDN'T DO THAT!

KLIK
KLIK
KLIK
KLIK

SOMETHING ELSE IS COMING. I CAN **FEEL** IT...

KRAKOOOOM

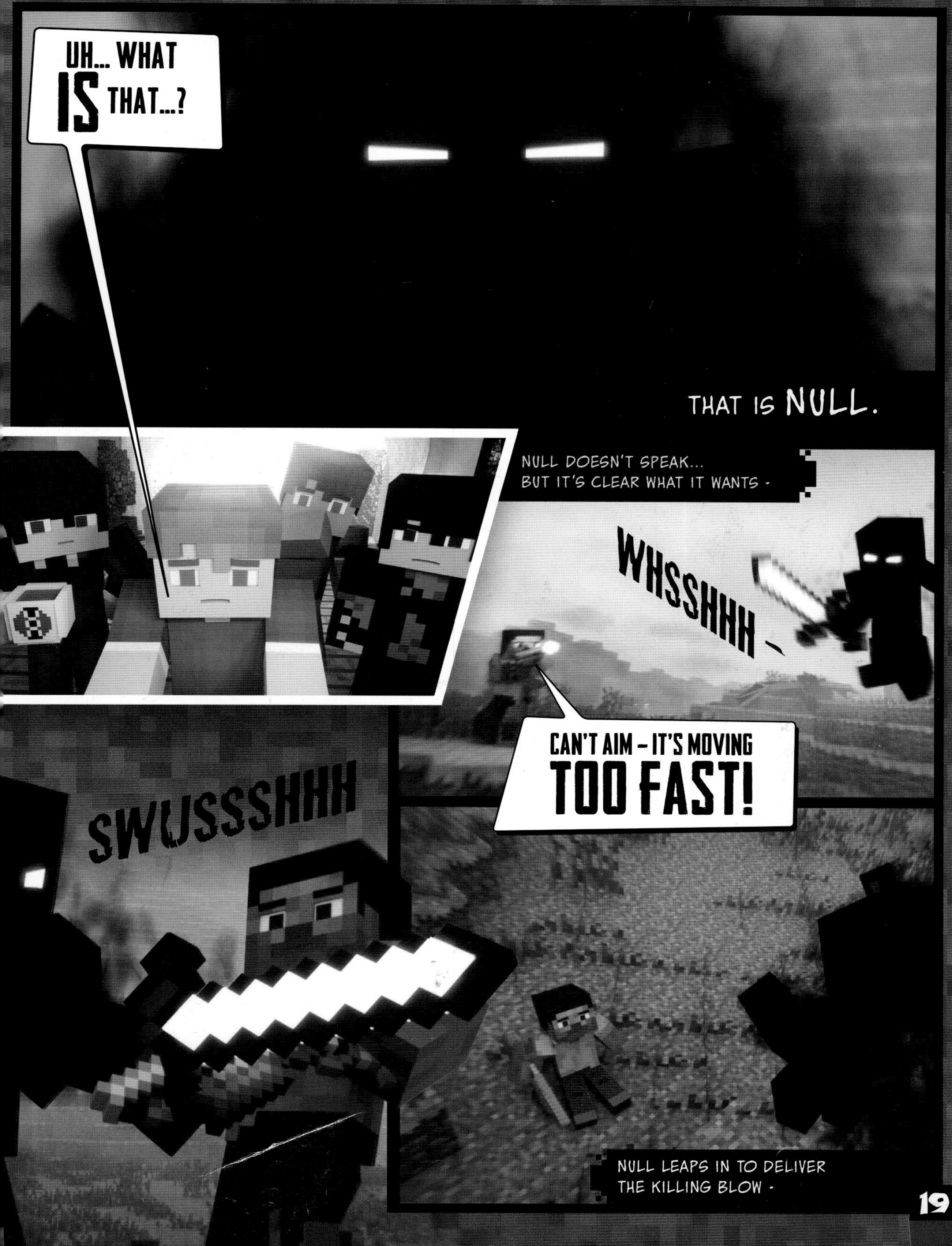
UH... WHAT IS THAT...?
THAT IS NULL.
NULL DOESN'T SPEAK... BUT IT'S CLEAR WHAT IT WANTS -
WHSSHHH -
CAN'T AIM – IT'S MOVING TOO FAST!
SWUSSSHHH
NULL LEAPS IN TO DELIVER THE KILLING BLOW -

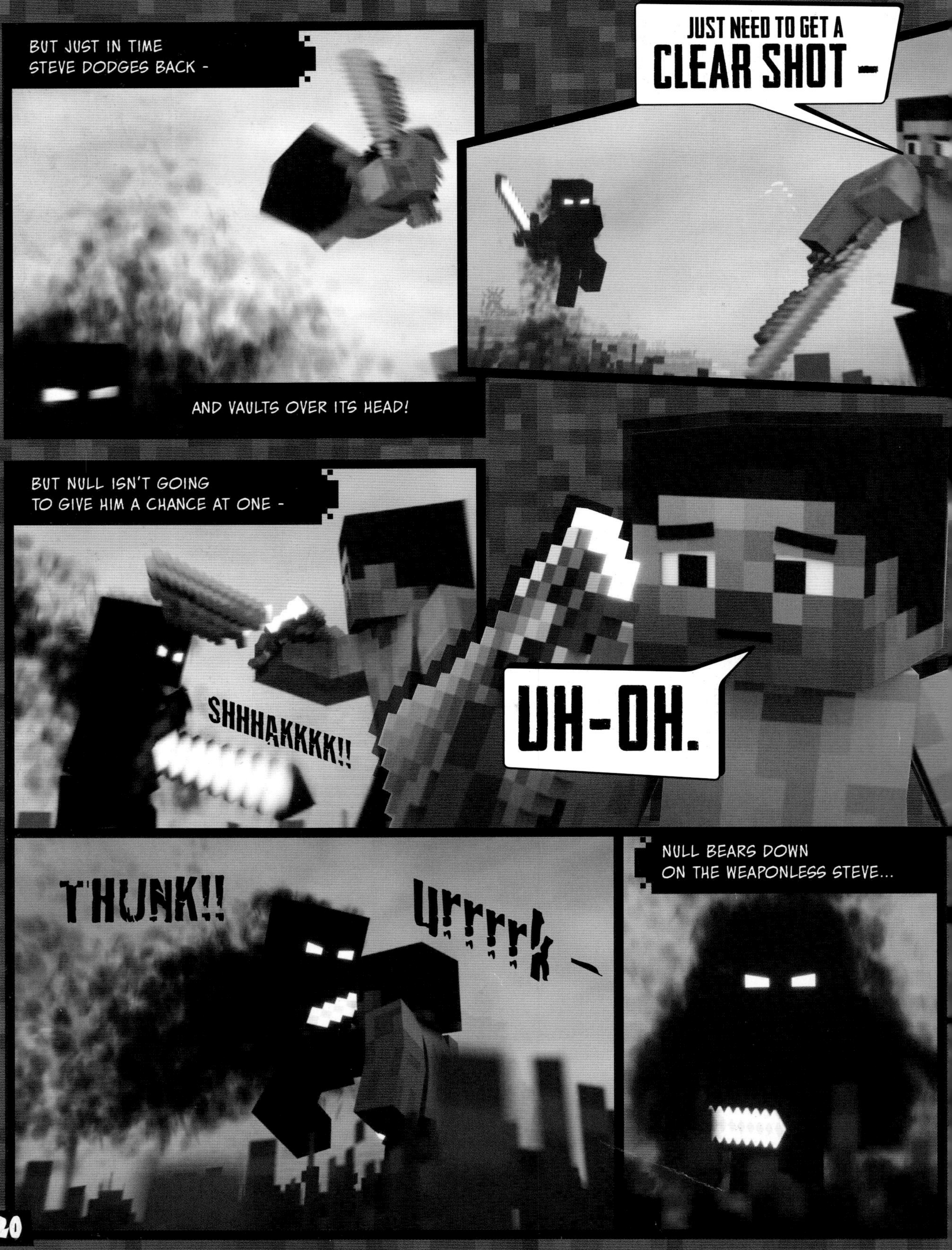
BUT JUST IN TIME
STEVE DODGES BACK -
AND VAULTS OVER ITS HEAD!
JUST NEED TO GET A CLEAR SHOT -
BUT NULL ISN'T GOING
TO GIVE HIM A CHANCE AT ONE -
SHHHAKKKK!!
UH-OH.
THUNK!!
Urrrrk -
NULL BEARS DOWN
ON THE WEAPONLESS STEVE...

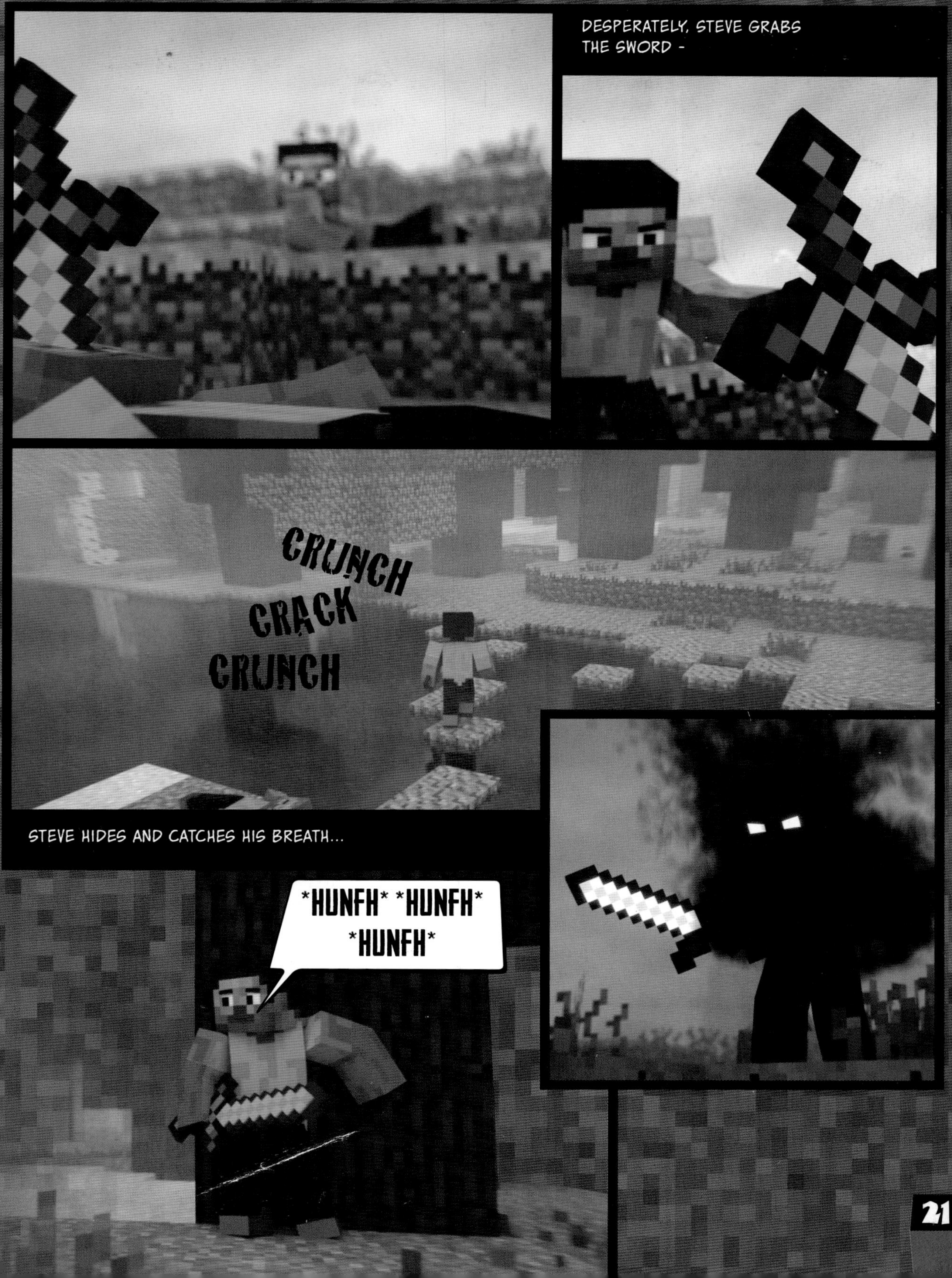
DESPERATELY, STEVE GRABS THE SWORD -
CRUNCH
CRACK
CRUNCH
STEVE HIDES AND CATCHES HIS BREATH...
HUNFH *HUNFH* *HUNFH*

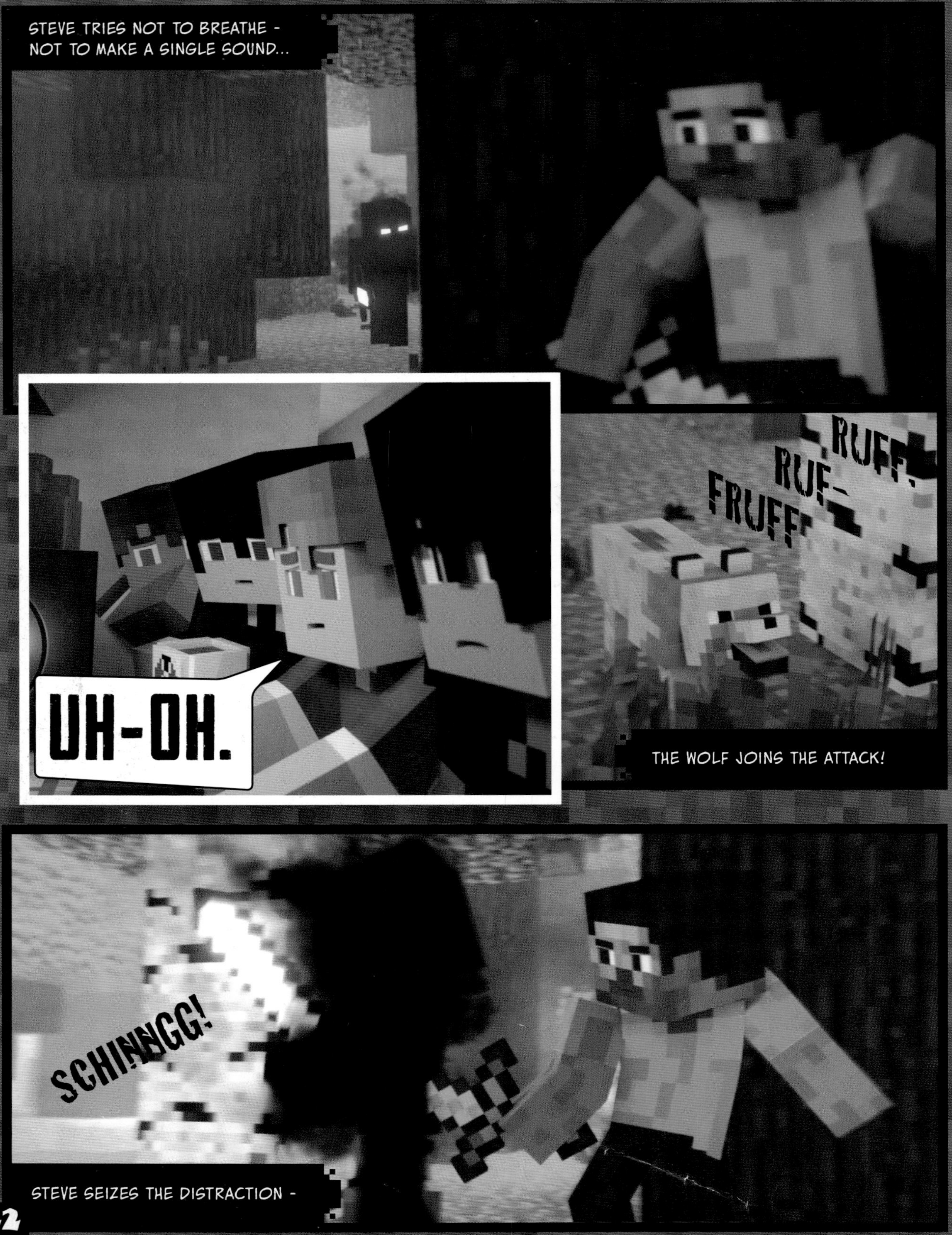

STEVE TRIES NOT TO BREATHE - NOT TO MAKE A SINGLE SOUND...
UH-OH.
RUFF. RUF-FRUFF!
THE WOLF JOINS THE ATTACK!
SCHINNGG!
STEVE SEIZES THE DISTRACTION -

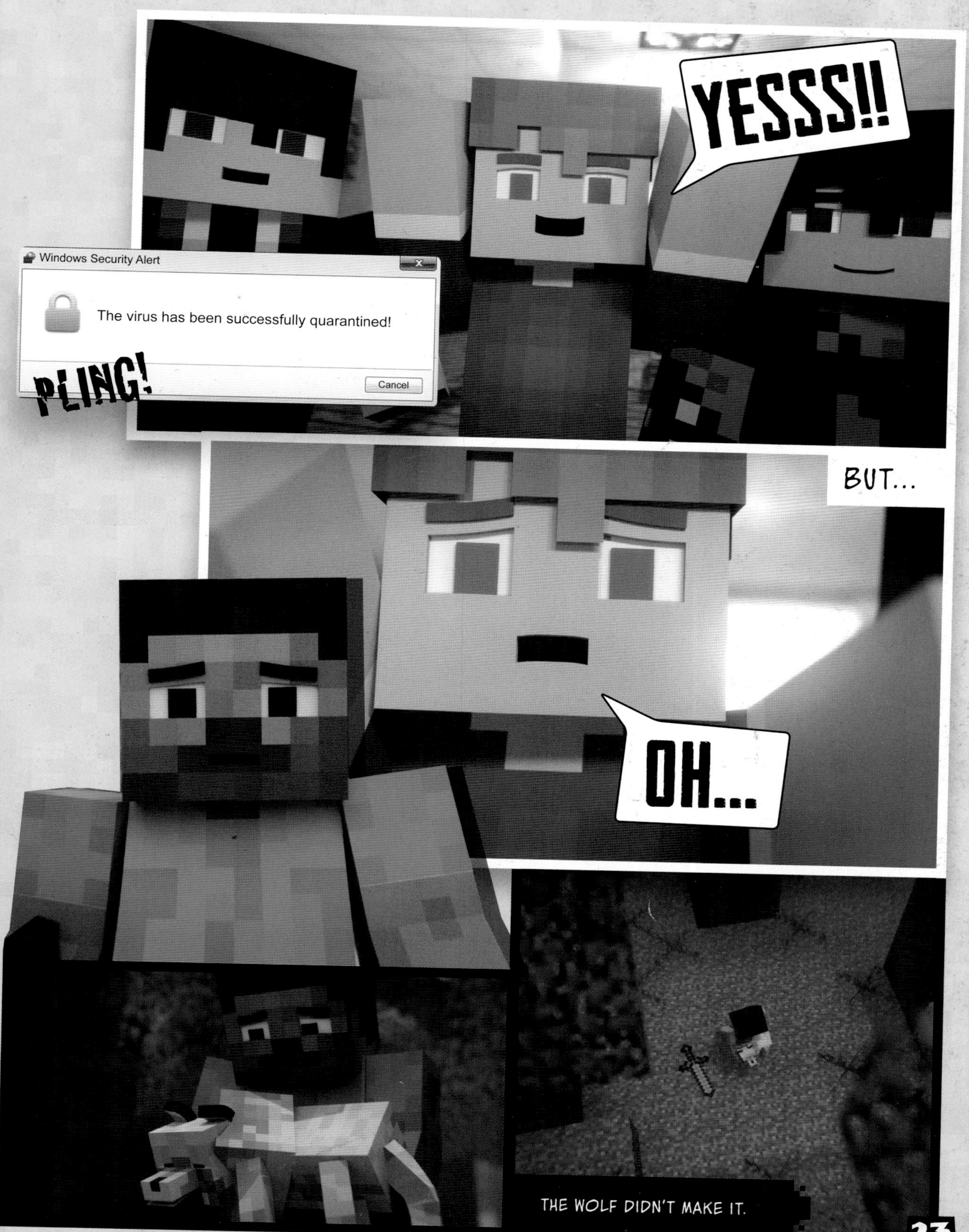
YESSS!!
Windows Security Alert
The virus has been successfully quarantined!
Cancel
PLING!
BUT...
OH...
THE WOLF DIDN'T MAKE IT.

CHAPTER 2

THE END OF THE FIRST DAY IN THIS NEW WORLD IS A **SAD** ONE...

AS STEVE SAYS FAREWELL TO A FAITHFUL FRIEND HE'D ONLY JUST MET –

BUT WHO SACRIFICED HIS LIFE TO SAVE HIS MASTER.

BEEP
BOOP
BIP

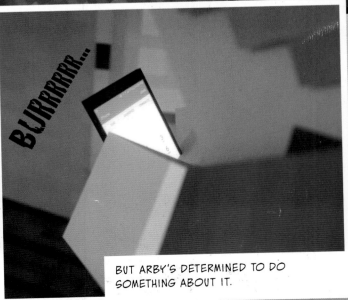

BURRRRRR...

STEVE'S PAIN IS SHARED IN ANOTHER WORLD...

BUT ARBY'S DETERMINED TO DO SOMETHING ABOUT IT.

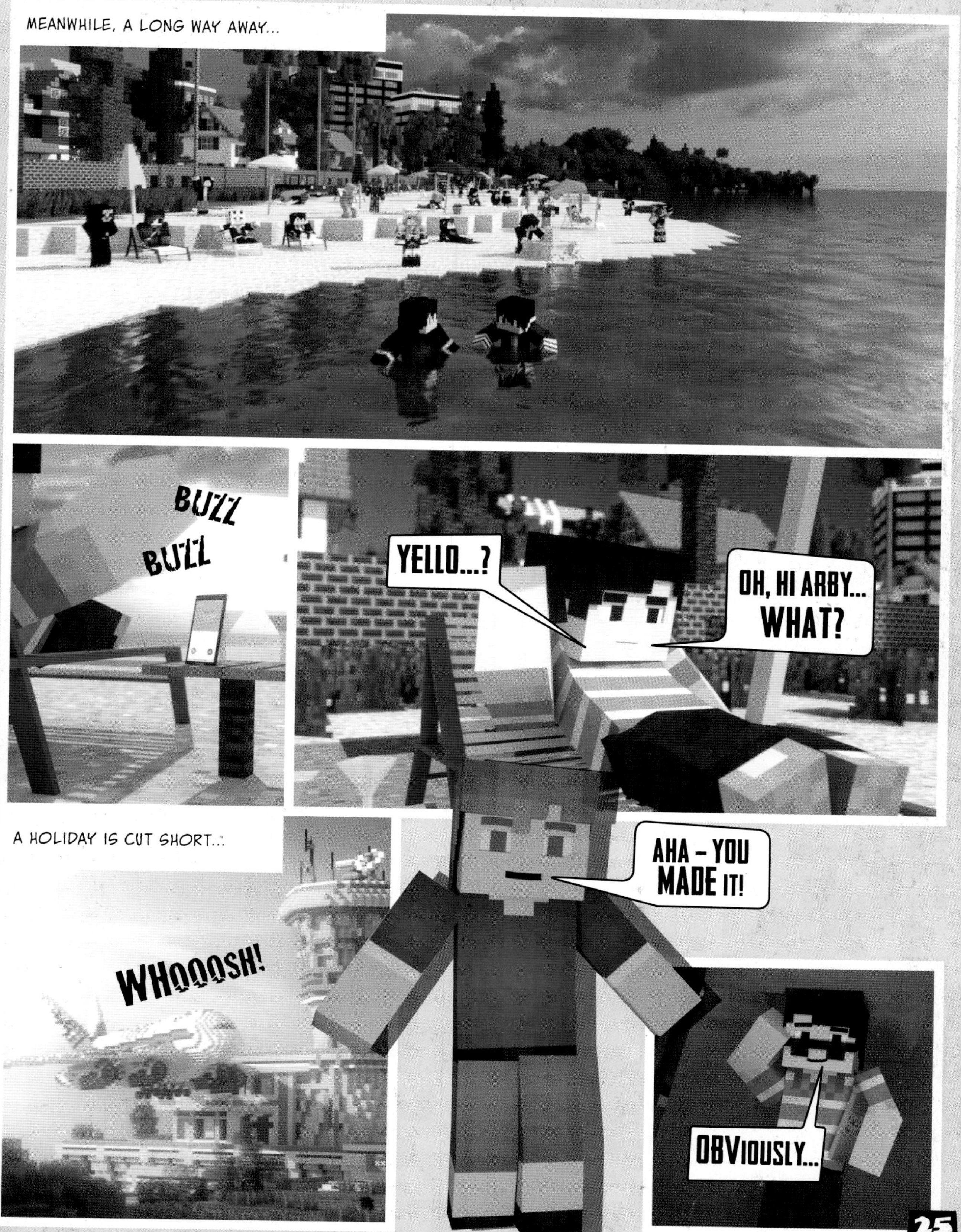

MEANWHILE, A LONG WAY AWAY...
BUZZ
BUZZ
YELLO...?
OH, HI ARBY...
WHAT?
A HOLIDAY IS CUT SHORT...
WHOOOSH!
AHA – YOU MADE IT!
OBVIOUSLY...

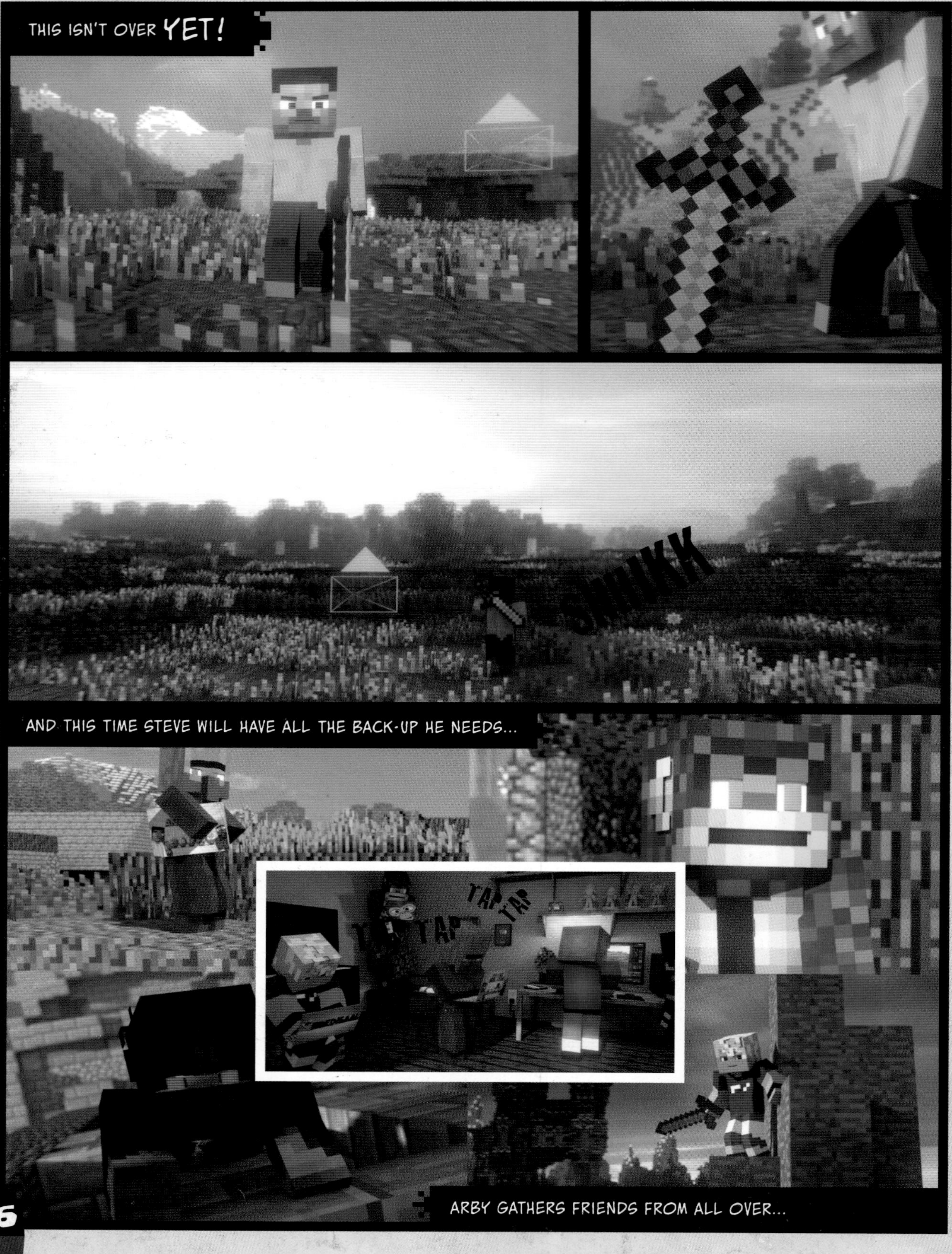

THIS ISN'T OVER YET!
SHIKK
AND THIS TIME STEVE WILL HAVE ALL THE BACK-UP HE NEEDS...
TAP TAP TAP TAP
ARBY GATHERS FRIENDS FROM ALL OVER...

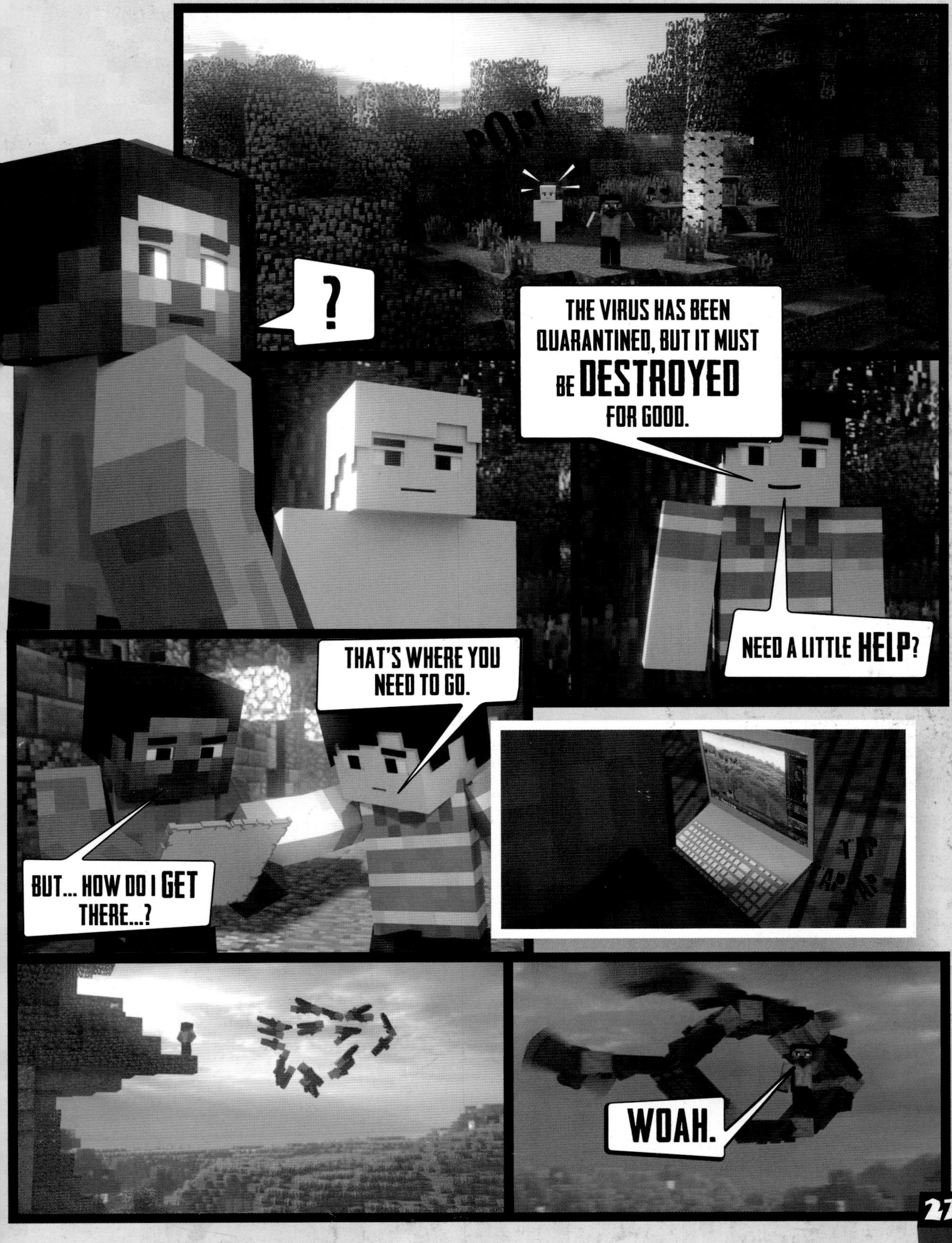

POP!
?
THE VIRUS HAS BEEN QUARANTINED, BUT IT MUST BE DESTROYED FOR GOOD.
NEED A LITTLE HELP?
THAT'S WHERE YOU NEED TO GO.
BUT... HOW DO I GET THERE...?
WOAH.

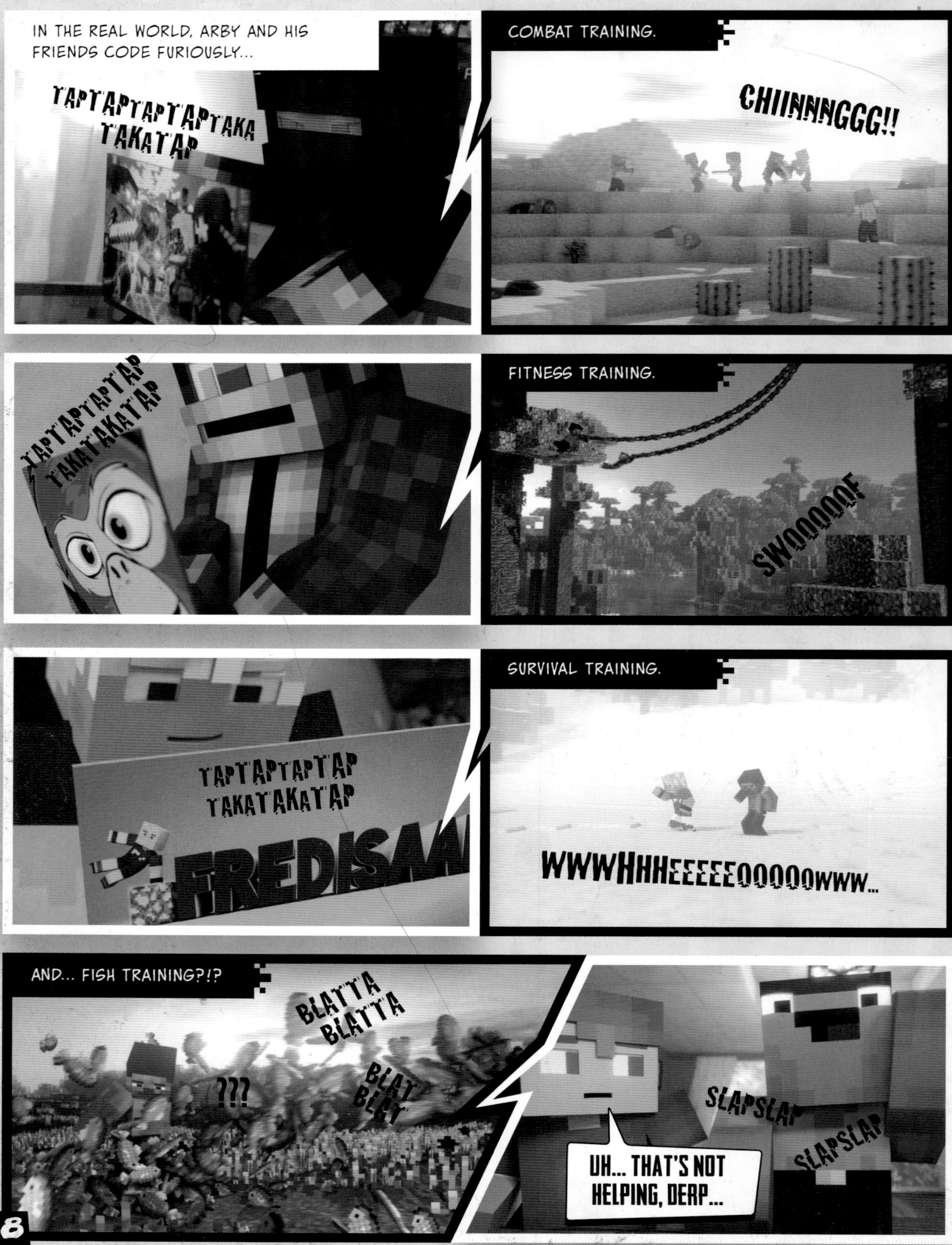

IN THE REAL WORLD, ARBY AND HIS FRIENDS CODE FURIOUSLY...
TAPTAPTAPTAPTAKA TAKATAP
COMBAT TRAINING.
CHIINNNGGG!!
TAPTAPTAPTAP TAKATAKATAP
FITNESS TRAINING.
SWOOOOOF
TAPTAPTAPTAP TAKATAKATAP
SURVIVAL TRAINING.
WWWHHHEEEEEOOOOOWWW...
AND... FISH TRAINING?!?
BLATTA BLATTA
???
BLAT BLAT
SLAPSLAP
SLAPSLAP
UH... THAT'S NOT HELPING, DERP...

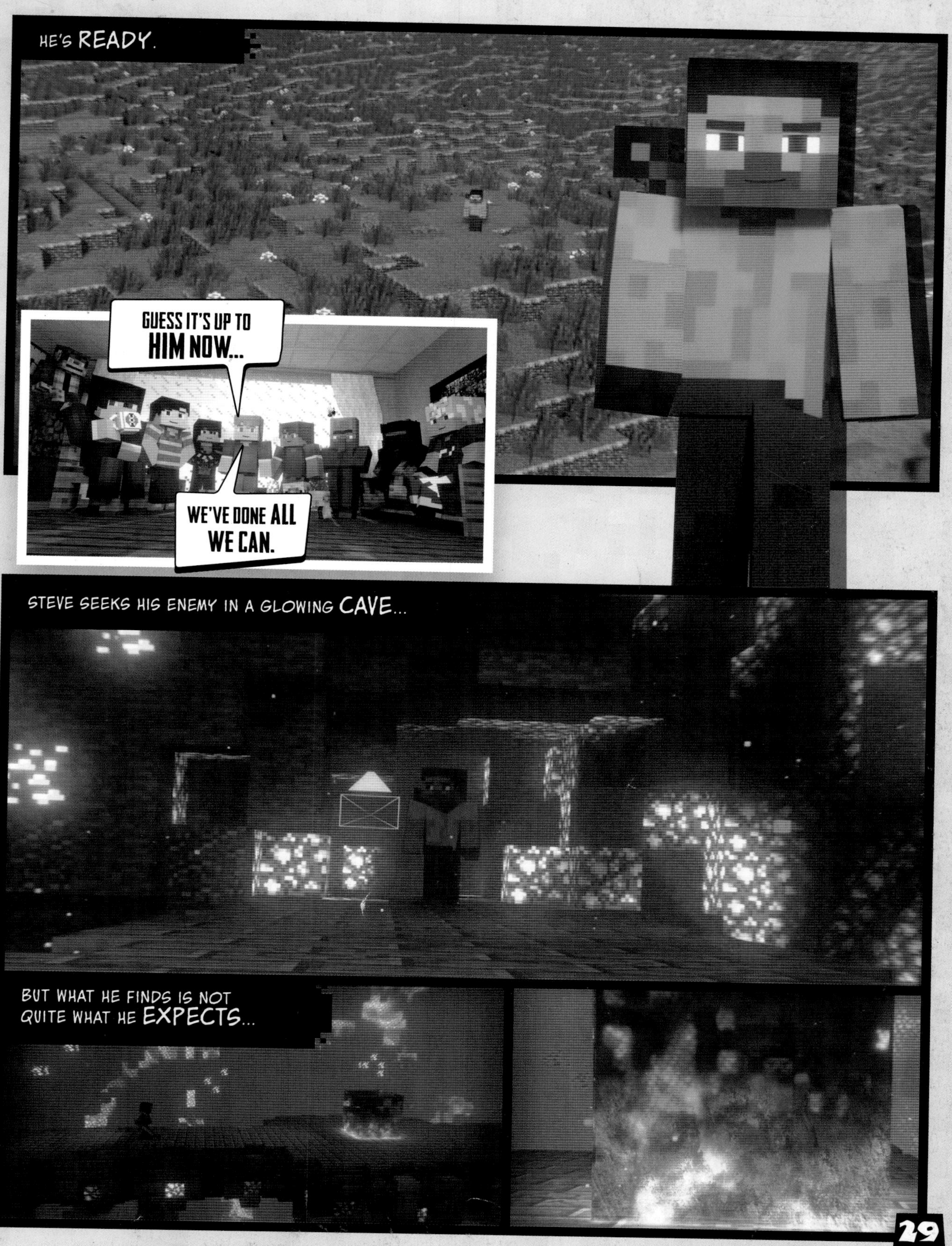

HE'S READY.
GUESS IT'S UP TO HIM NOW...
WE'VE DONE ALL WE CAN.
STEVE SEEKS HIS ENEMY IN A GLOWING CAVE...
BUT WHAT HE FINDS IS NOT QUITE WHAT HE EXPECTS...

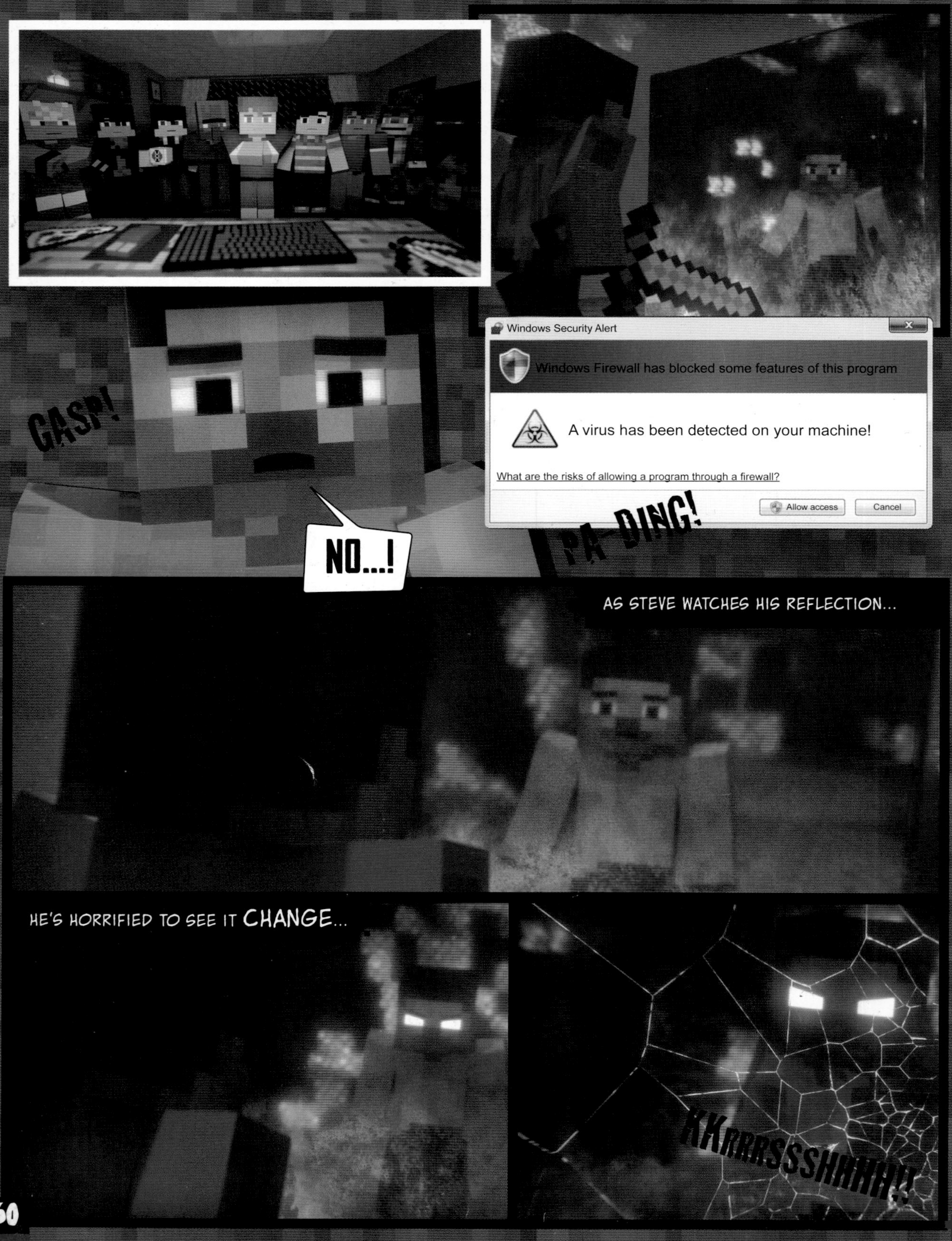
GASP!
NO...!
Windows Security Alert
Windows Firewall has blocked some features of this program
A virus has been detected on your machine!
What are the risks of allowing a program through a firewall?
Allow access
Cancel
PA-DING!
AS STEVE WATCHES HIS REFLECTION...
HE'S HORRIFIED TO SEE IT CHANGE...
KKRRRSSSHHHH!!

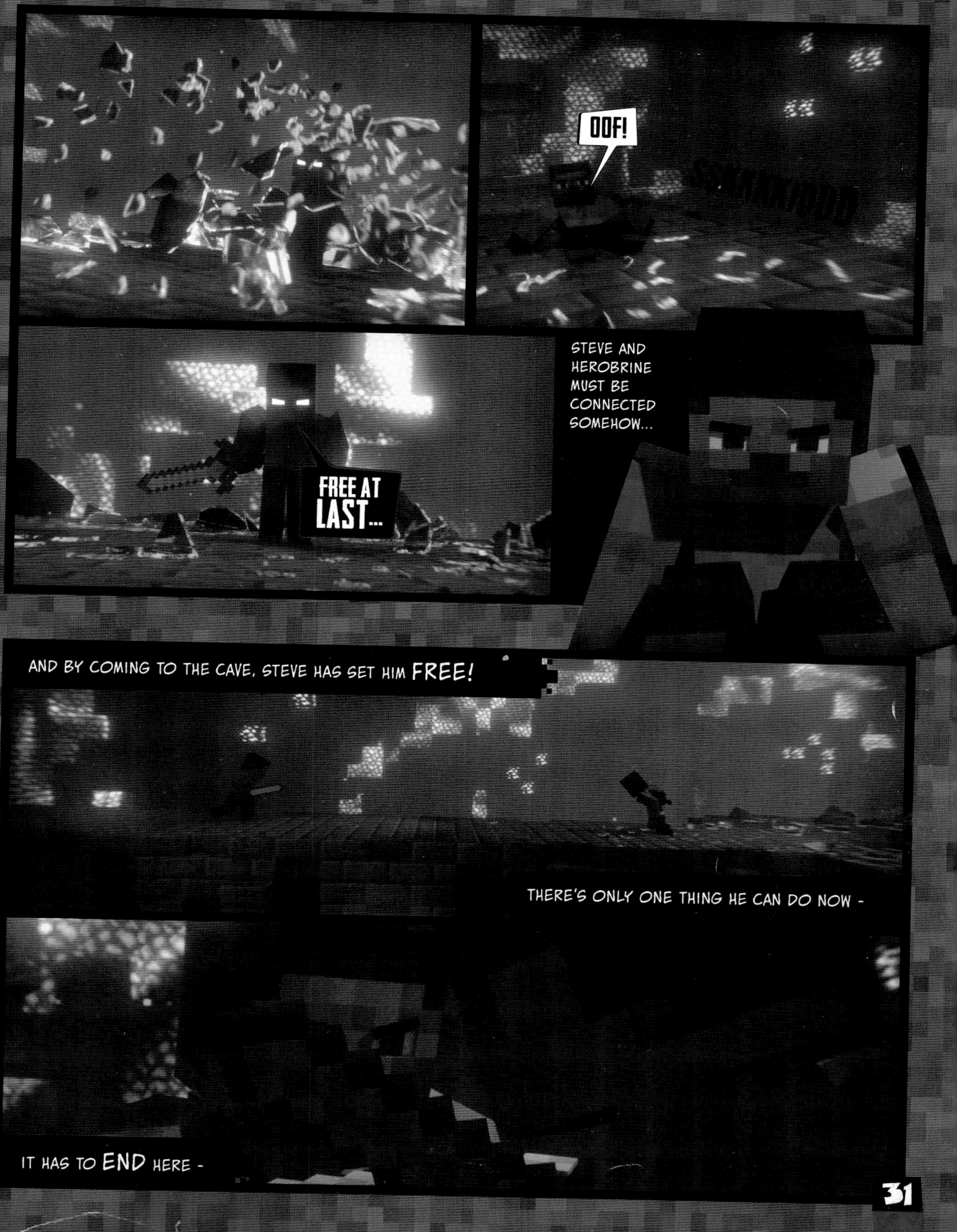
OOF!
STEVE AND HEROBRINE MUST BE CONNECTED SOMEHOW...
FREE AT LAST...
AND BY COMING TO THE CAVE, STEVE HAS SET HIM FREE!
THERE'S ONLY ONE THING HE CAN DO NOW -
IT HAS TO END HERE -

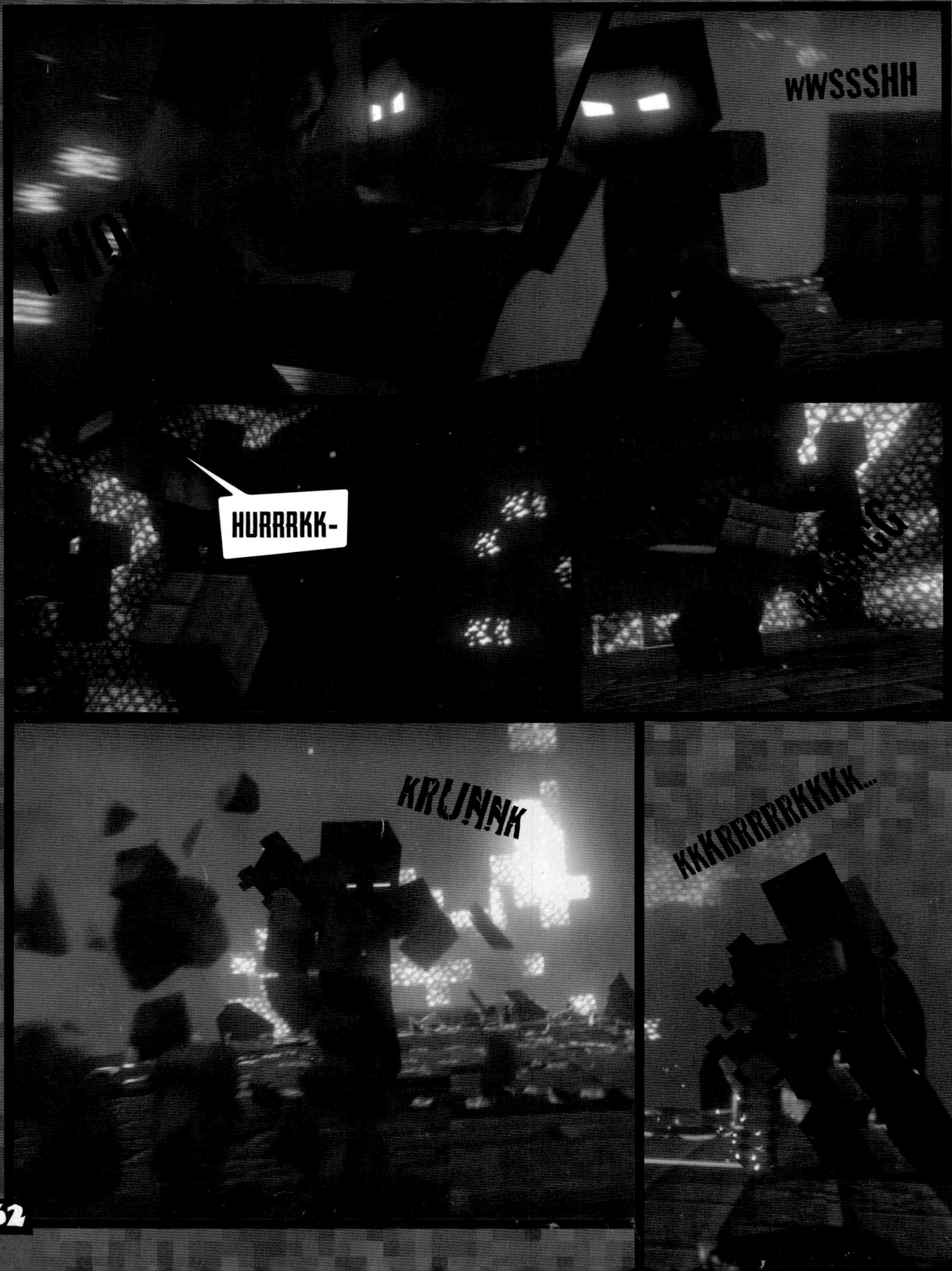
WWSSSHH
HURRRKK-
KRUNNK
KKKRRRRRKKKK...

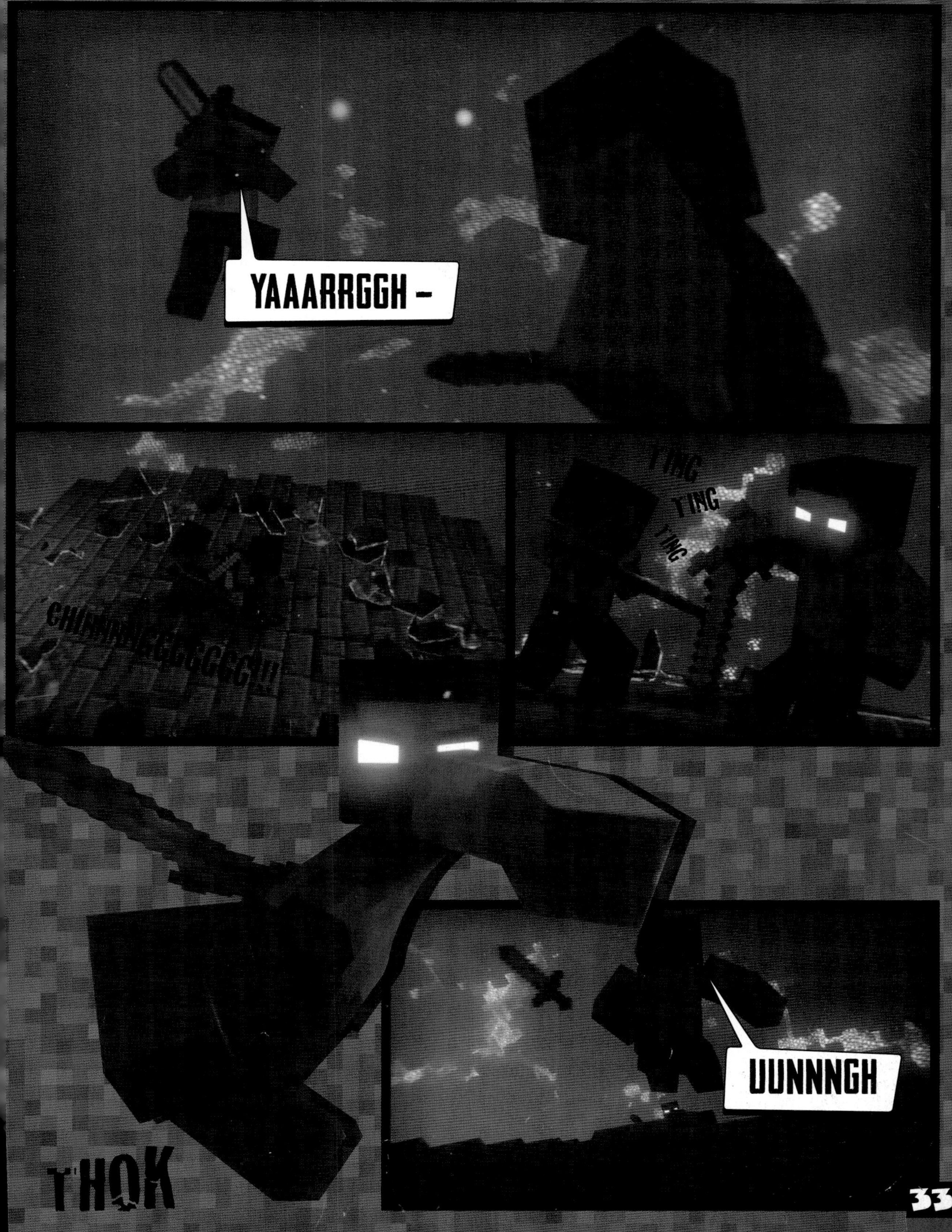
YAAARRGGH –
TING
UUNNNGH
THOK

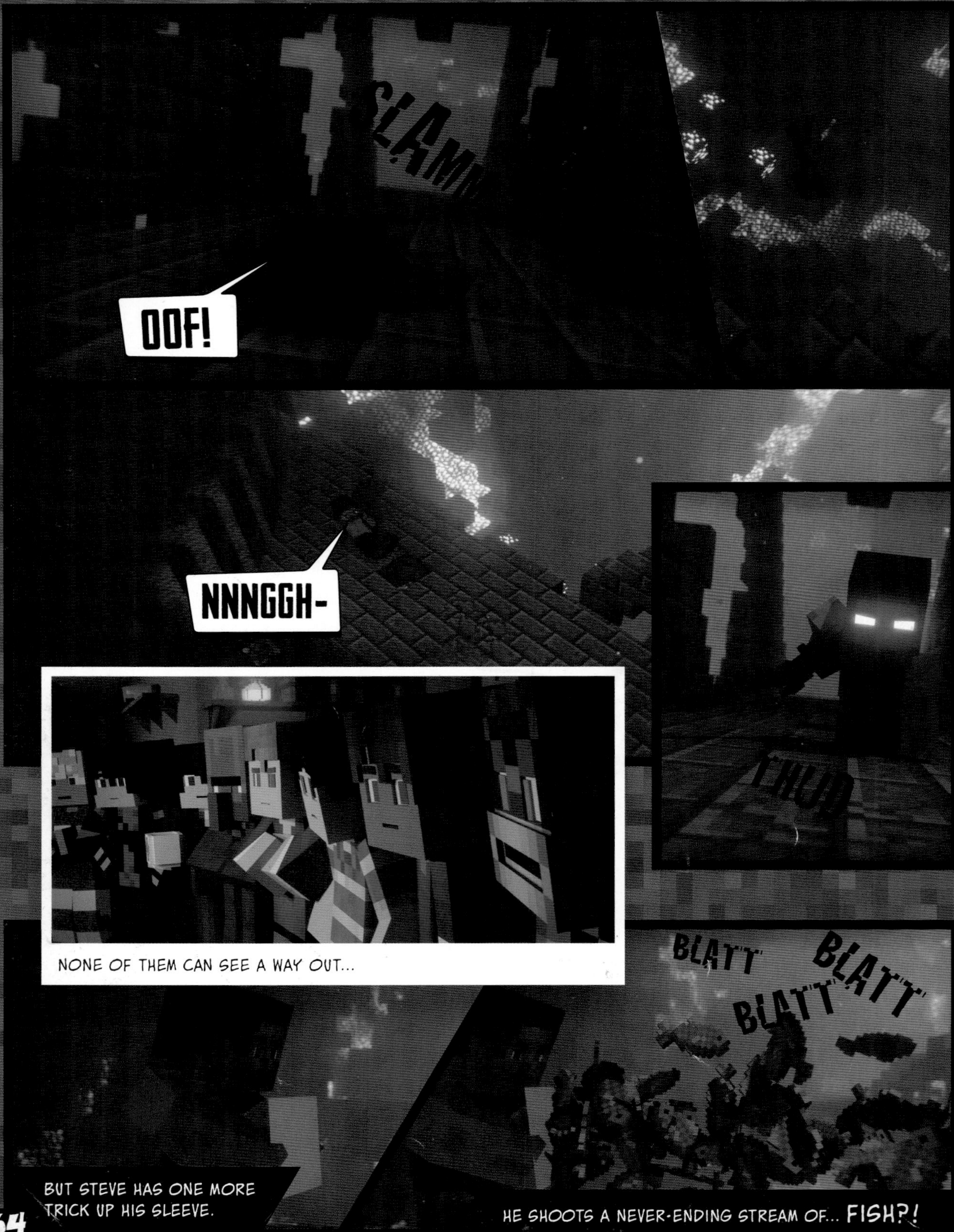

SLAM
OOF!
NNNGGH-
THUD
NONE OF THEM CAN SEE A WAY OUT...
BLATT
BLATT
BLATT
BUT STEVE HAS ONE MORE TRICK UP HIS SLEEVE.
HE SHOOTS A NEVER-ENDING STREAM OF... FISH?!

UNFORTUNATELY IT'LL TAKE MORE THAN FISH TO STOP HEROBRINE...

BLATT BLATT

OR WILL IT...?

THE FISH START TO PILE UP...

STOMP

SYSTEM RESOURCES PING

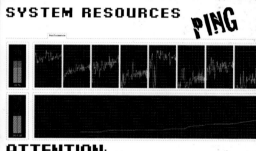

ATTENTION:
TOO MANY OBJECTS IN WORLD

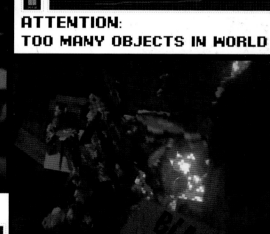

BLATT BLATT

HEROBRINE KEEPS COMING -
BUT SO DO THE FISH... UNTIL SUDDENLY -

WARNING! CRASH IMMINENT!

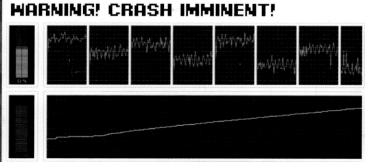

DONG DDDONG DONG

35

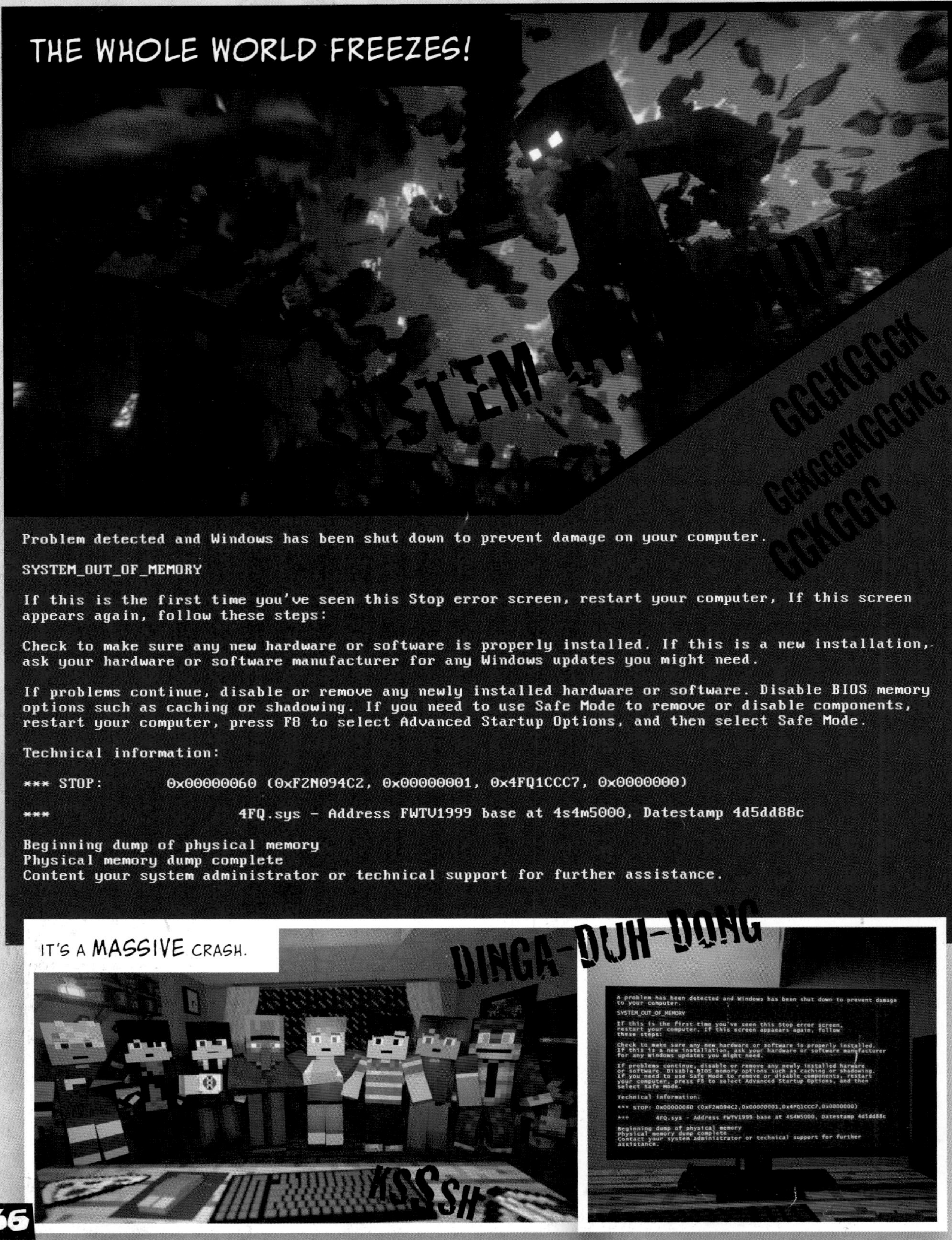
THE WHOLE WORLD FREEZES!
SYSTEM
GGGKGGGK
GGKGGGKGGGKG
GGKGGG
Problem detected and Windows has been shut down to prevent damage on your computer.
SYSTEM_OUT_OF_MEMORY
If this is the first time you've seen this Stop error screen, restart your computer, If this screen appears again, follow these steps:
Check to make sure any new hardware or software is properly installed. If this is a new installation, ask your hardware or software manufacturer for any Windows updates you might need.
If problems continue, disable or remove any newly installed hardware or software. Disable BIOS memory options such as caching or shadowing. If you need to use Safe Mode to remove or disable components, restart your computer, press F8 to select Advanced Startup Options, and then select Safe Mode.
Technical information:
*** STOP: 0x00000060 (0xF2N094C2, 0x00000001, 0x4FQ1CCC7, 0x0000000)
*** 4FQ.sys - Address FWTV1999 base at 4s4m5000, Datestamp 4d5dd88c
Beginning dump of physical memory
Physical memory dump complete
Content your system administrator or technical support for further assistance.
IT'S A MASSIVE CRASH.
DINGA-DUH-DONG
KSSSH

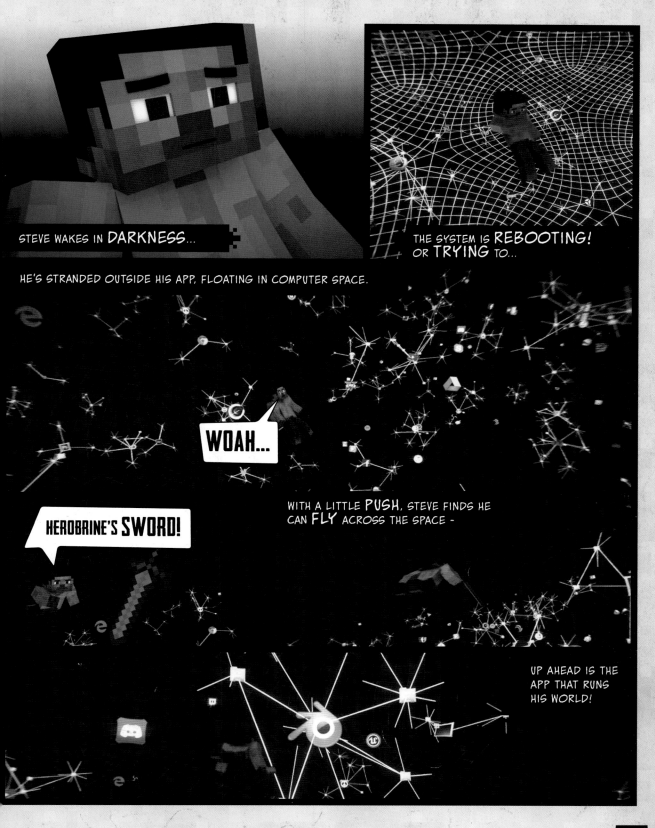

STEVE WAKES IN **DARKNESS**...

THE SYSTEM IS **REBOOTING!** OR **TRYING** TO...

HE'S STRANDED OUTSIDE HIS APP, FLOATING IN COMPUTER SPACE.

WOAH...

HEROBRINE'S SWORD!

WITH A LITTLE **PUSH**, STEVE FINDS HE CAN **FLY** ACROSS THE SPACE –

UP AHEAD IS THE APP THAT RUNS HIS WORLD!

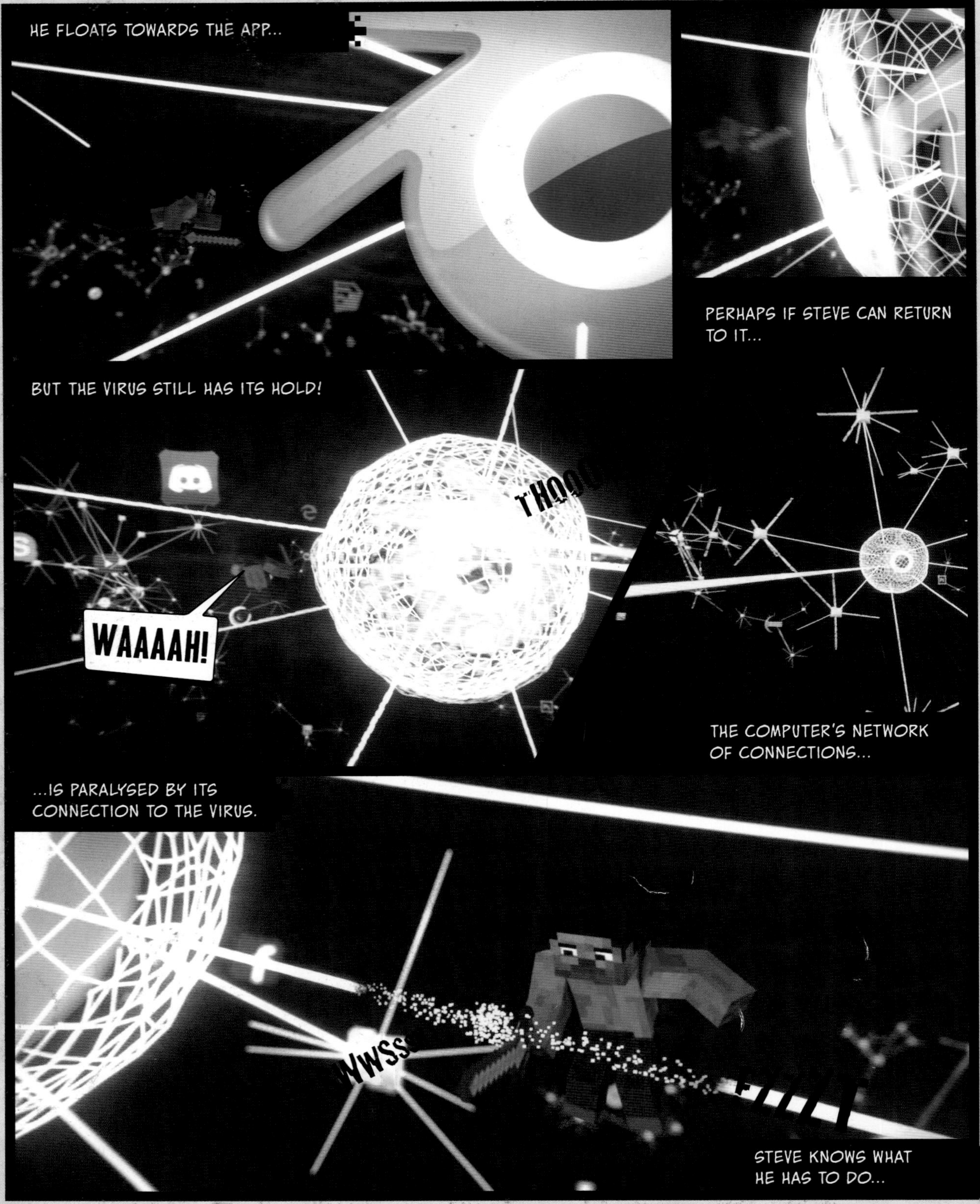
HE FLOATS TOWARDS THE APP...
PERHAPS IF STEVE CAN RETURN TO IT...
BUT THE VIRUS STILL HAS ITS HOLD!
WAAAAH!
THE COMPUTER'S NETWORK OF CONNECTIONS...
...IS PARALYSED BY ITS CONNECTION TO THE VIRUS.
STEVE KNOWS WHAT HE HAS TO DO...

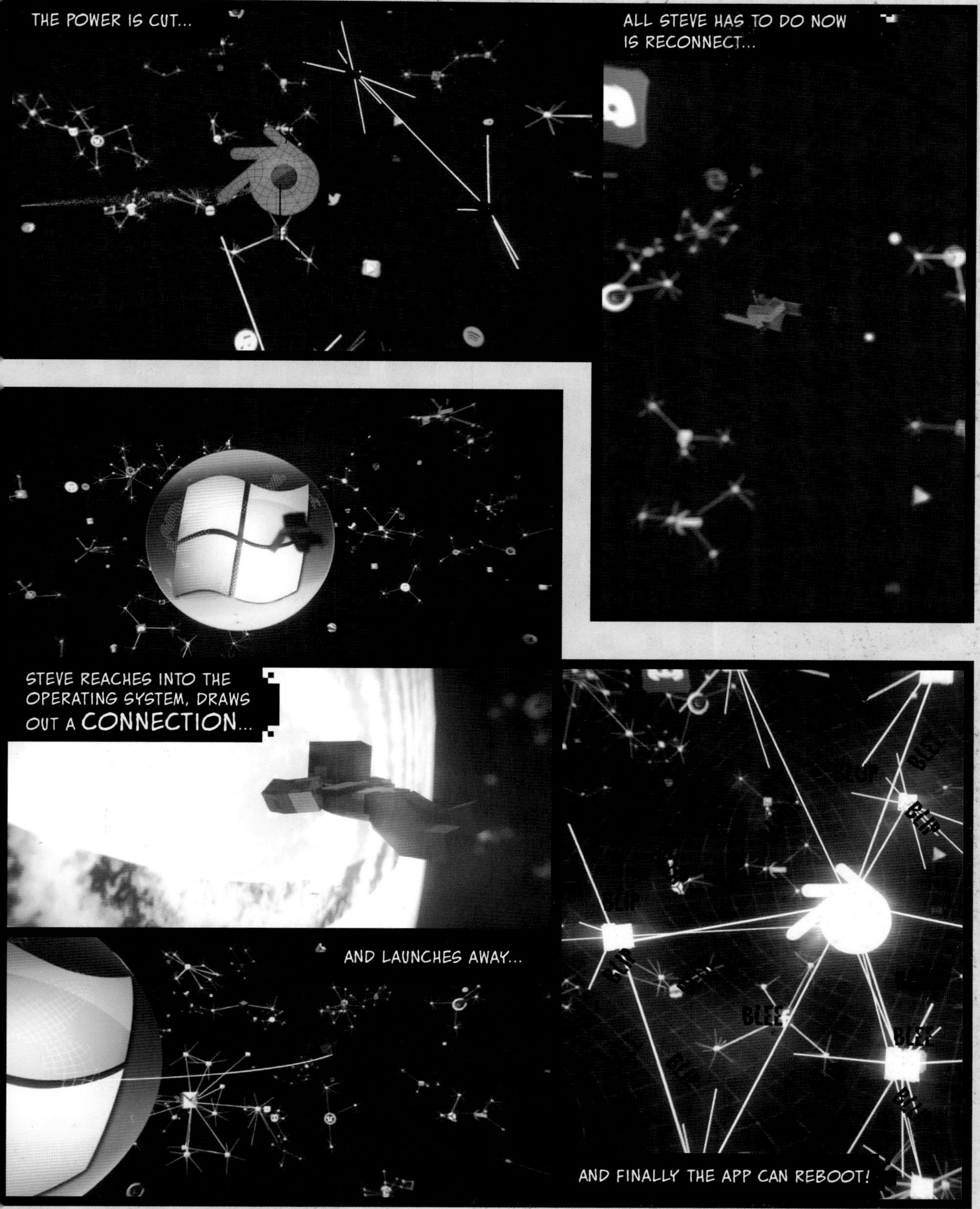
THE POWER IS CUT...
ALL STEVE HAS TO DO NOW IS RECONNECT...
STEVE REACHES INTO THE OPERATING SYSTEM, DRAWS OUT A CONNECTION...
AND LAUNCHES AWAY...
BLIP
BLEE
BLEE
AND FINALLY THE APP CAN REBOOT!

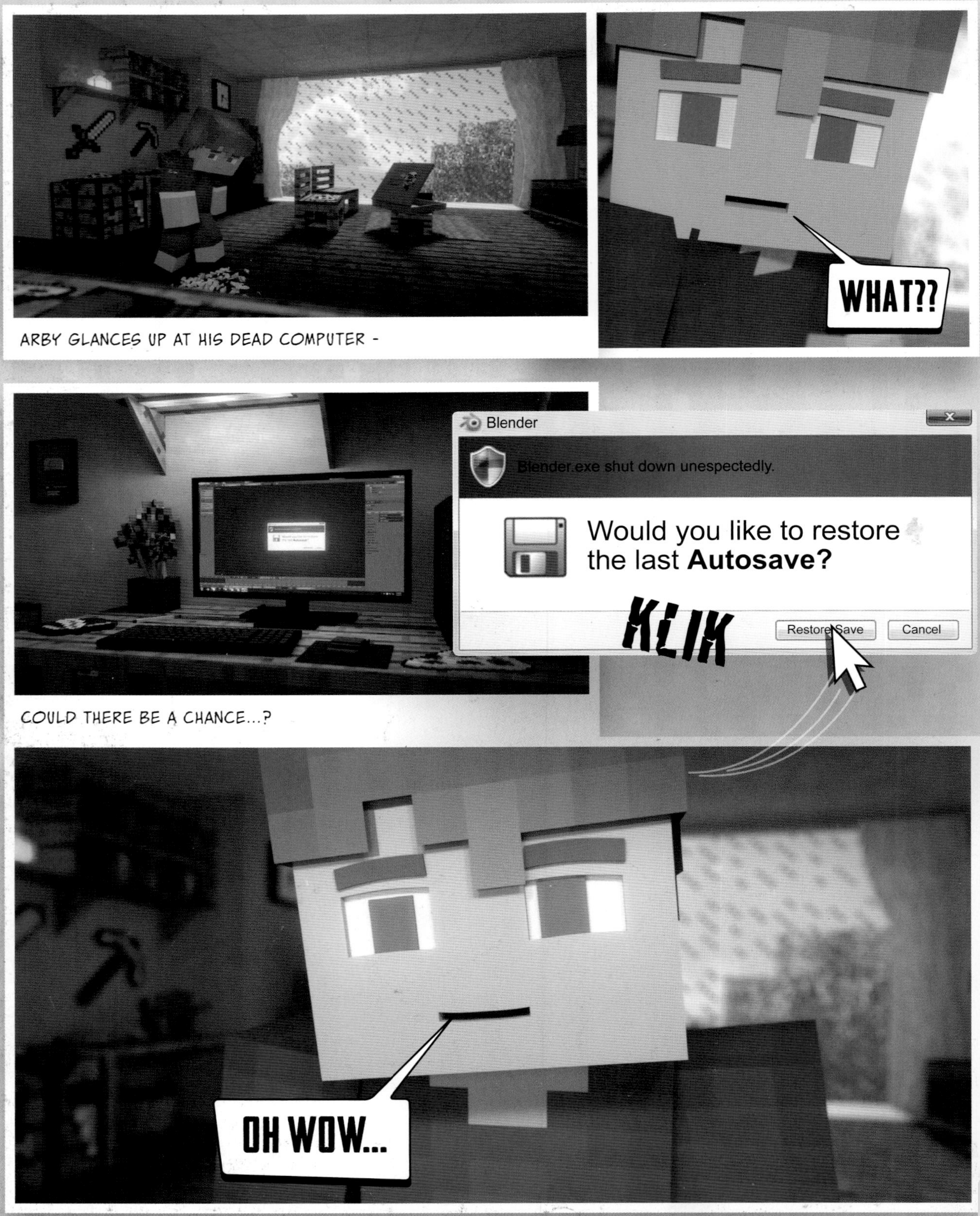
ARBY GLANCES UP AT HIS DEAD COMPUTER -
WHAT??
COULD THERE BE A CHANCE...?
Blender
Blender.exe shut down unespectedly.
Would you like to restore the last **Autosave?**
KLIK
Restore Save
Cancel
OH WOW...

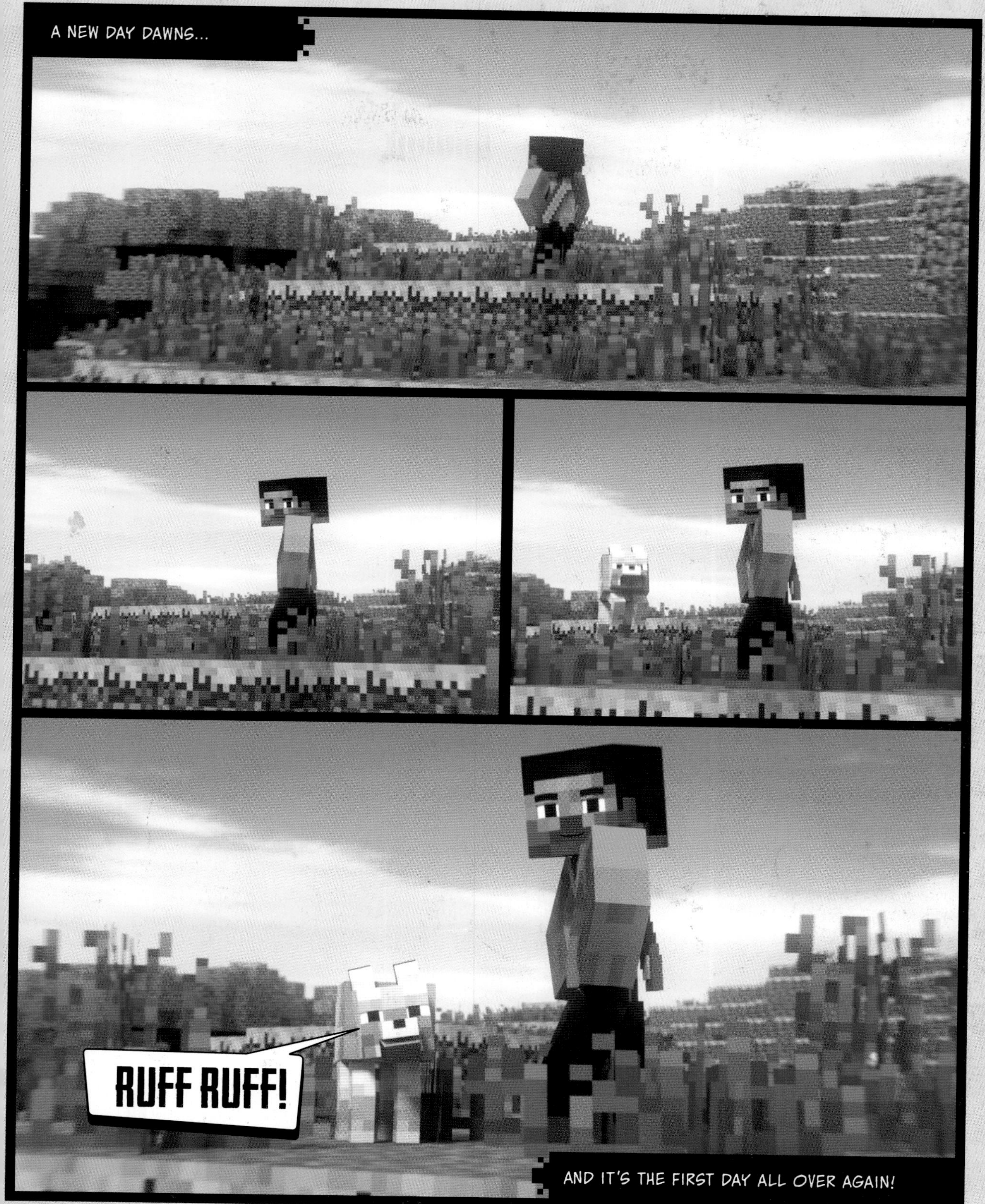
A NEW DAY DAWNS...
RUFF RUFF!
AND IT'S THE FIRST DAY ALL OVER AGAIN!

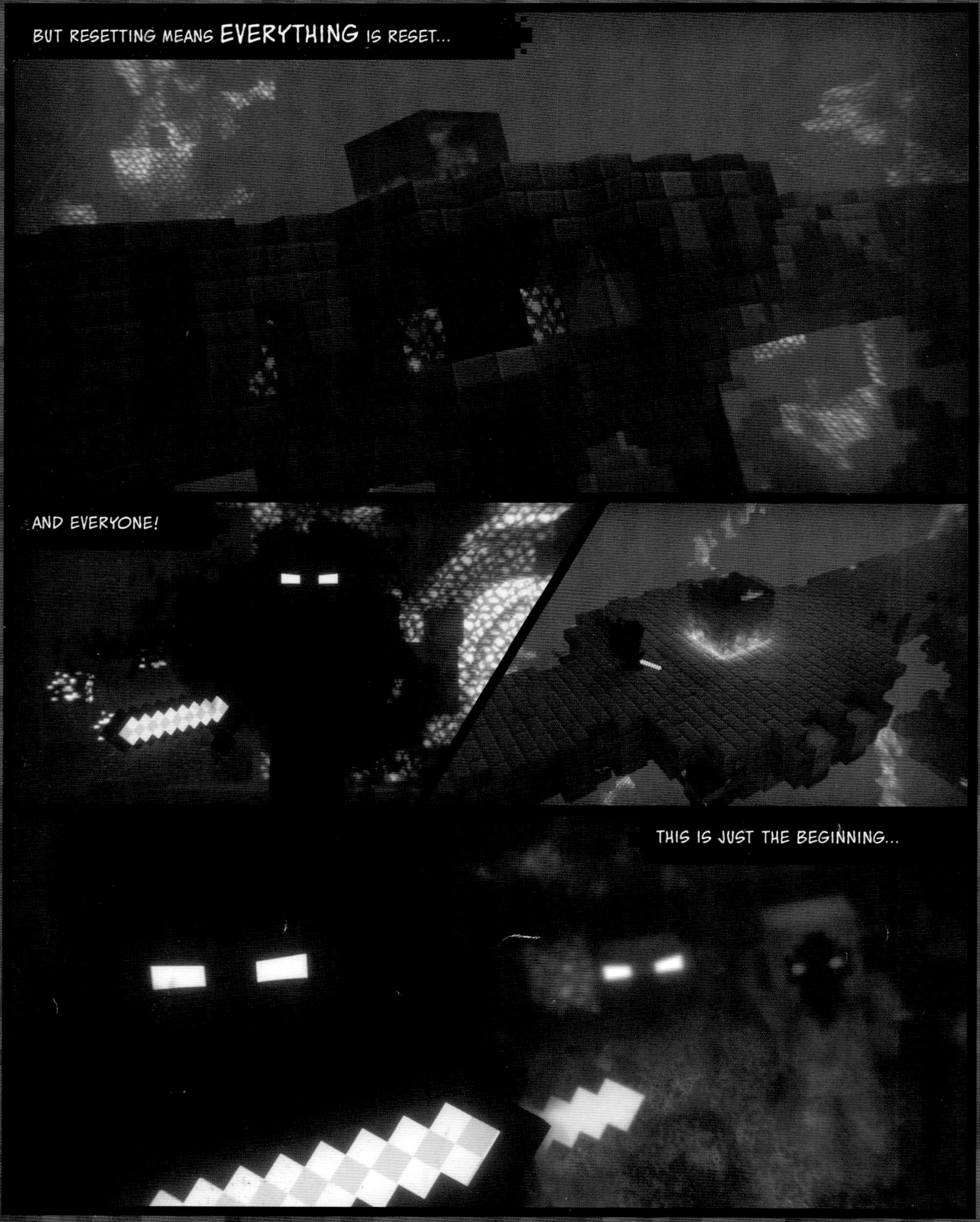
BUT RESETTING MEANS EVERYTHING IS RESET...
AND EVERYONE!
THIS IS JUST THE BEGINNING...

CHAPTER 3

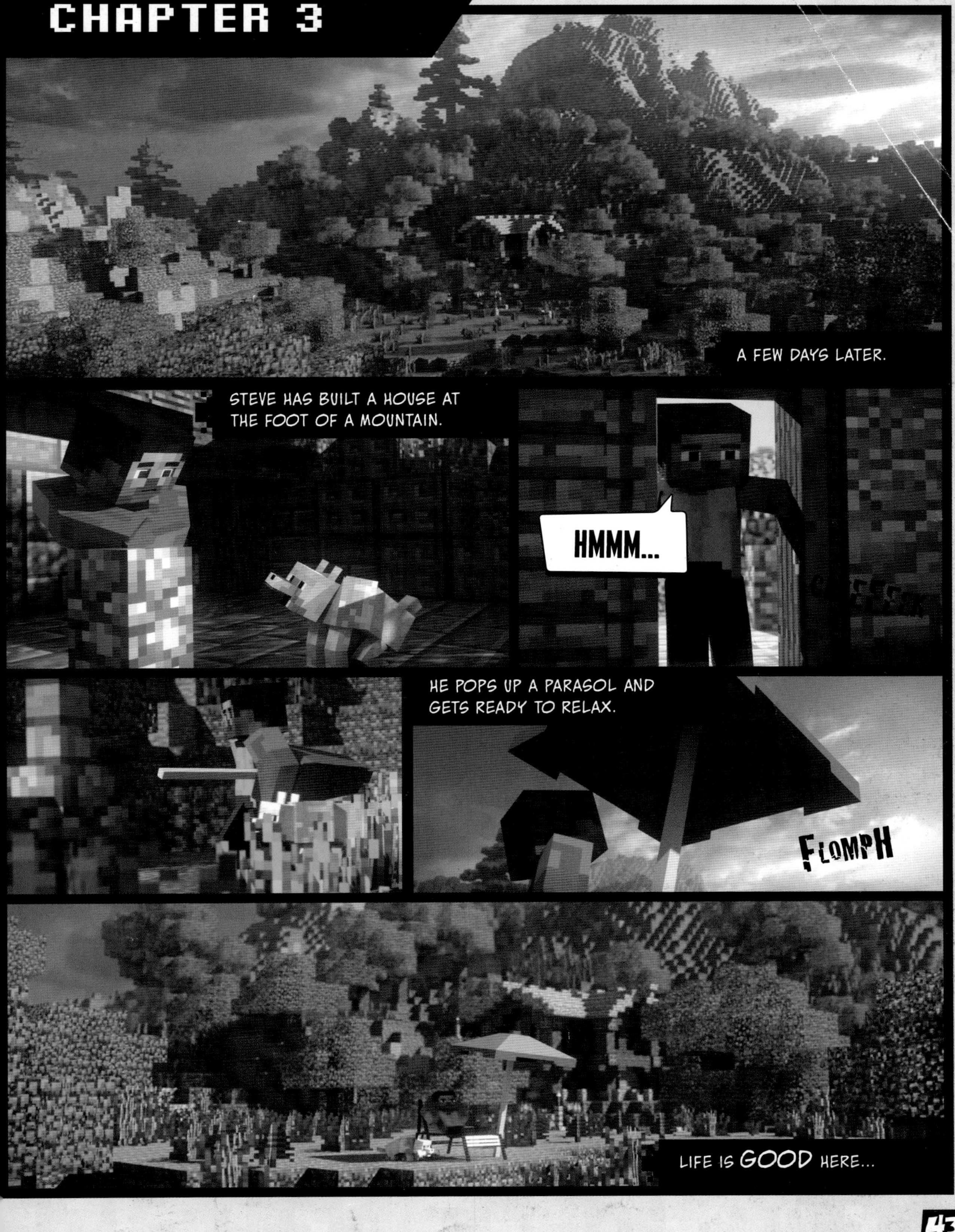
A FEW DAYS LATER.
STEVE HAS BUILT A HOUSE AT THE FOOT OF A MOUNTAIN.
HMMM...
HE POPS UP A PARASOL AND GETS READY TO RELAX.
FLOMPH
LIFE IS GOOD HERE...

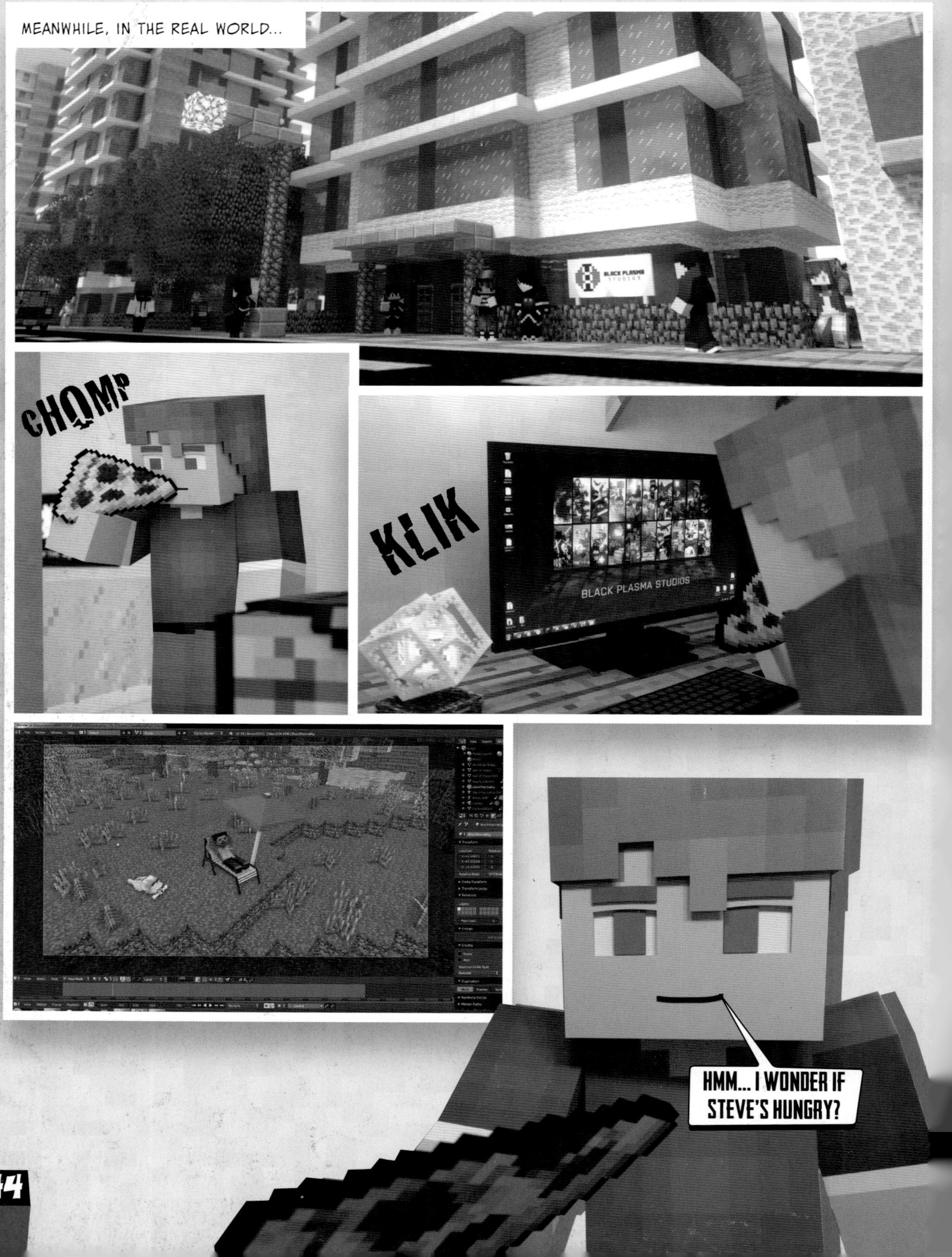

MEANWHILE, IN THE REAL WORLD...
BLACK PLASMA STUDIOS
CHOMP
KLIK
BLACK PLASMA STUDIOS
HMM... I WONDER IF STEVE'S HUNGRY?

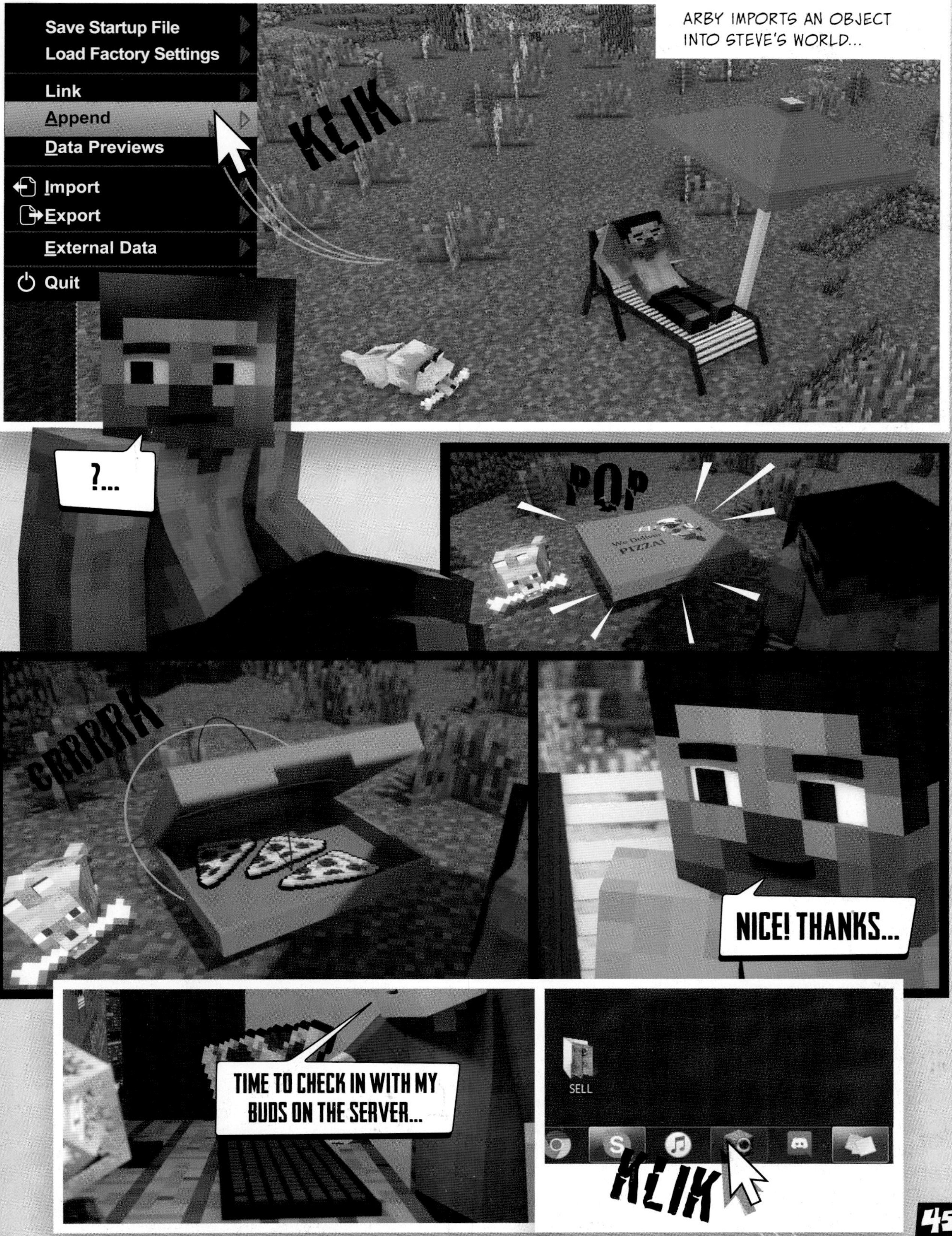
Save Startup File
Load Factory Settings
Link
Append
Data Previews
Import
Export
External Data
Quit
ARBY IMPORTS AN OBJECT INTO STEVE'S WORLD...
KLIK
?...
POP
We Deliver PIZZA!
GRRRRK
NICE! THANKS...
TIME TO CHECK IN WITH MY BUDS ON THE SERVER...
SELL
KLIK

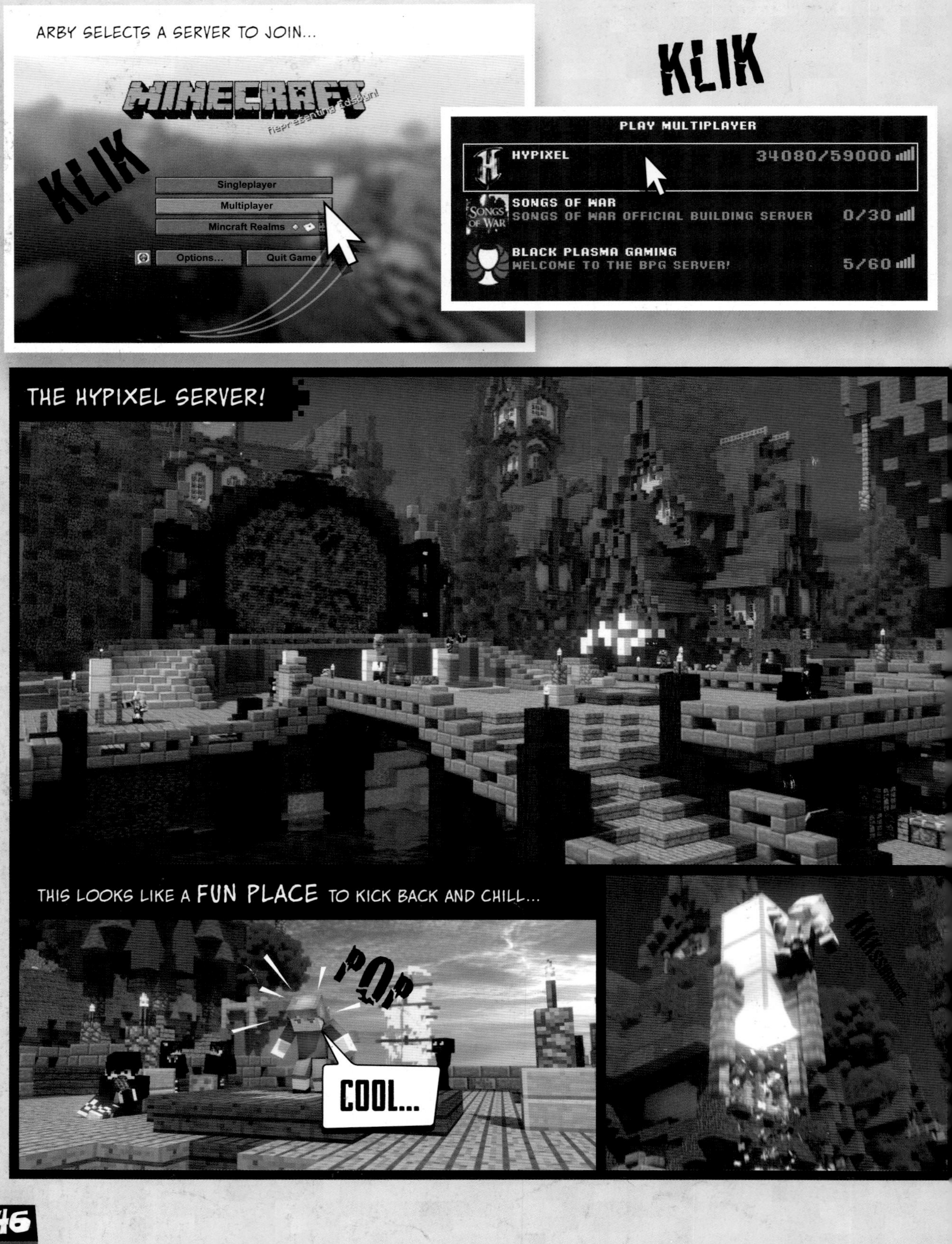
ARBY SELECTS A SERVER TO JOIN...
MINECRAFT
KLIK
Singleplayer
Multiplayer
Mincraft Realms
Options...
Quit Game
KLIK
PLAY MULTIPLAYER
HYPIXEL 34080/59000
SONGS OF WAR
SONGS OF WAR OFFICIAL BUILDING SERVER 0/30
BLACK PLASMA GAMING
WELCOME TO THE BPG SERVER! 5/60
THE HYPIXEL SERVER!
THIS LOOKS LIKE A FUN PLACE TO KICK BACK AND CHILL...
POP
COOL...

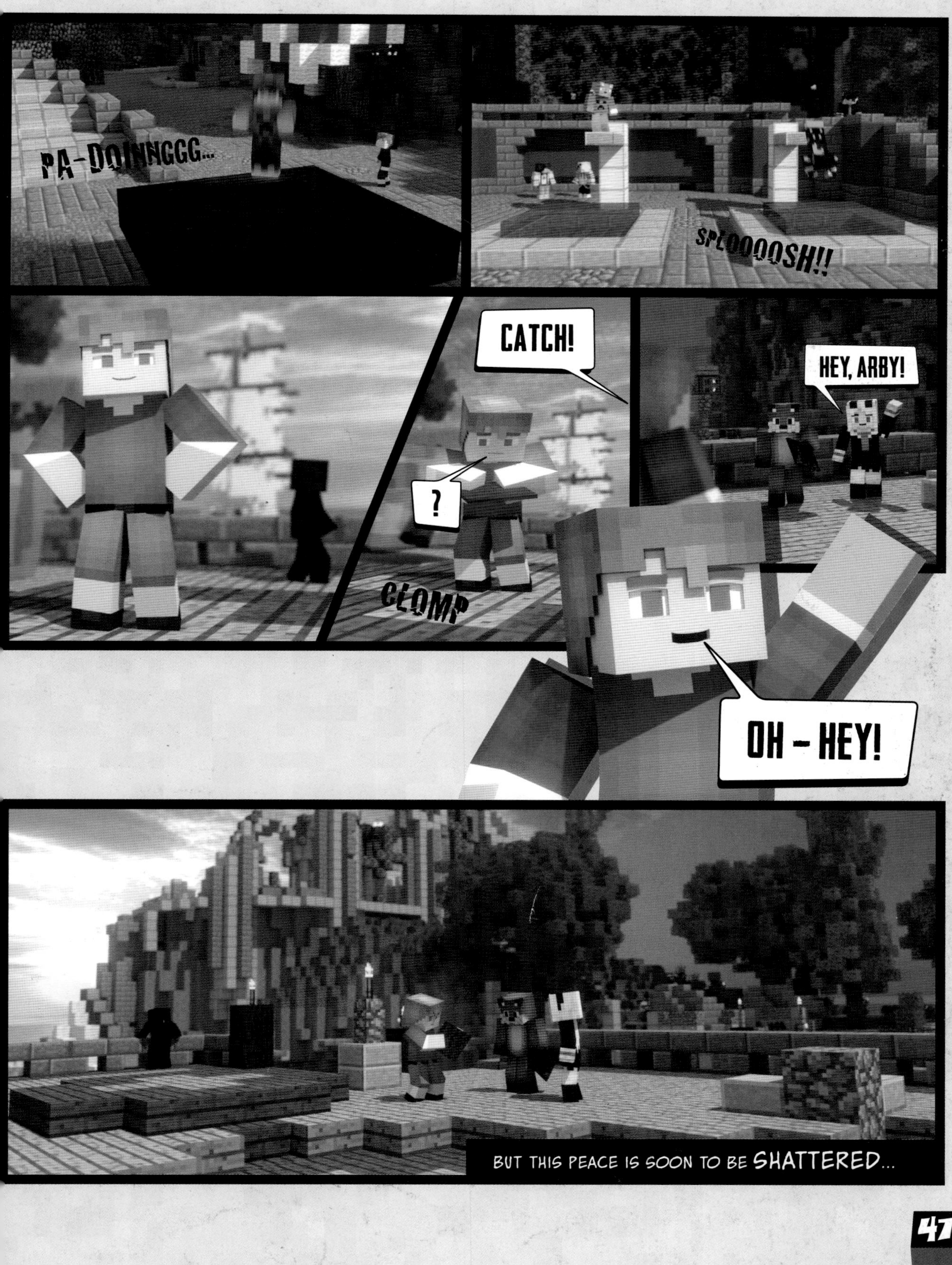

PA-DOINNGGG...
SPLOOOOOSH!!
CATCH!
?
CLOMP
HEY, ARBY!
OH – HEY!
BUT THIS PEACE IS SOON TO BE SHATTERED...

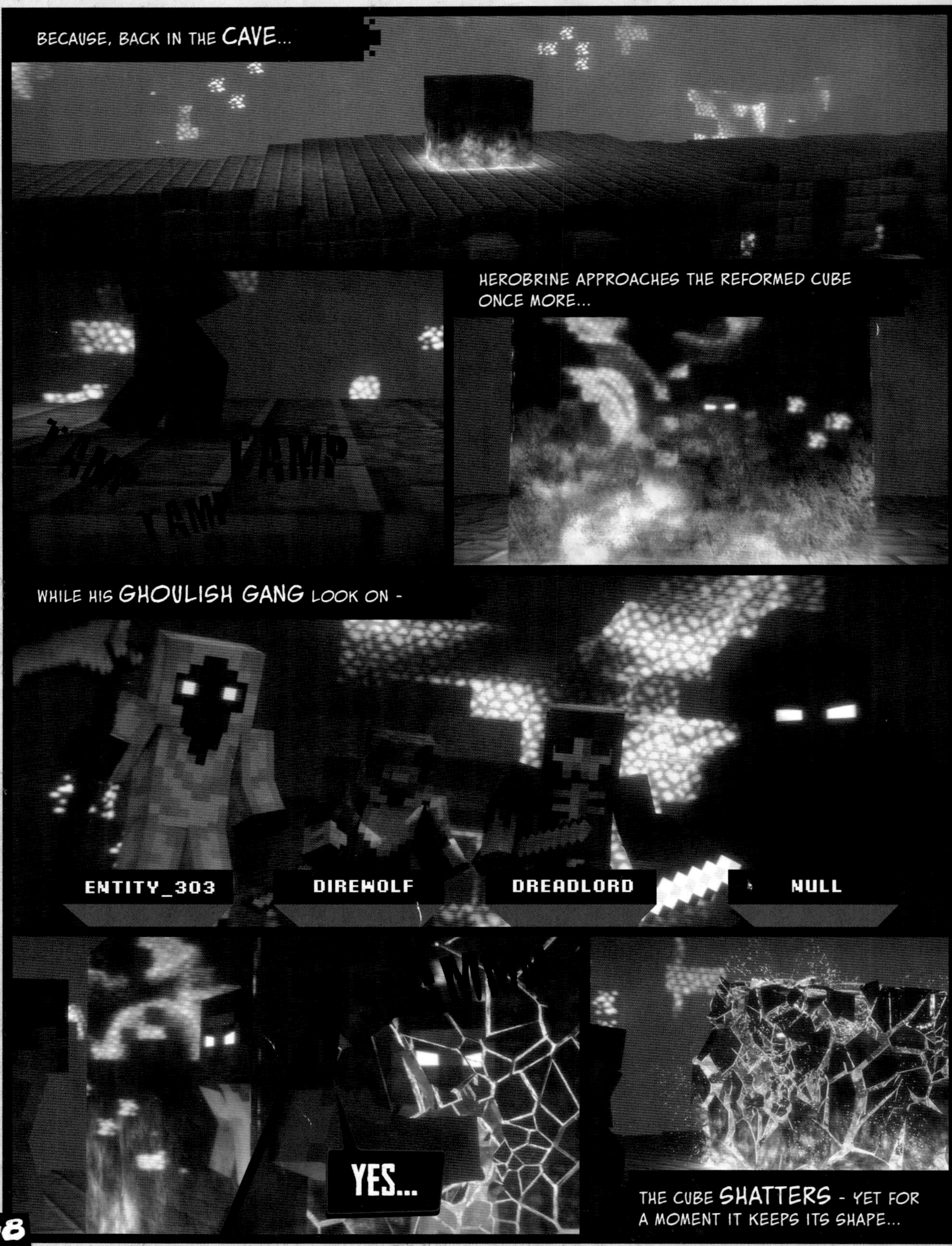
BECAUSE, BACK IN THE CAVE...
TAMP
TAMP
TAMP
HEROBRINE APPROACHES THE REFORMED CUBE ONCE MORE...
WHILE HIS GHOULISH GANG LOOK ON -
ENTITY_303
DIREWOLF
DREADLORD
NULL
YES...
THE CUBE SHATTERS - YET FOR A MOMENT IT KEEPS ITS SHAPE...

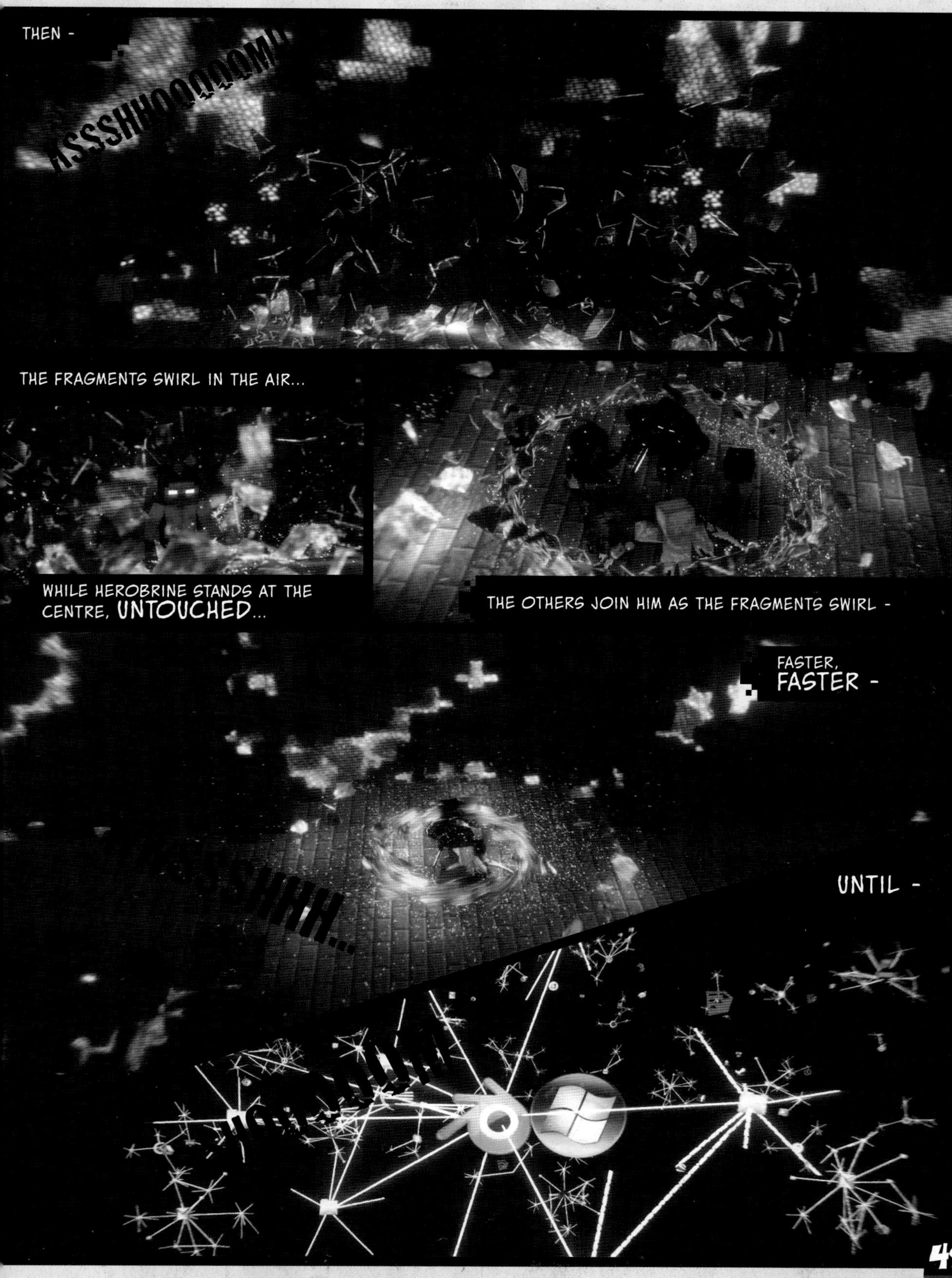
THEN -
THE FRAGMENTS SWIRL IN THE AIR...
WHILE HEROBRINE STANDS AT THE CENTRE, UNTOUCHED...
THE OTHERS JOIN HIM AS THE FRAGMENTS SWIRL -
FASTER, FASTER -
UNTIL -

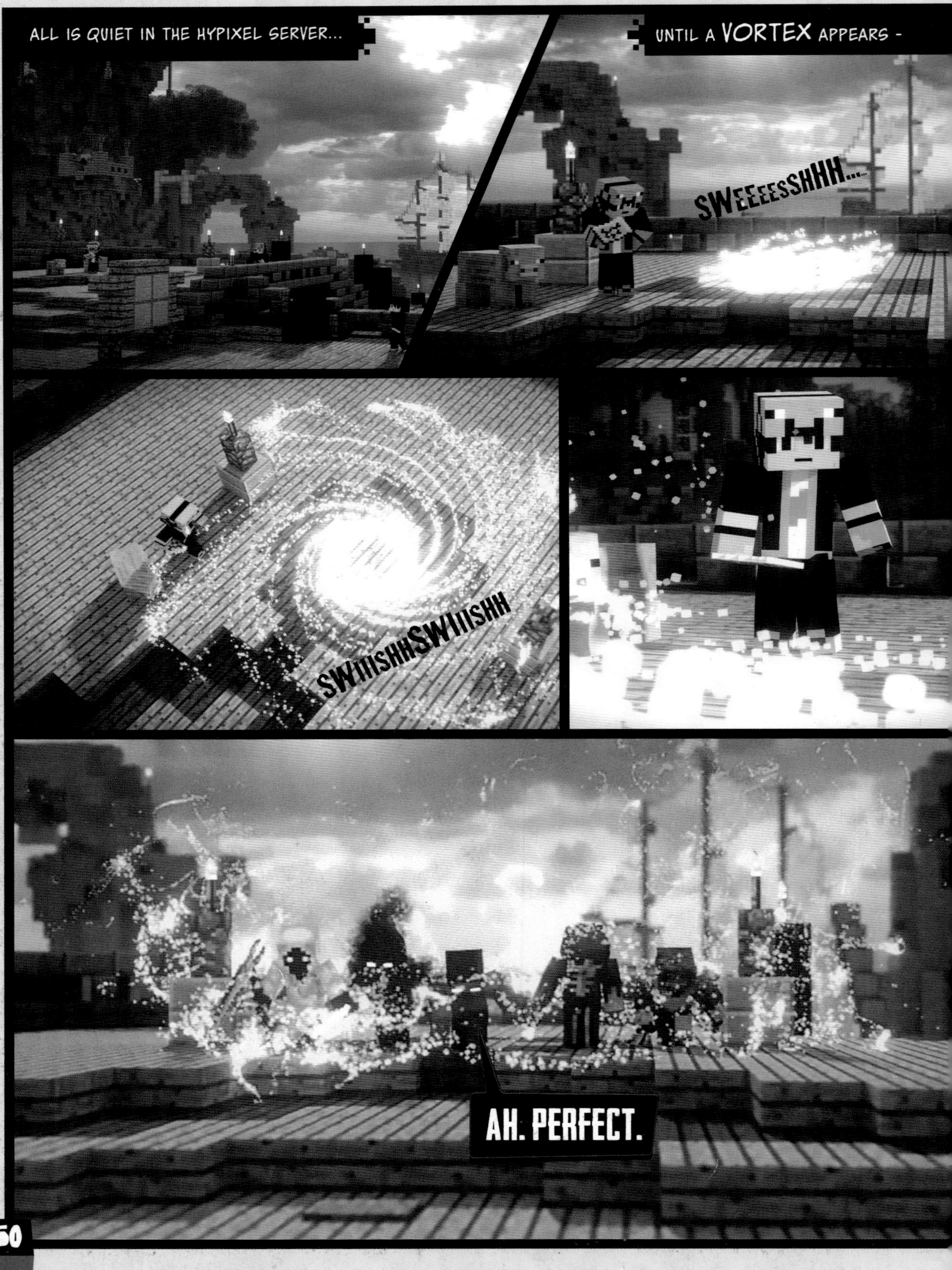
ALL IS QUIET IN THE HYPIXEL SERVER...
UNTIL A VORTEX APPEARS -
SWEEEEESSHHH.....
SWIIISHHSWIIISHH
AH. PERFECT.

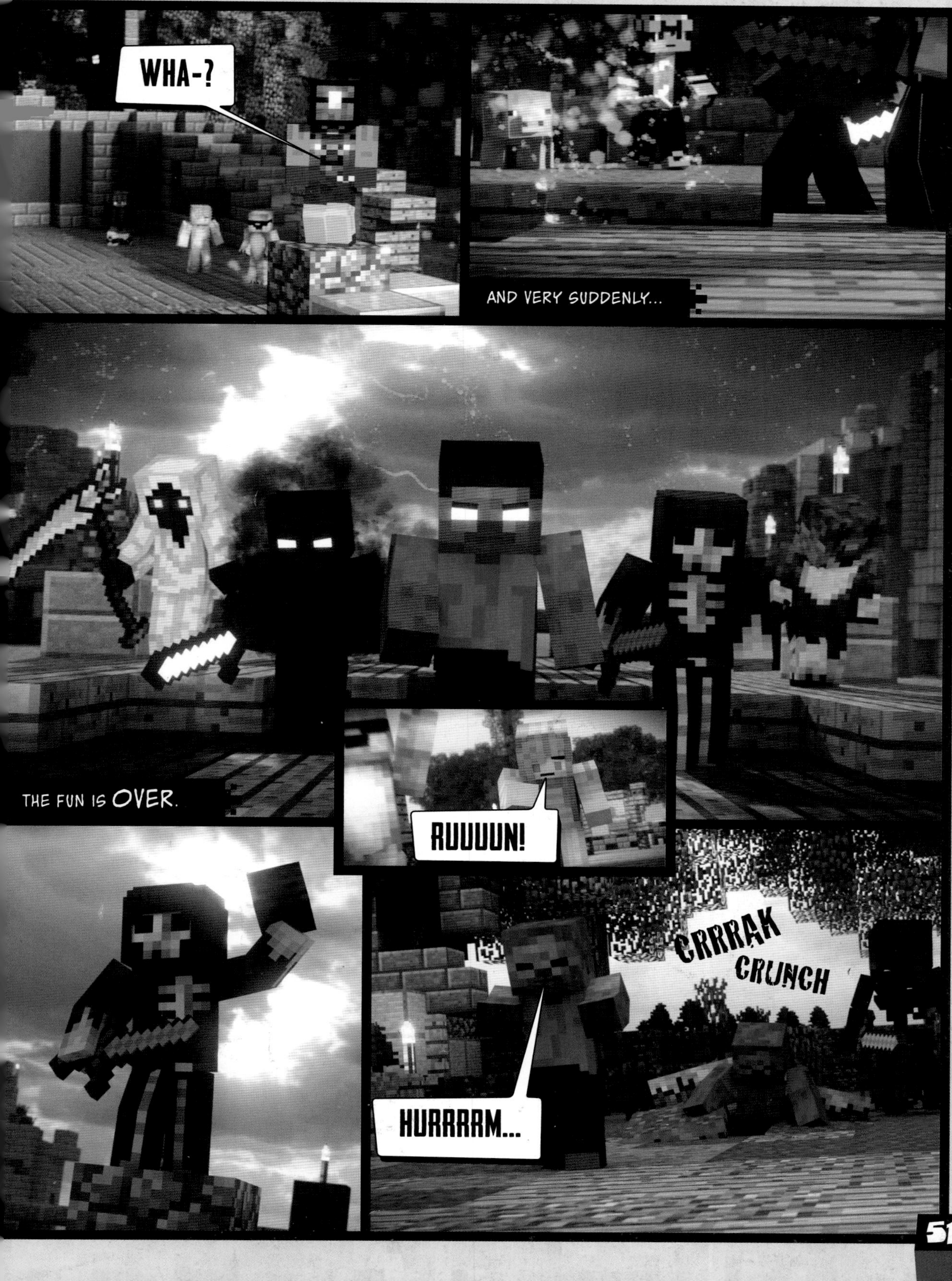
WHA-?
AND VERY SUDDENLY...
THE FUN IS OVER.
RUUUUN!
CRRRAK
CRUNCH
HURRRRM...

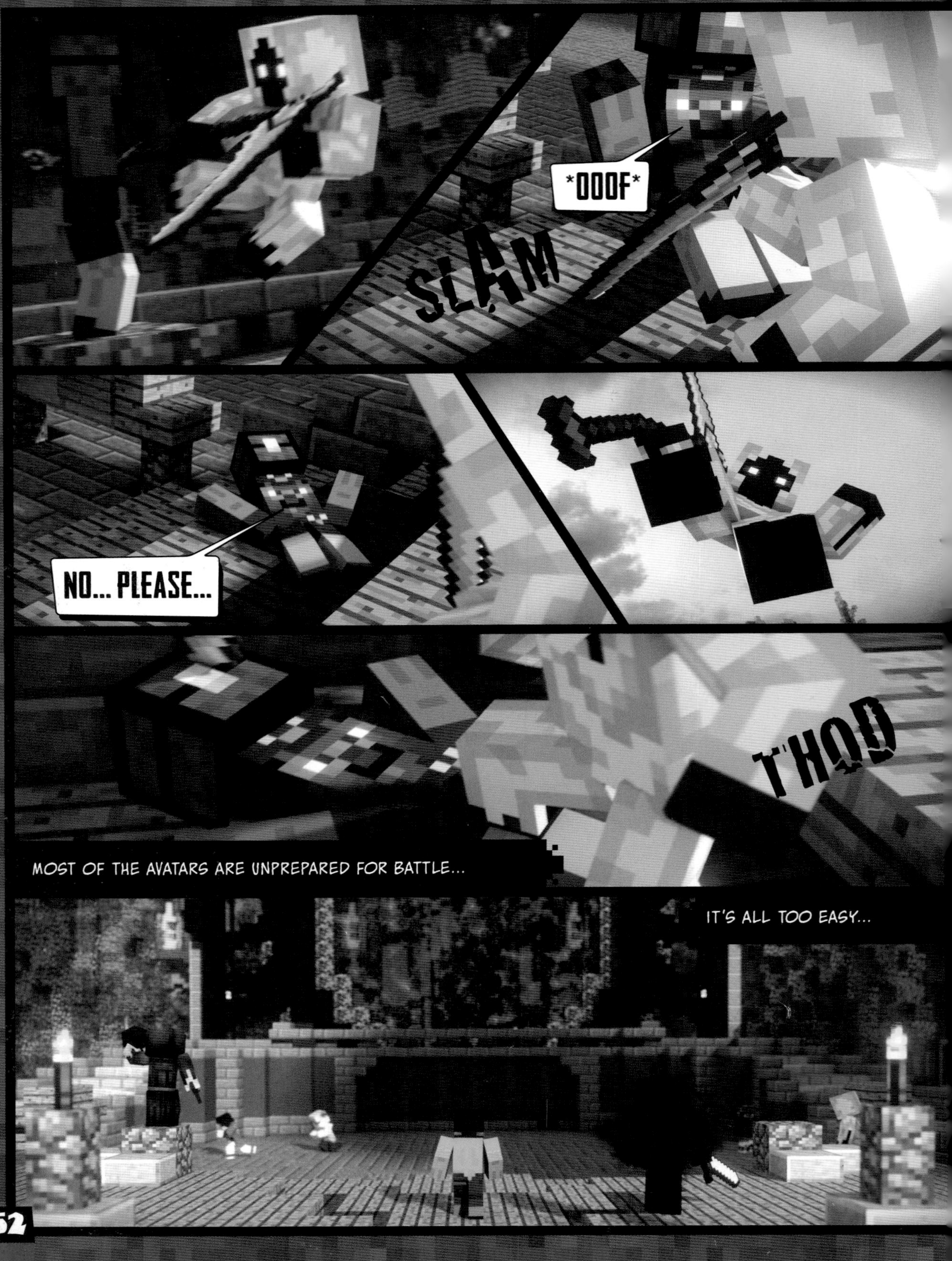

OOOF
SLAM
NO... PLEASE...
THOD
MOST OF THE AVATARS ARE UNPREPARED FOR BATTLE...
IT'S ALL TOO EASY...

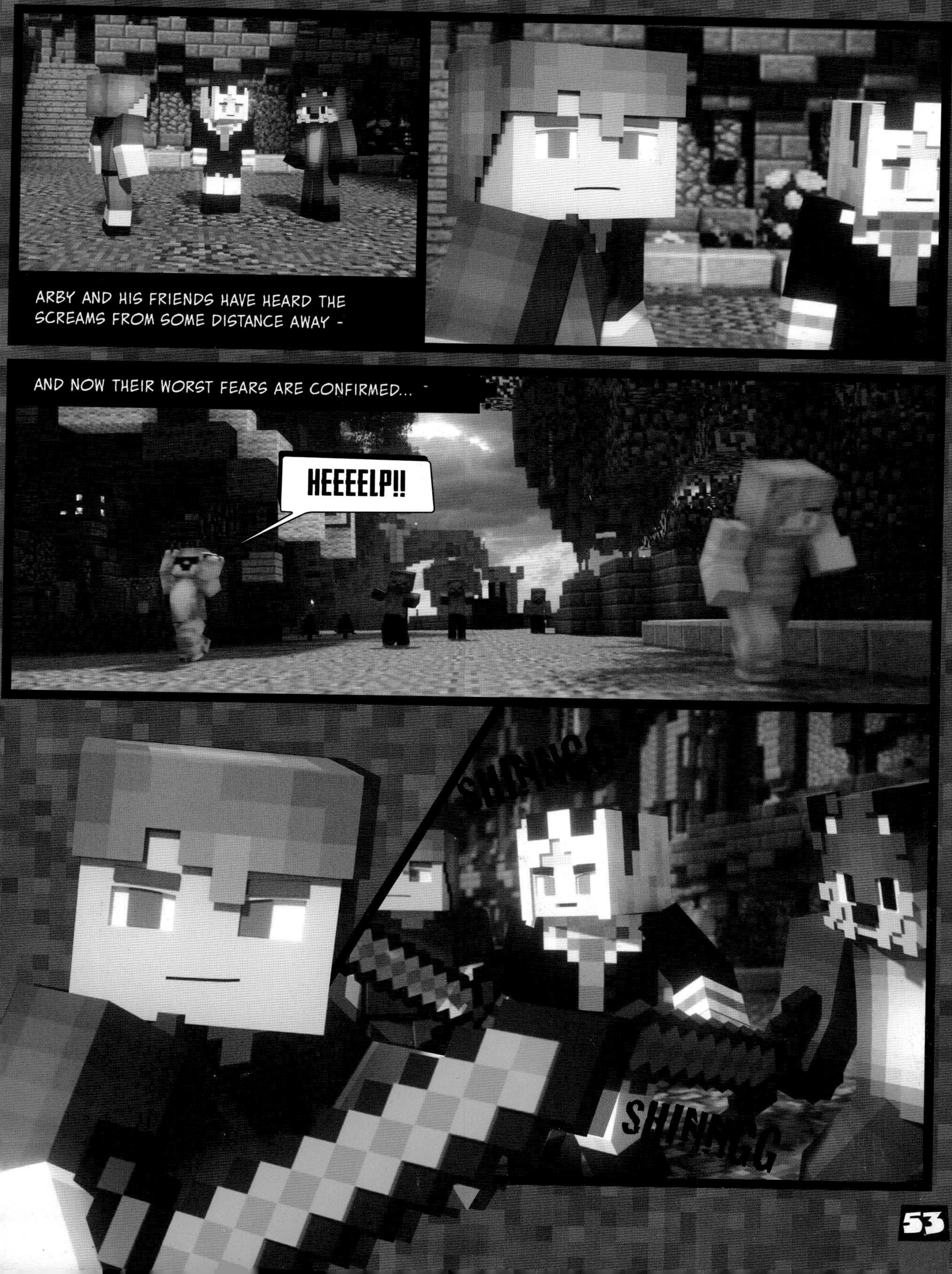
ARBY AND HIS FRIENDS HAVE HEARD THE SCREAMS FROM SOME DISTANCE AWAY -
AND NOW THEIR WORST FEARS ARE CONFIRMED...
HEEEELP!!
SHINNGG
SHINNGG

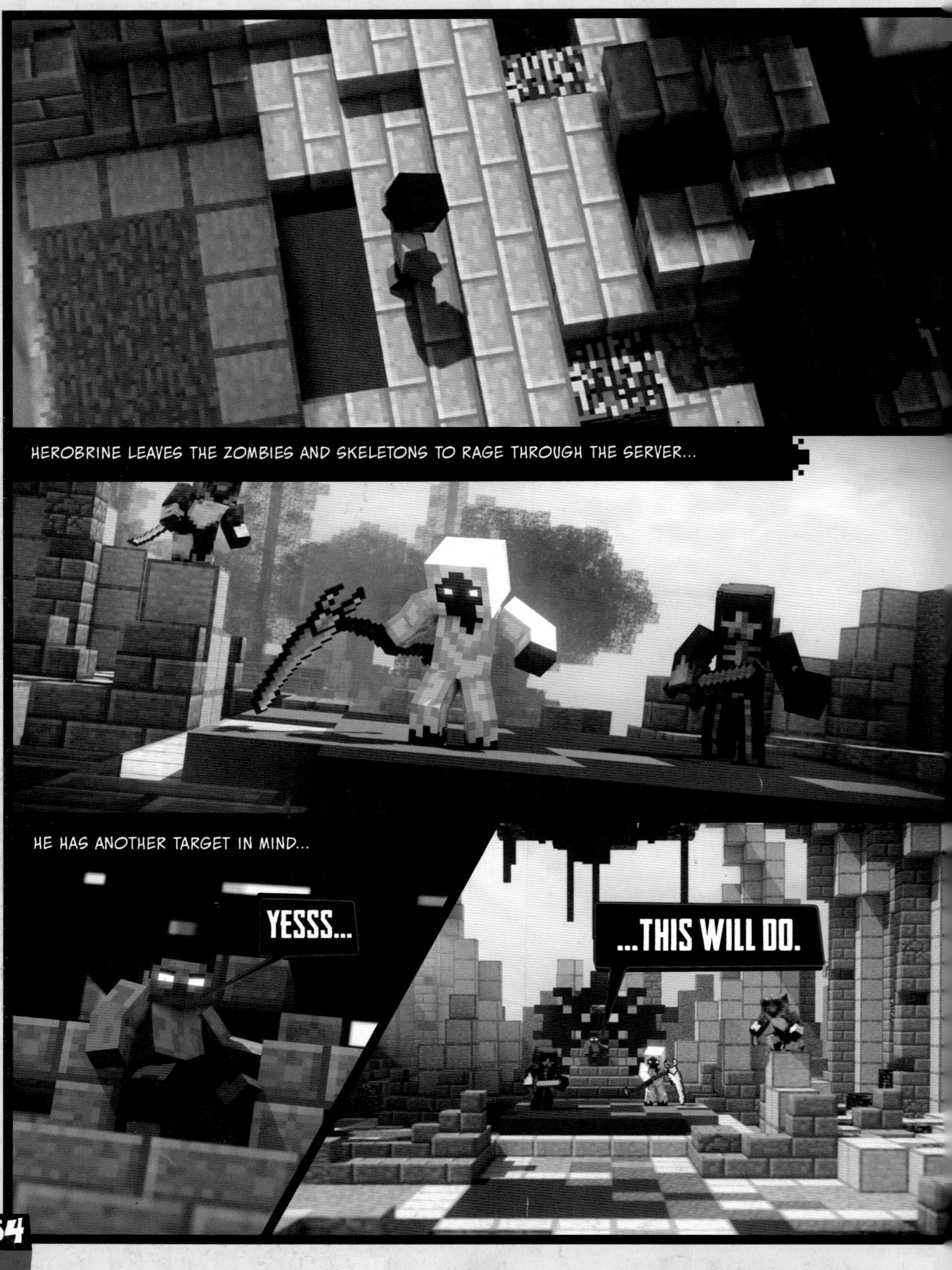
HEROBRINE LEAVES THE ZOMBIES AND SKELETONS TO RAGE THROUGH THE SERVER...
HE HAS ANOTHER TARGET IN MIND...
YESSS...
...THIS WILL DO.

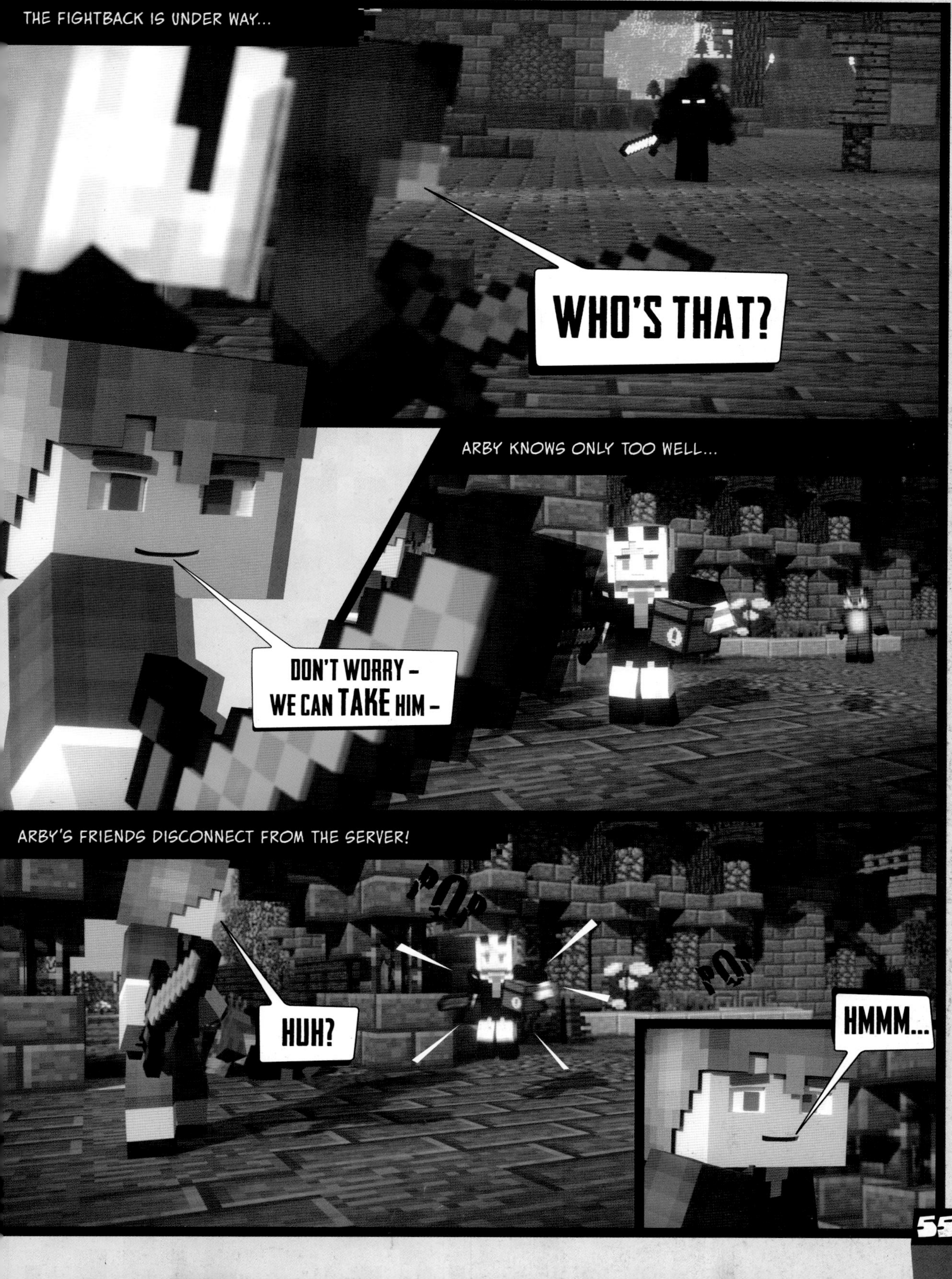
THE FIGHTBACK IS UNDER WAY...
WHO'S THAT?
ARBY KNOWS ONLY TOO WELL...
DON'T WORRY – WE CAN TAKE HIM –
ARBY'S FRIENDS DISCONNECT FROM THE SERVER!
HUH?
HMMM...

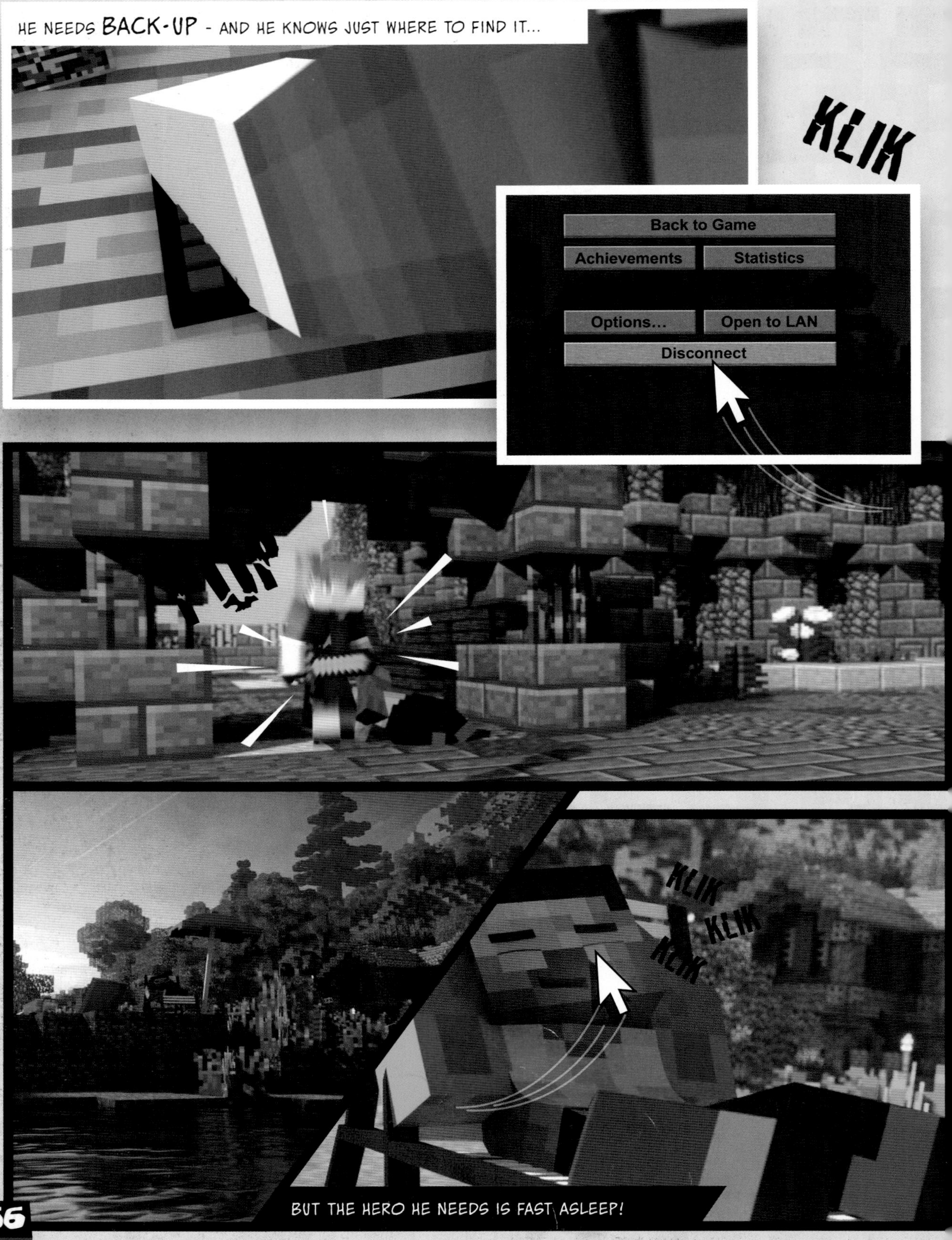

HE NEEDS BACK-UP - AND HE KNOWS JUST WHERE TO FIND IT...
KLIK
Back to Game
Achievements
Statistics
Options...
Open to LAN
Disconnect
KLIK
KLIK
KLIK
BUT THE HERO HE NEEDS IS FAST ASLEEP!

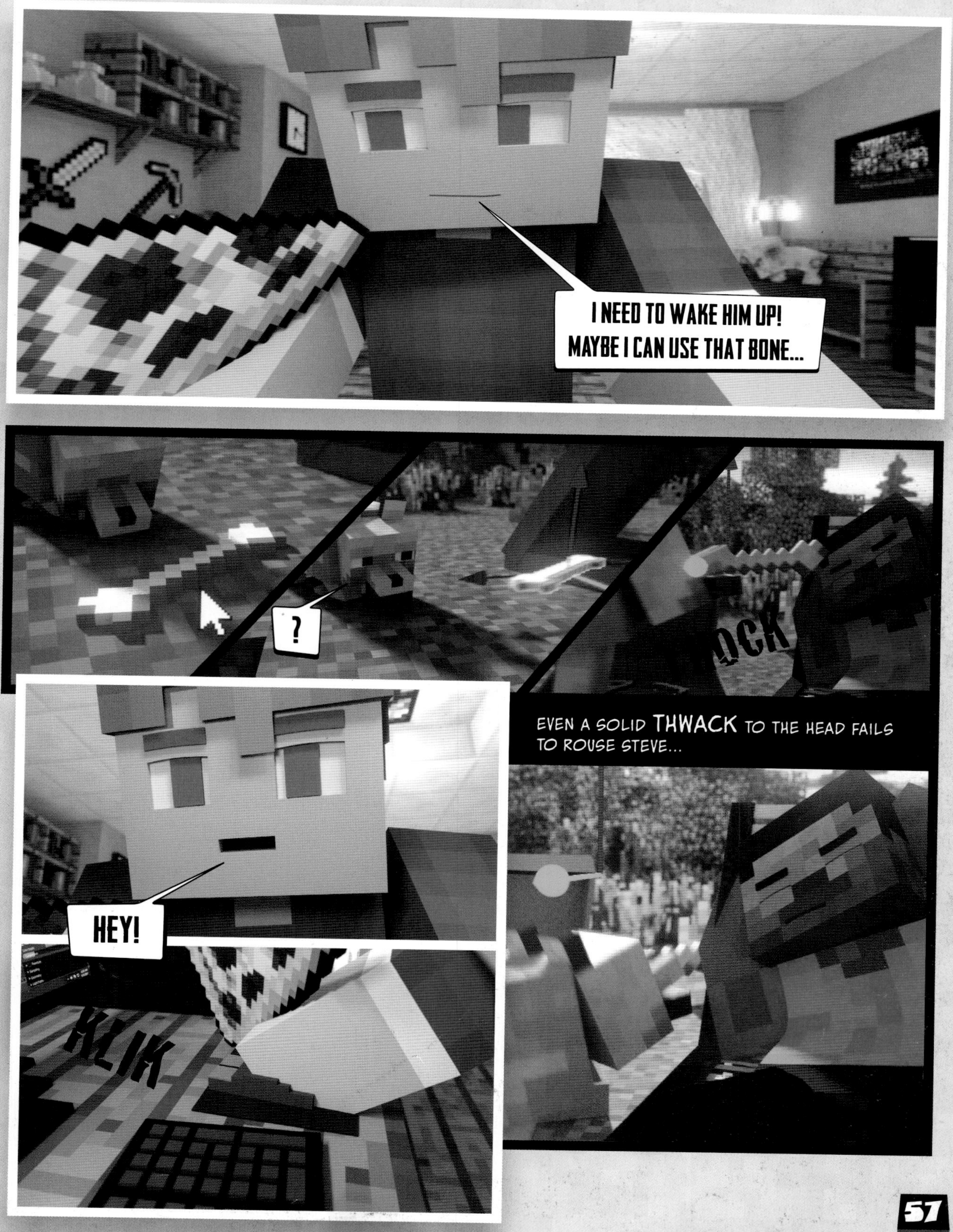

I NEED TO WAKE HIM UP!
MAYBE I CAN USE THAT BONE...
?
EVEN A SOLID THWACK TO THE HEAD FAILS TO ROUSE STEVE...
HEY!
KLIK

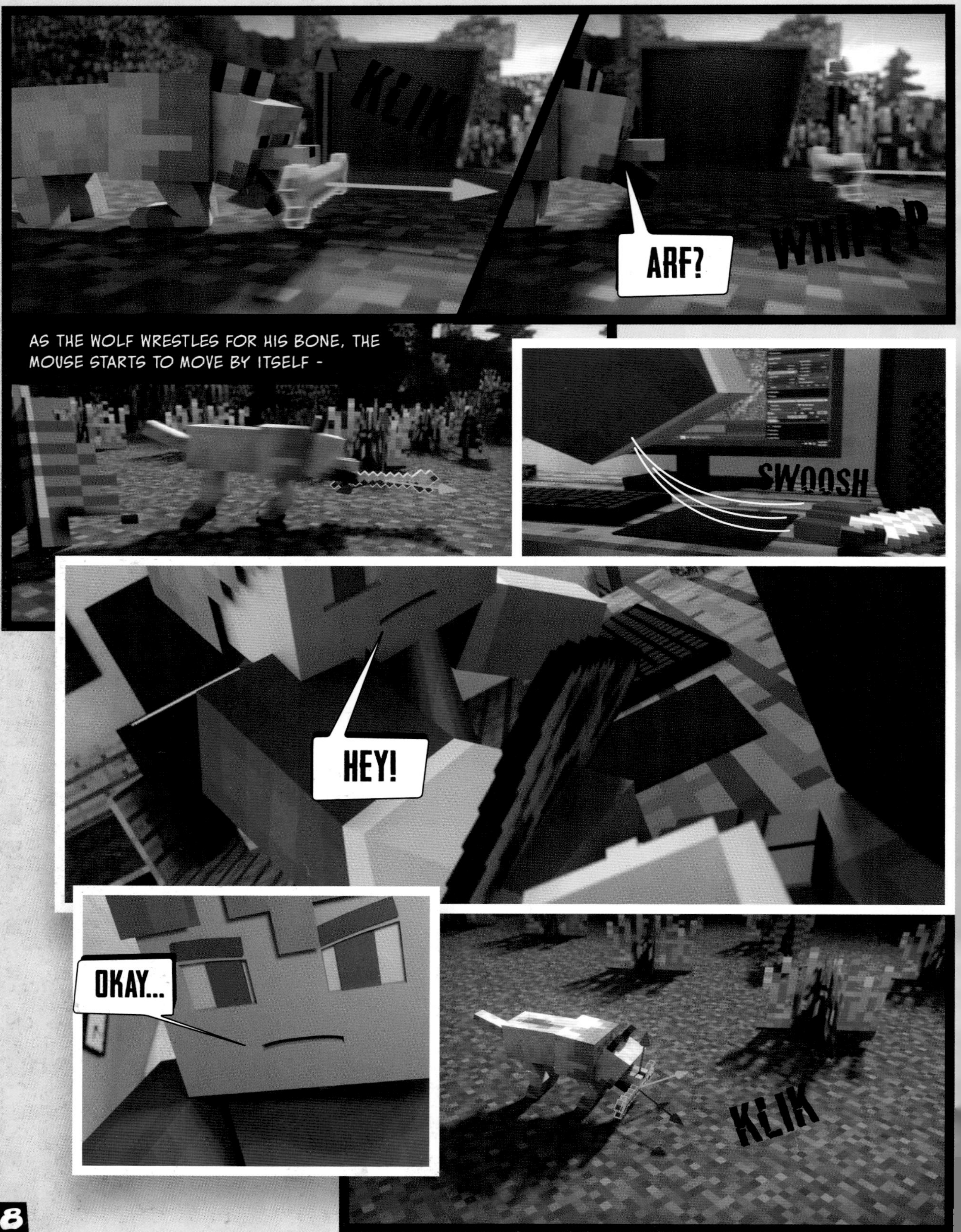
KLIK
ARF?
WHIPP
AS THE WOLF WRESTLES FOR HIS BONE, THE MOUSE STARTS TO MOVE BY ITSELF -
SWOOSH
HEY!
OKAY...
KLIK

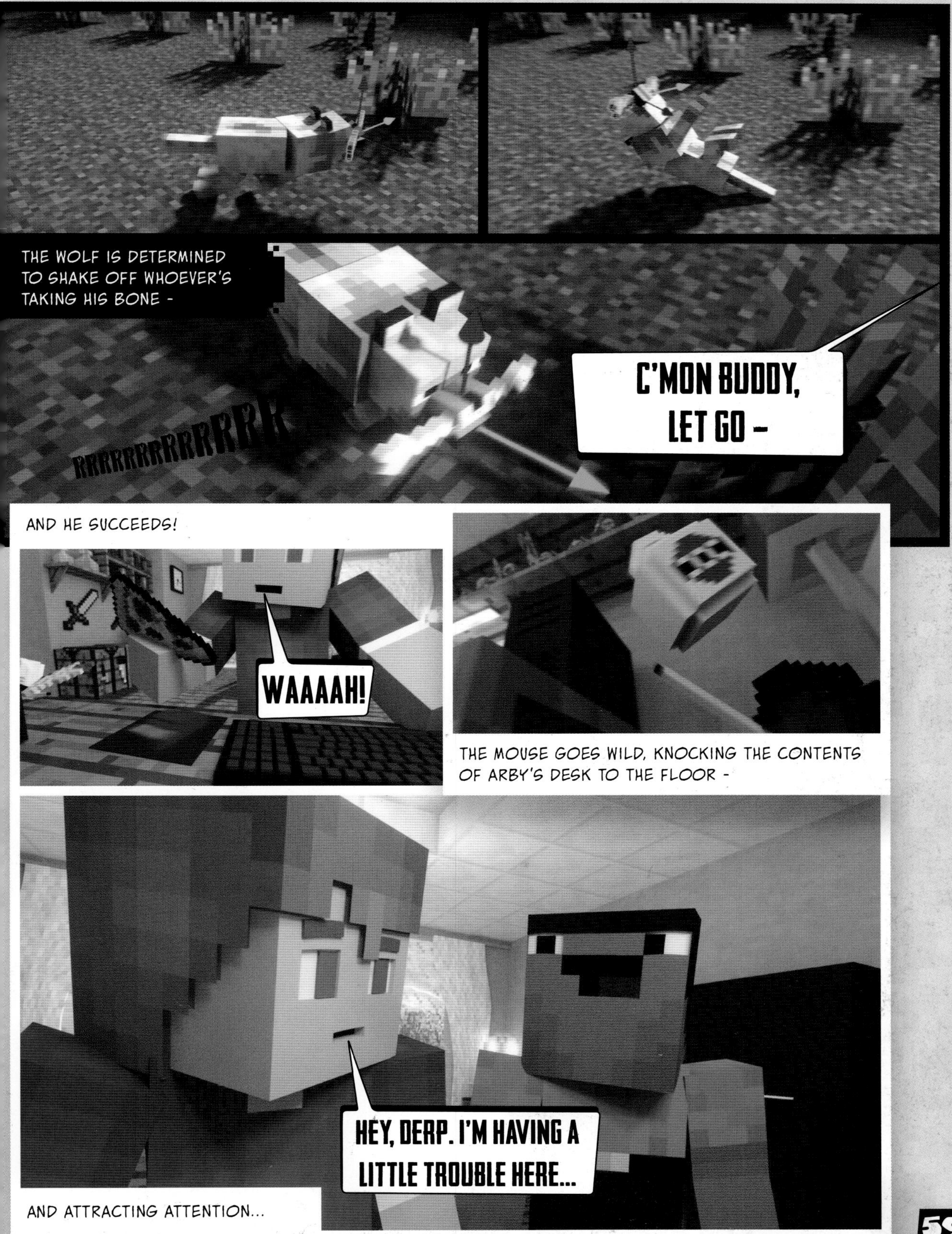
THE WOLF IS DETERMINED TO SHAKE OFF WHOEVER'S TAKING HIS BONE -
C'MON BUDDY, LET GO -
RRRRRRRRRRRRRRRK
AND HE SUCCEEDS!
WAAAAH!
THE MOUSE GOES WILD, KNOCKING THE CONTENTS OF ARBY'S DESK TO THE FLOOR -
HEY, DERP. I'M HAVING A LITTLE TROUBLE HERE...
AND ATTRACTING ATTENTION...

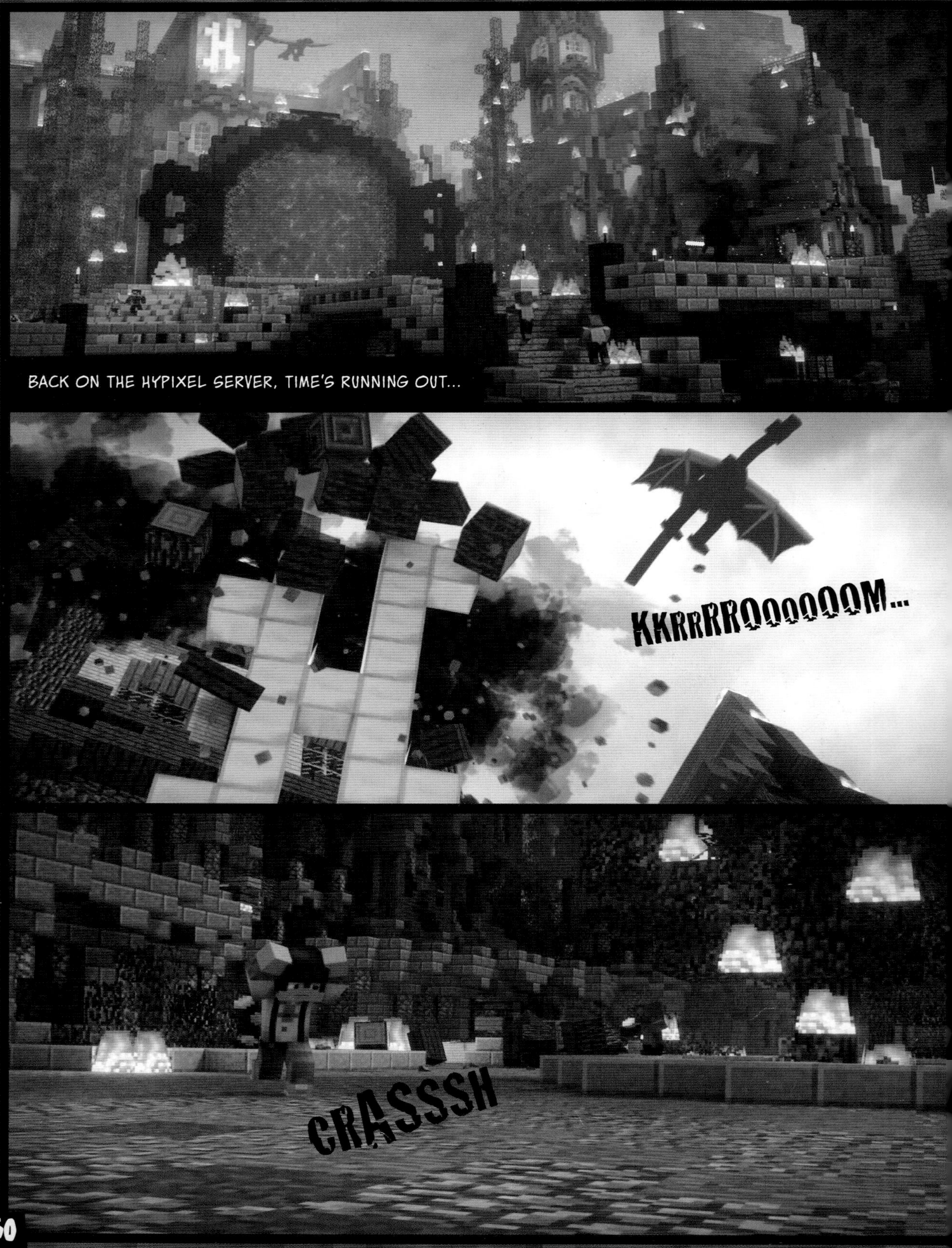
BACK ON THE HYPIXEL SERVER, TIME'S RUNNING OUT...
KKRRRROOOOOOOM...
CRASSSH

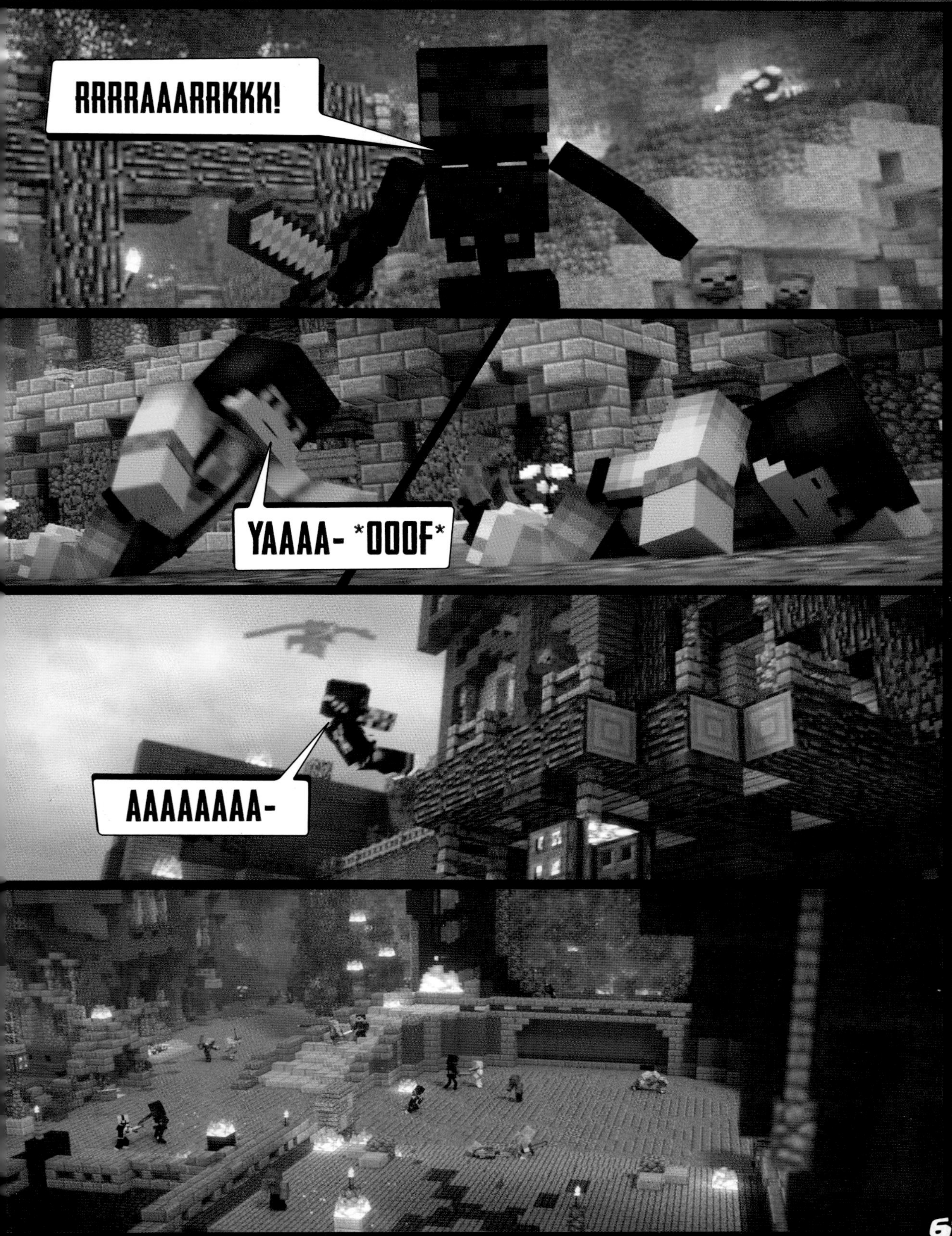
RRRRAAARRRKKK!
YAAAA- *OOOF*
AAAAAAAA-

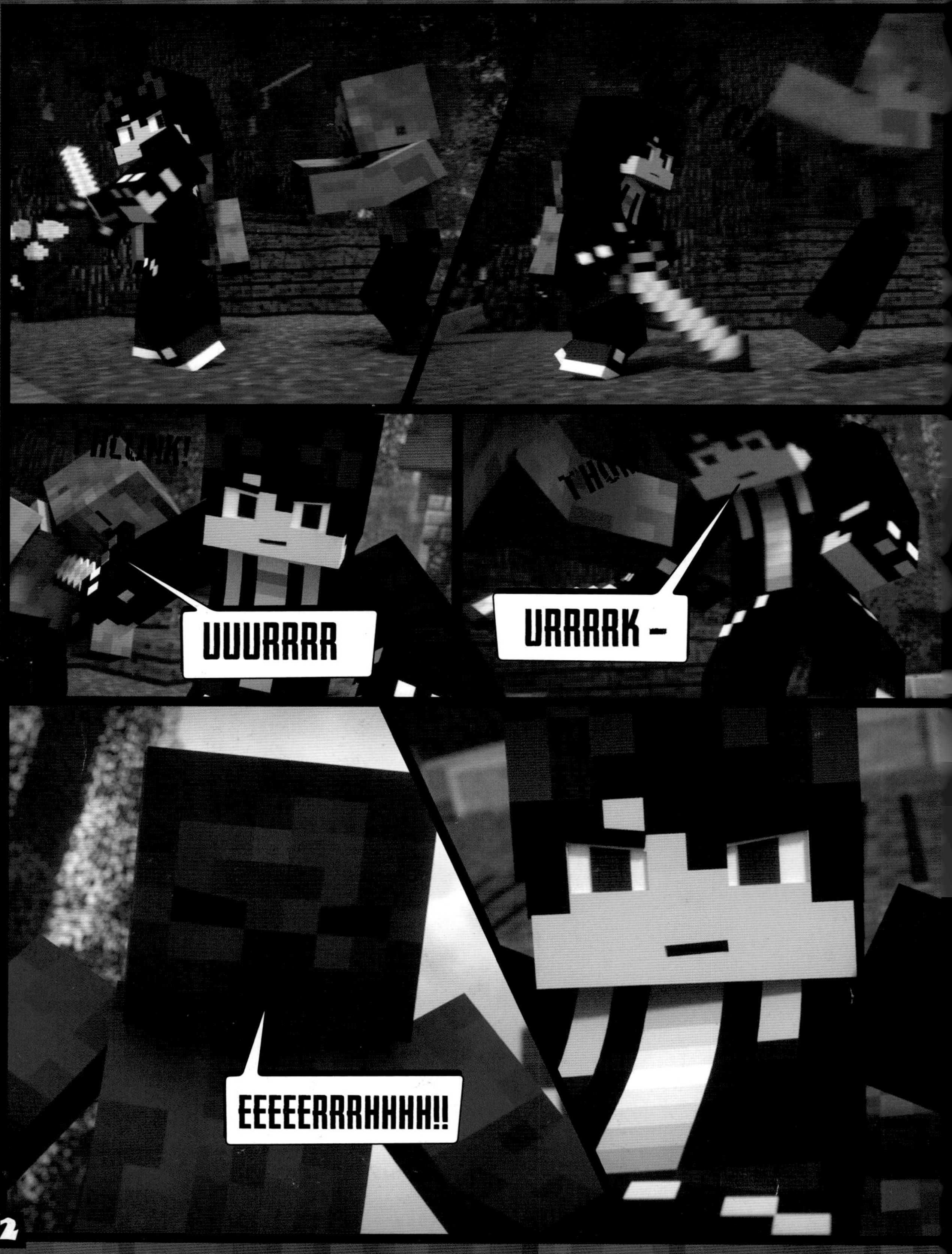
UUURRRR
URRRRK -
EEEEERRRHHHH!!

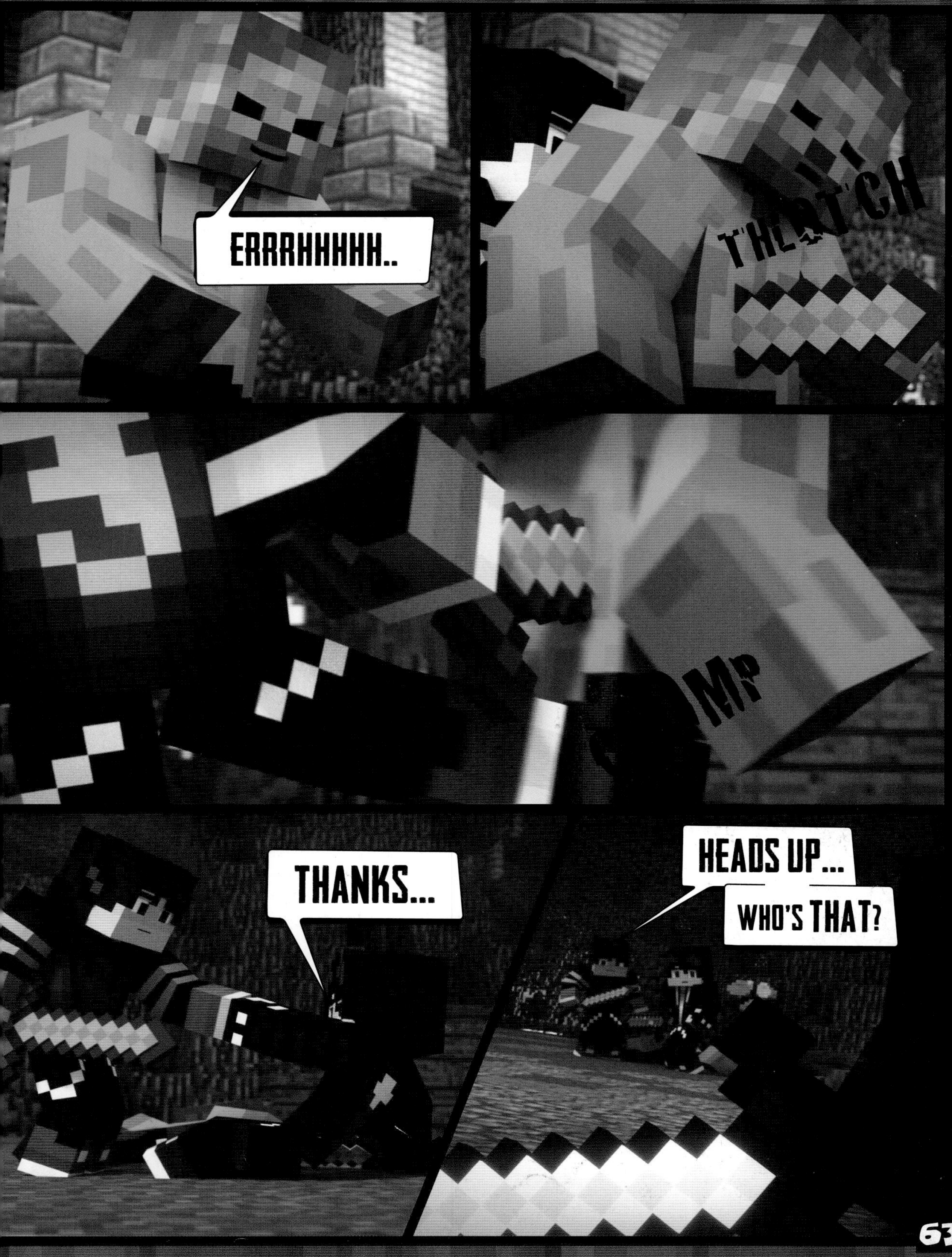
ERRRHHHHH..
THANKS...
HEADS UP...
WHO'S THAT?

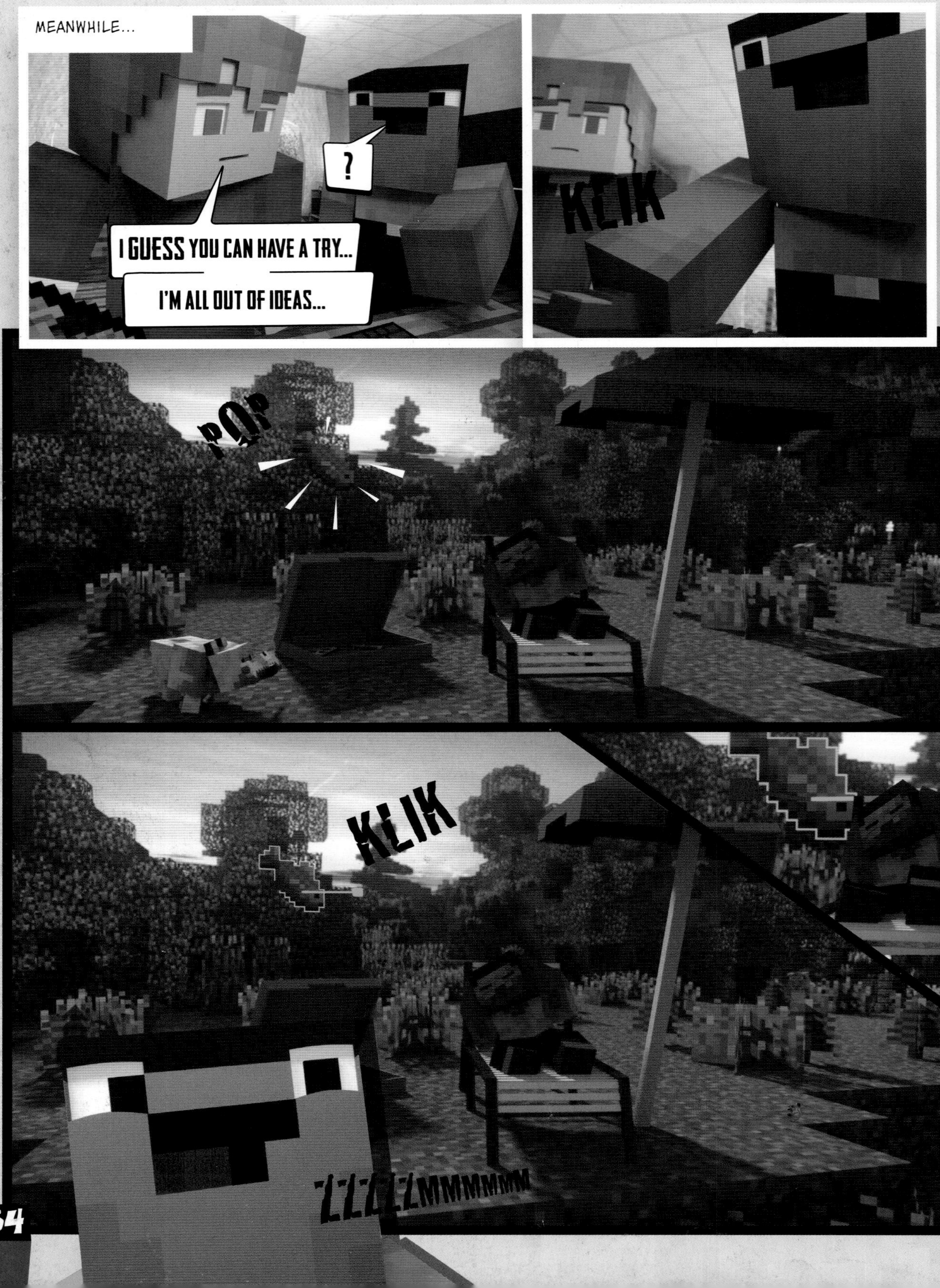
MEANWHILE...
I GUESS YOU CAN HAVE A TRY...
I'M ALL OUT OF IDEAS...
?
KLIK
POP
KLIK
ZZZZZZMMMMMM

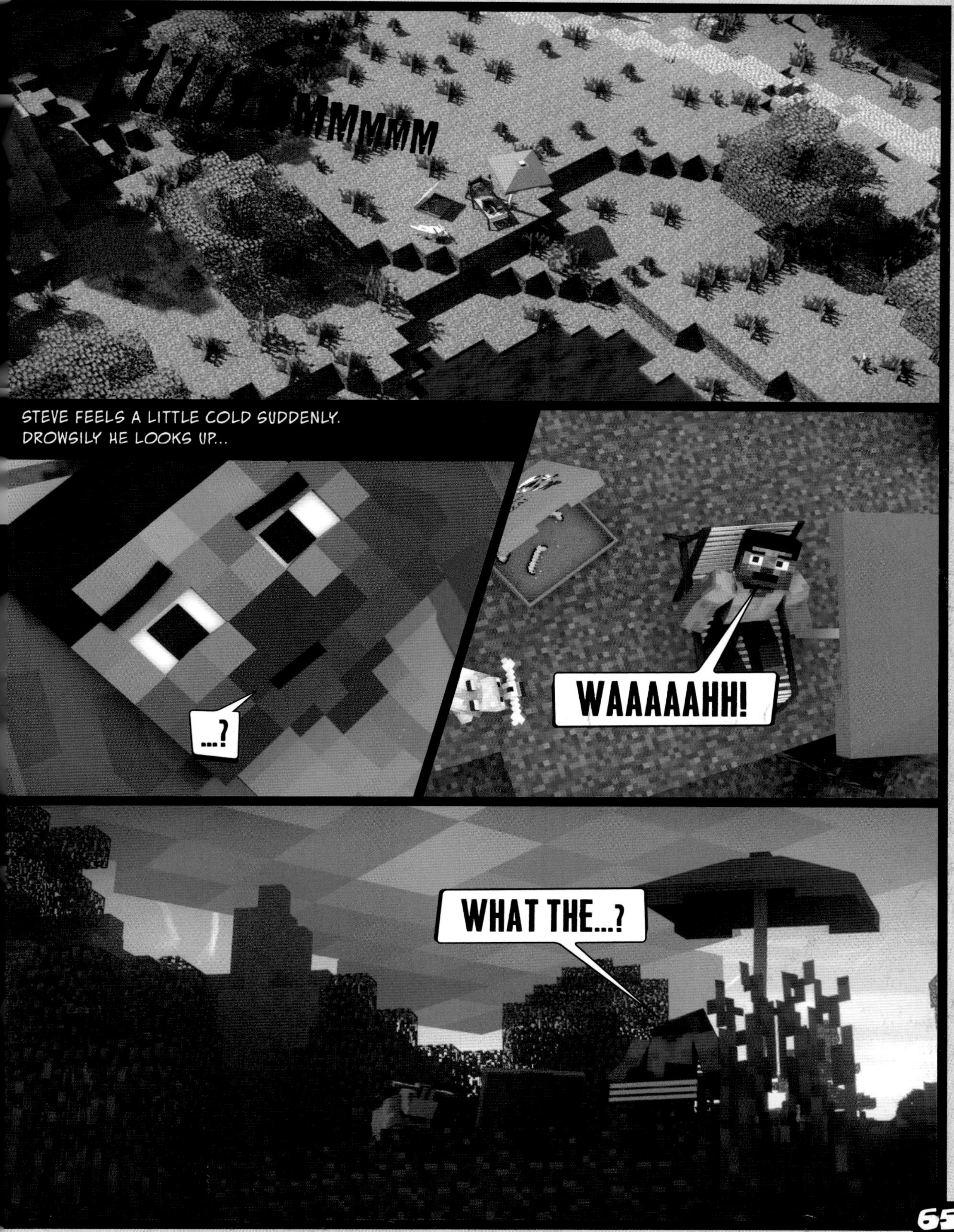
STEVE FEELS A LITTLE COLD SUDDENLY.
DROWSILY HE LOOKS UP...
...?
WAAAAAHH!
WHAT THE...?

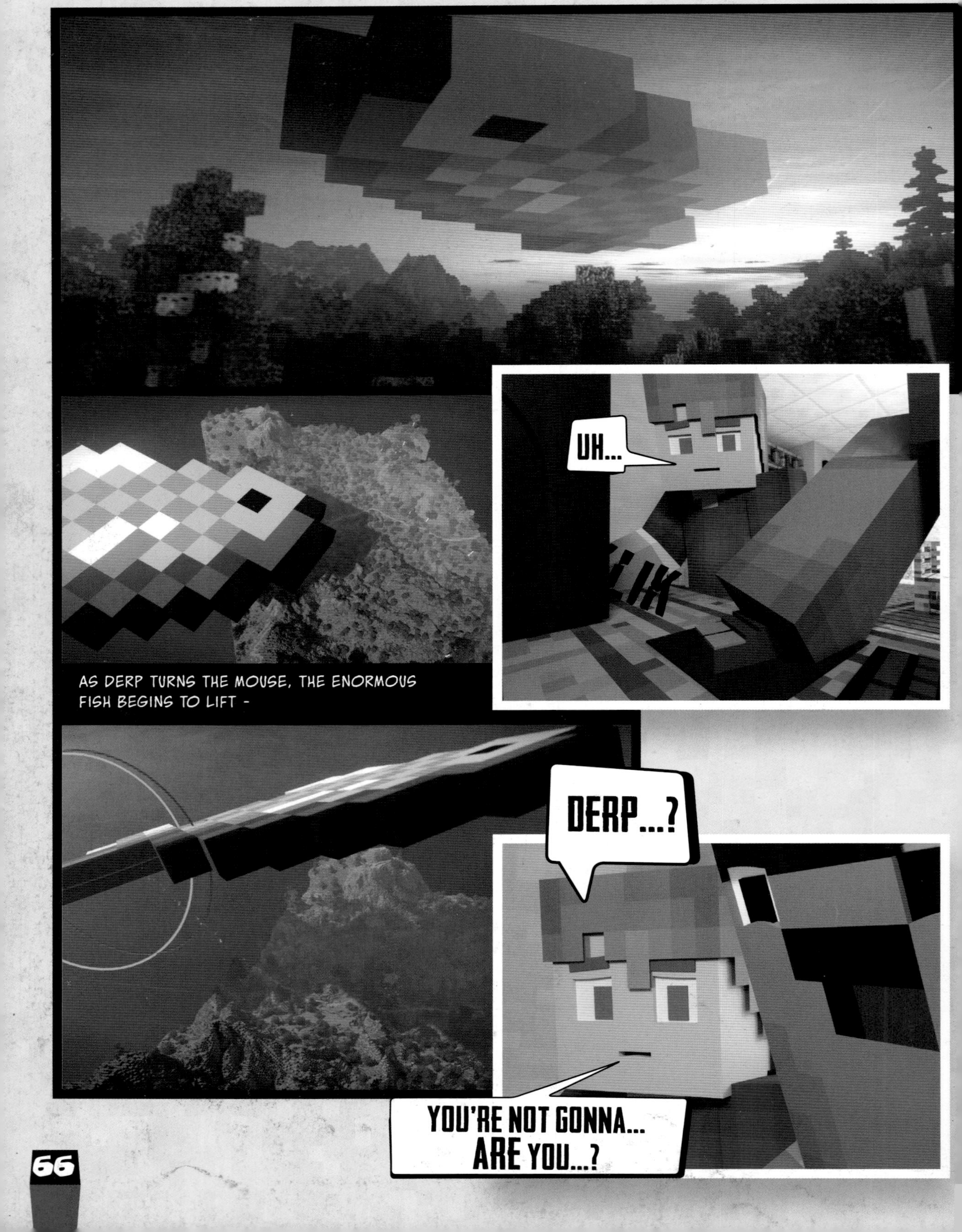

AS DERP TURNS THE MOUSE, THE ENORMOUS FISH BEGINS TO LIFT -
UH...
DERP...?
YOU'RE NOT GONNA... ARE YOU...?

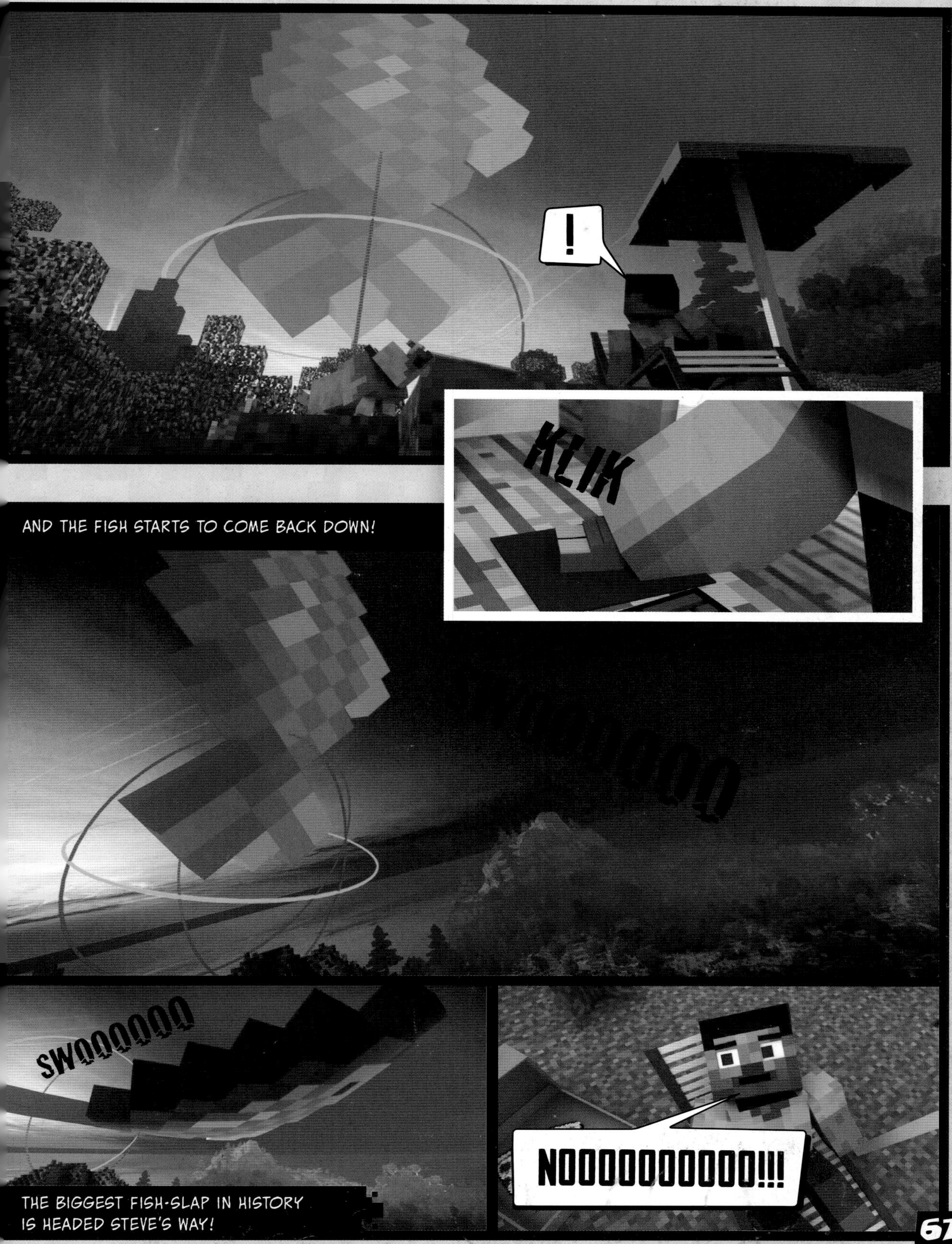
!
KLIK
AND THE FISH STARTS TO COME BACK DOWN!
SWOOOOOO
THE BIGGEST FISH-SLAP IN HISTORY IS HEADED STEVE'S WAY!
NOOOOOOOOOO!!!

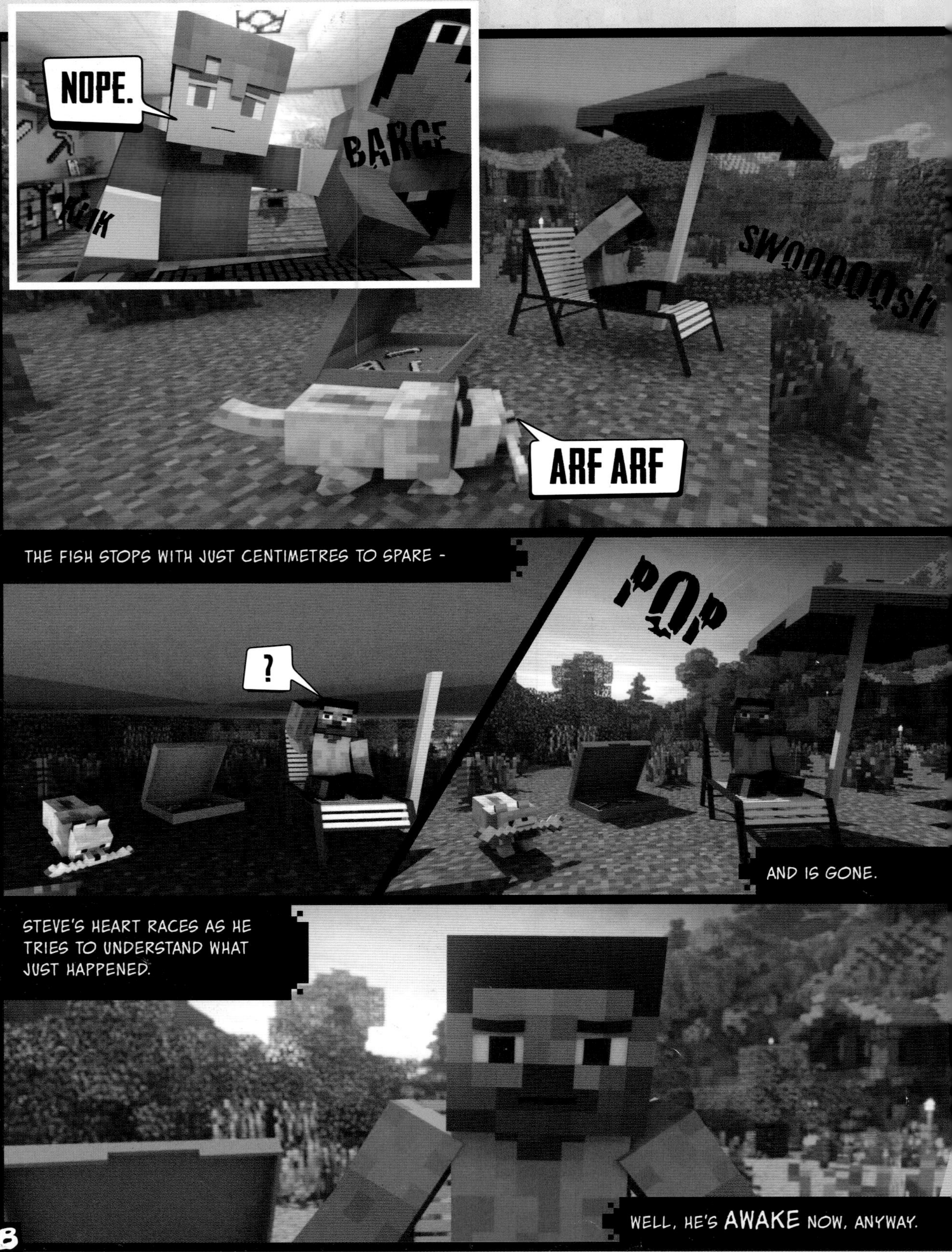

NOPE.
BARGE
SWOOOOOsh
ARF ARF
THE FISH STOPS WITH JUST CENTIMETRES TO SPARE -
?
POP
AND IS GONE.
STEVE'S HEART RACES AS HE TRIES TO UNDERSTAND WHAT JUST HAPPENED.
WELL, HE'S AWAKE NOW, ANYWAY.

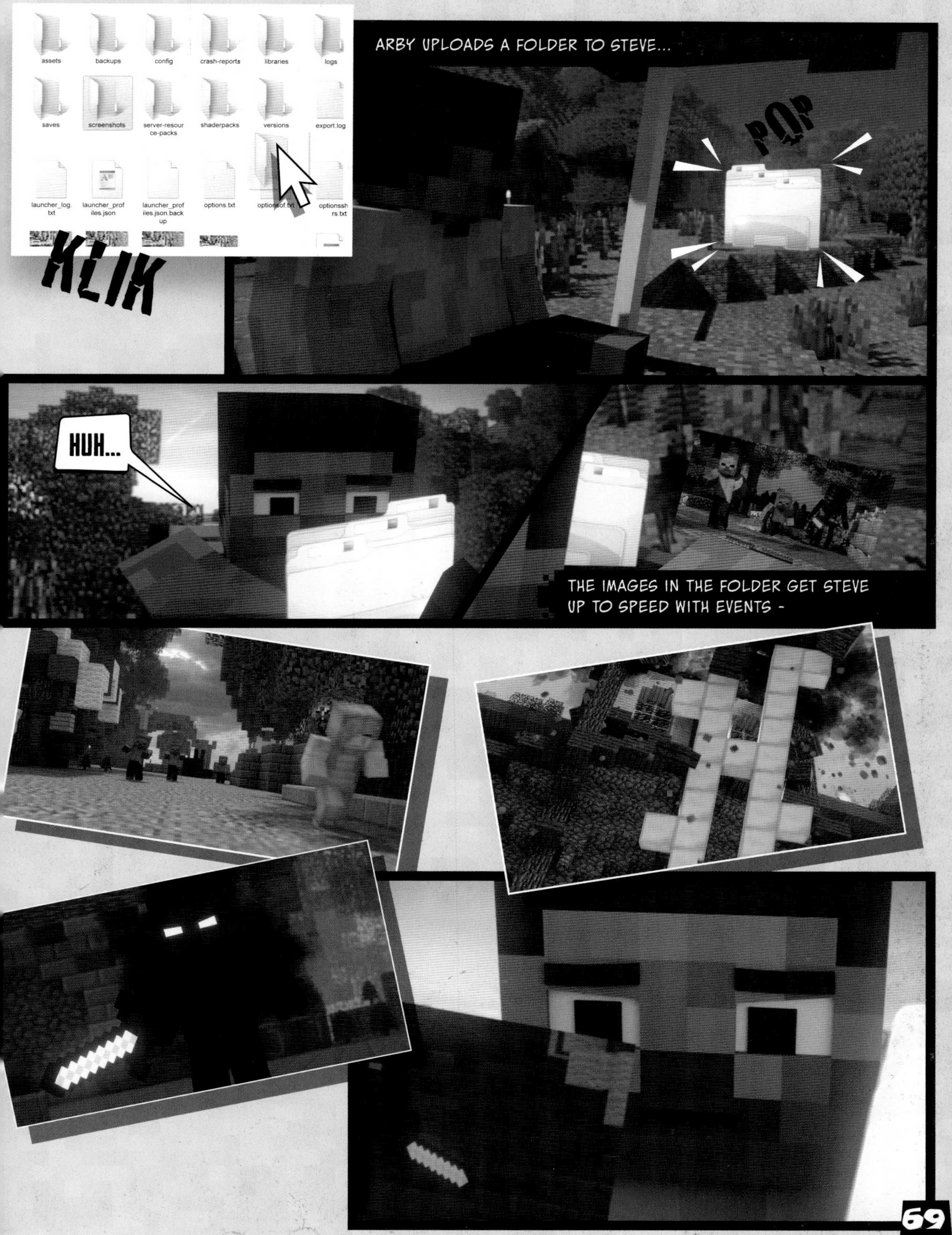
assets
backups
config
crash-reports
libraries
logs
saves
screenshots
server-resource-packs
shaderpacks
versions
export.log
launcher_log.txt
launcher_profiles.json
launcher_profiles.json.backup
options.txt
optionsof.txt
optionsshrs.txt
KLIK
ARBY UPLOADS A FOLDER TO STEVE...
POP
HUH...
THE IMAGES IN THE FOLDER GET STEVE UP TO SPEED WITH EVENTS -

AND THERE'S NO QUESTION ABOUT WHAT HE'S GOING TO DO.

HE'S GOING TO PICK **THIS** UP AGAIN...

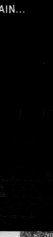

AND ANSWER THE CALL...

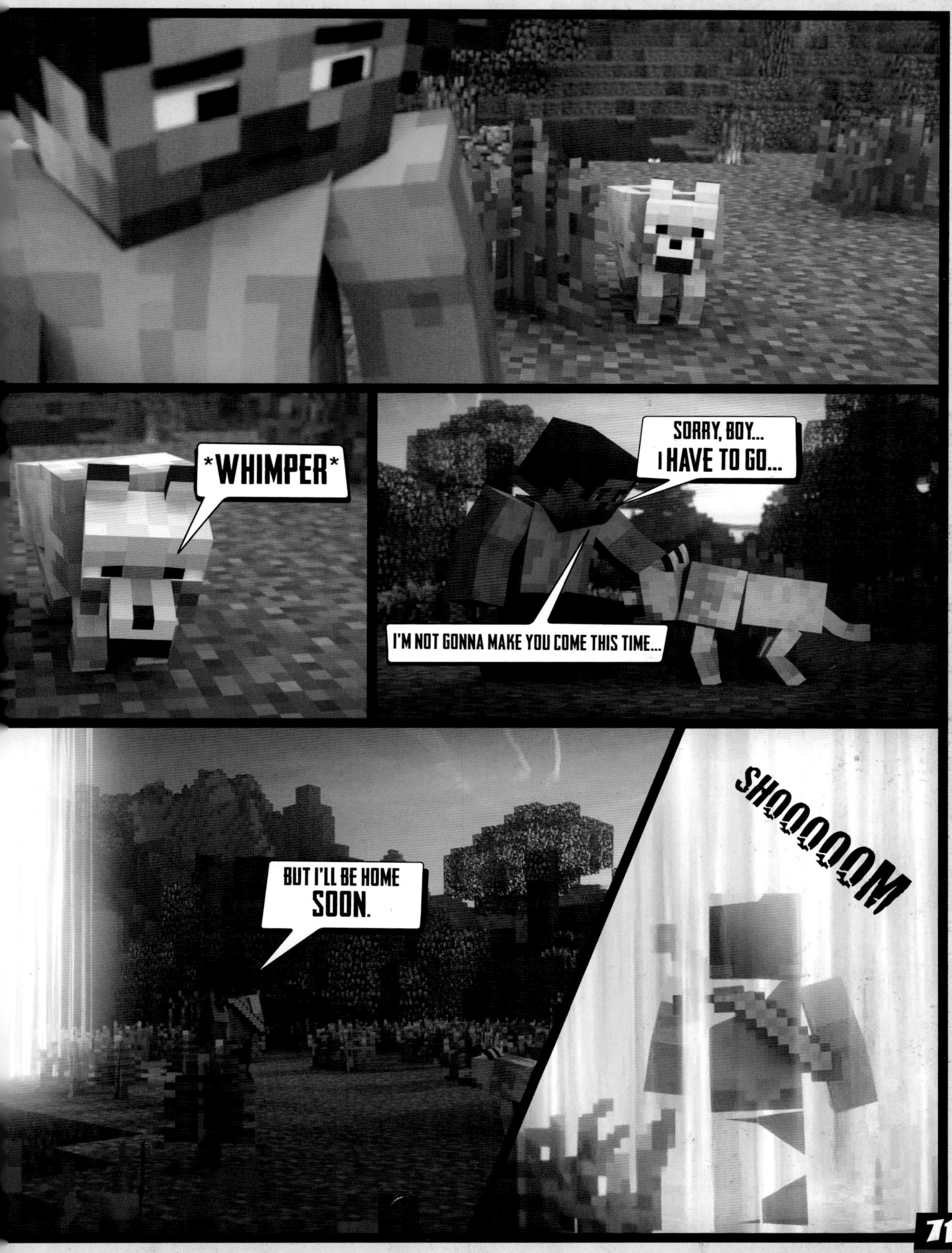
WHIMPER
SORRY, BOY...
I HAVE TO GO...
I'M NOT GONNA MAKE YOU COME THIS TIME...
BUT I'LL BE HOME
SOON.
SHOOOOOOM

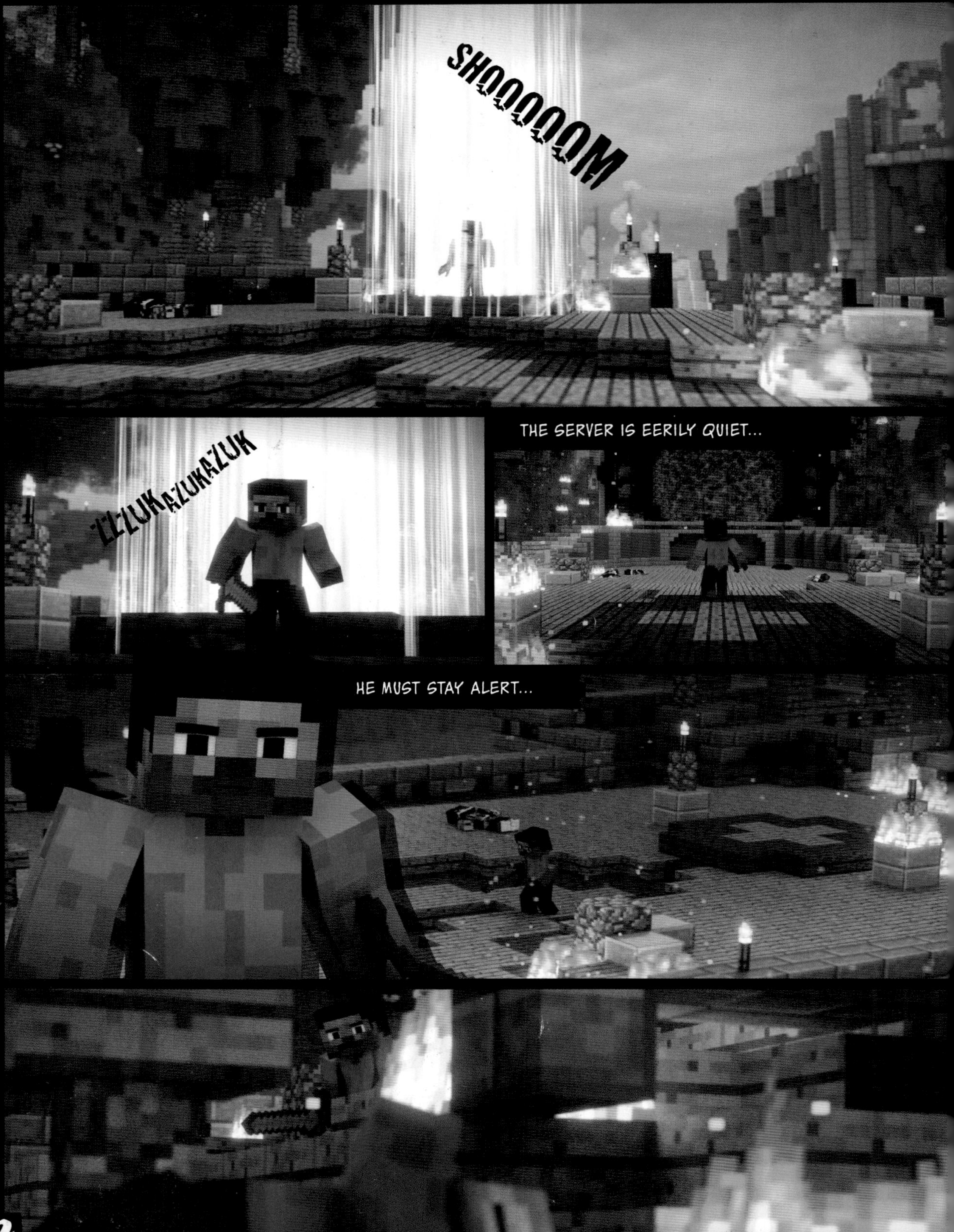
SHOOOOOM
ZZZUKAZUKAZUK
THE SERVER IS EERILY QUIET...
HE MUST STAY ALERT...

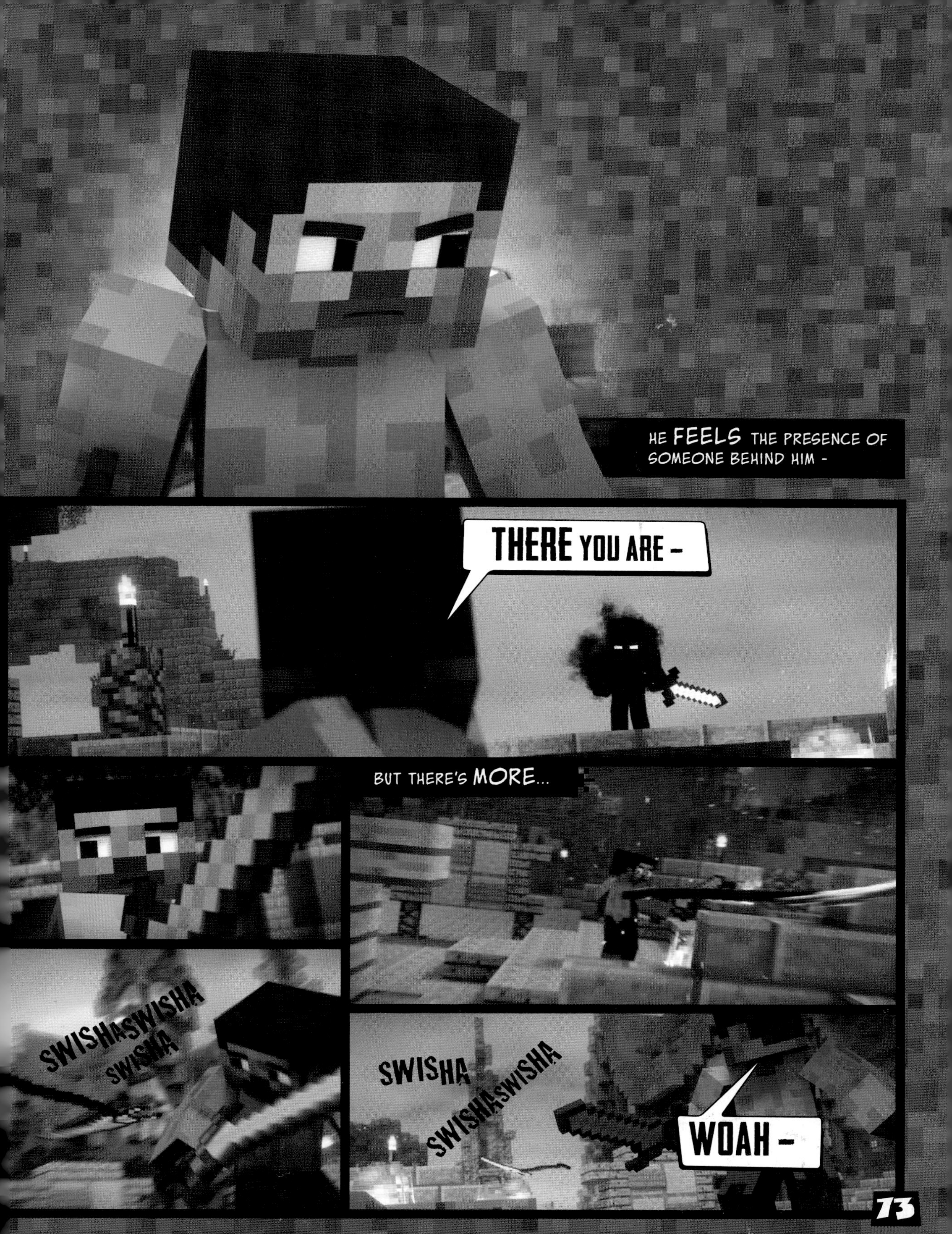
HE FEELS THE PRESENCE OF SOMEONE BEHIND HIM -
THERE YOU ARE -
BUT THERE'S MORE...
SWISHA SWISHA SWISHA
SWISHA SWISHA SWISHA
WOAH -

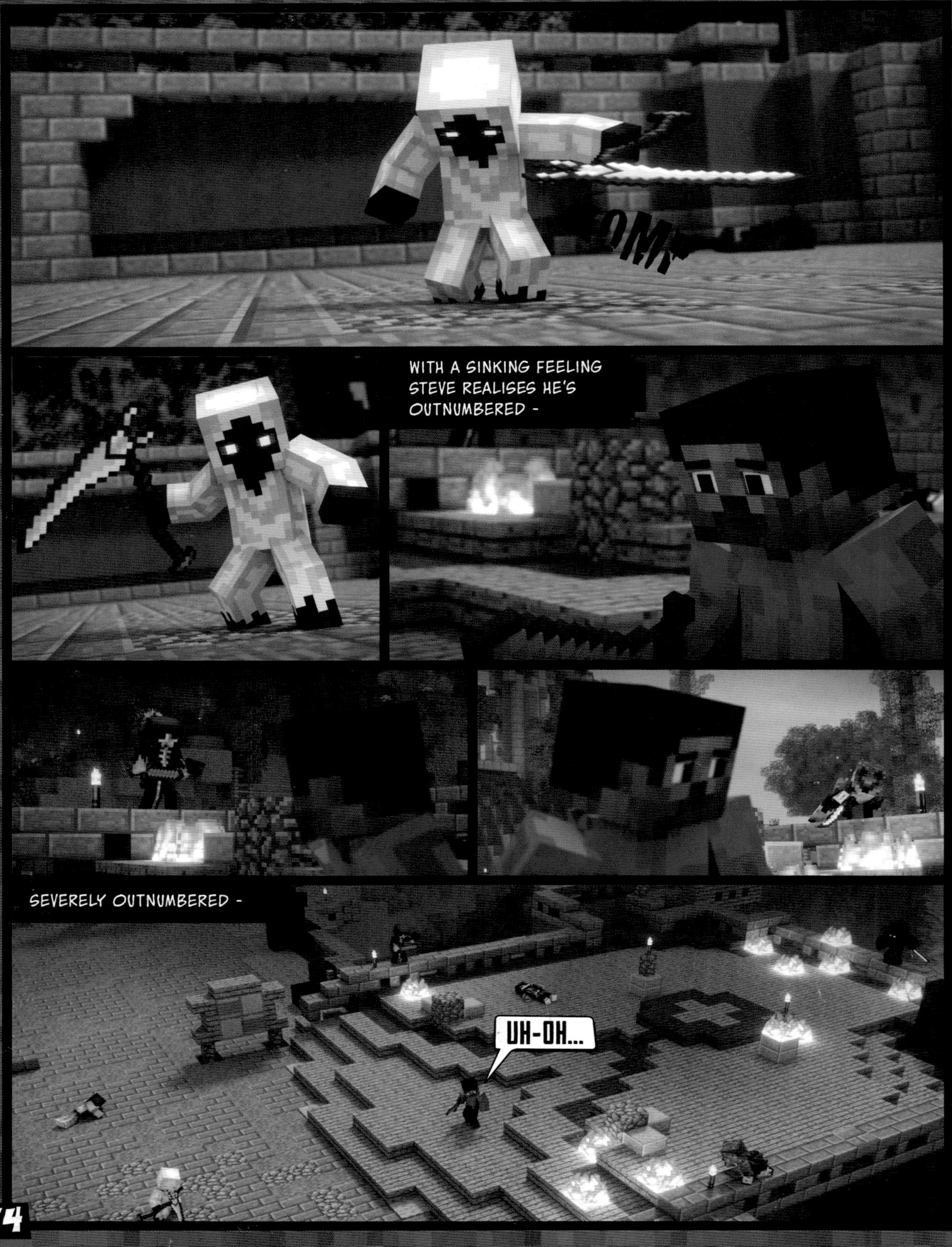
WITH A SINKING FEELING
STEVE REALISES HE'S
OUTNUMBERED -
SEVERELY OUTNUMBERED -
UH-OH...

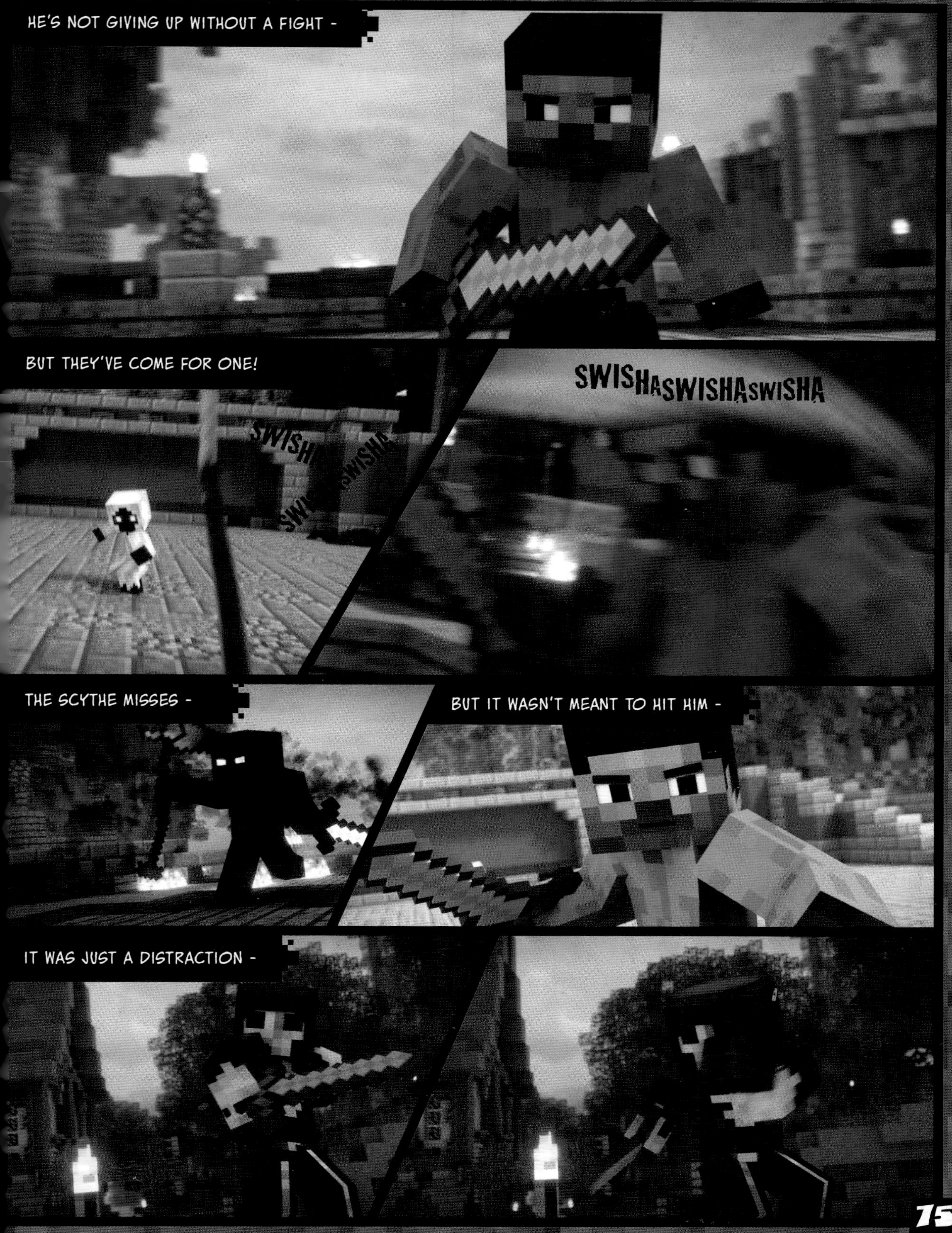
HE'S NOT GIVING UP WITHOUT A FIGHT -
BUT THEY'VE COME FOR ONE!
SWISHASWISHASWISHA
THE SCYTHE MISSES -
BUT IT WASN'T MEANT TO HIT HIM -
IT WAS JUST A DISTRACTION -

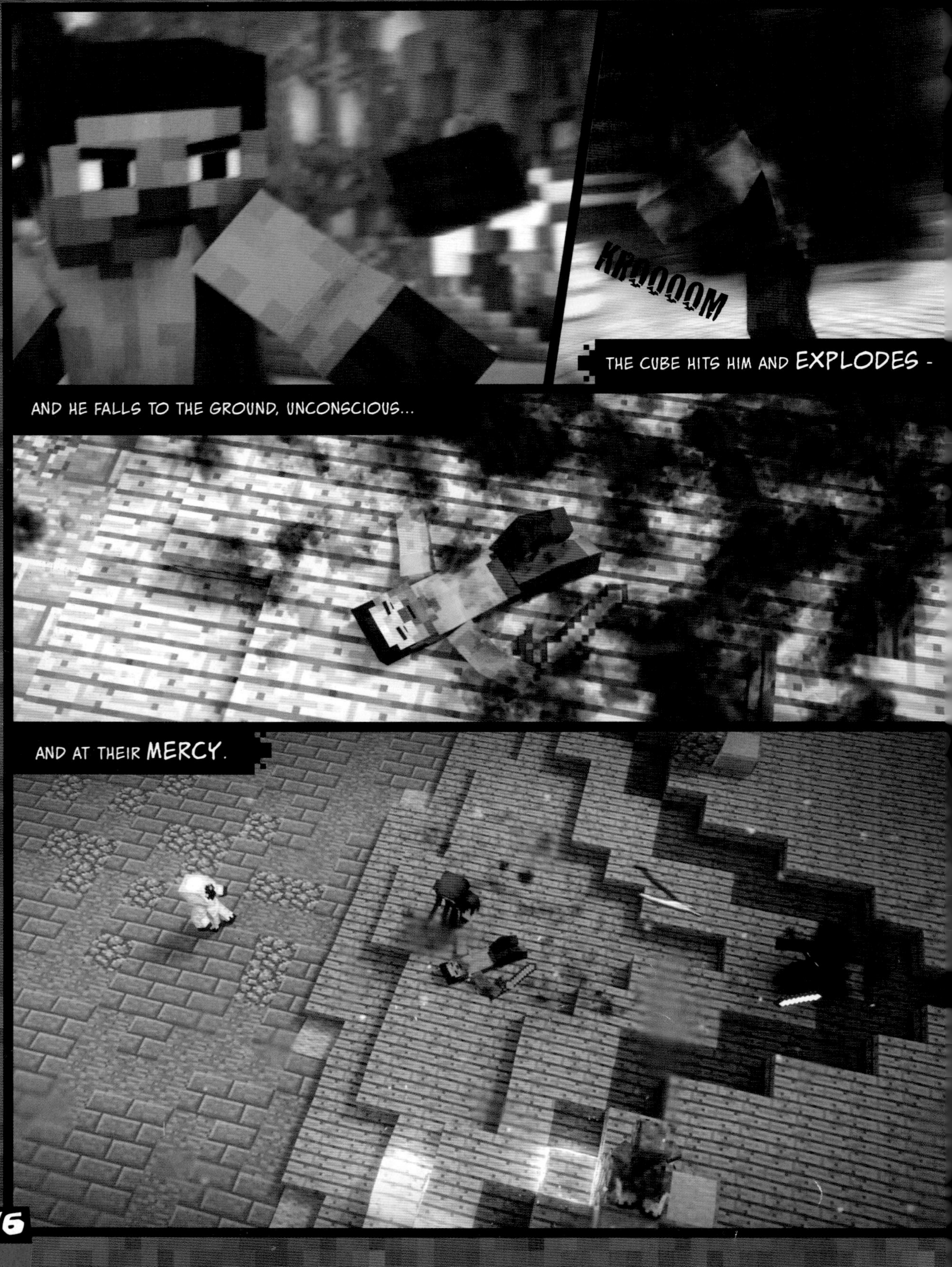
KROOOOM
THE CUBE HITS HIM AND EXPLODES -
AND HE FALLS TO THE GROUND, UNCONSCIOUS...
AND AT THEIR MERCY.

CHAPTER 4

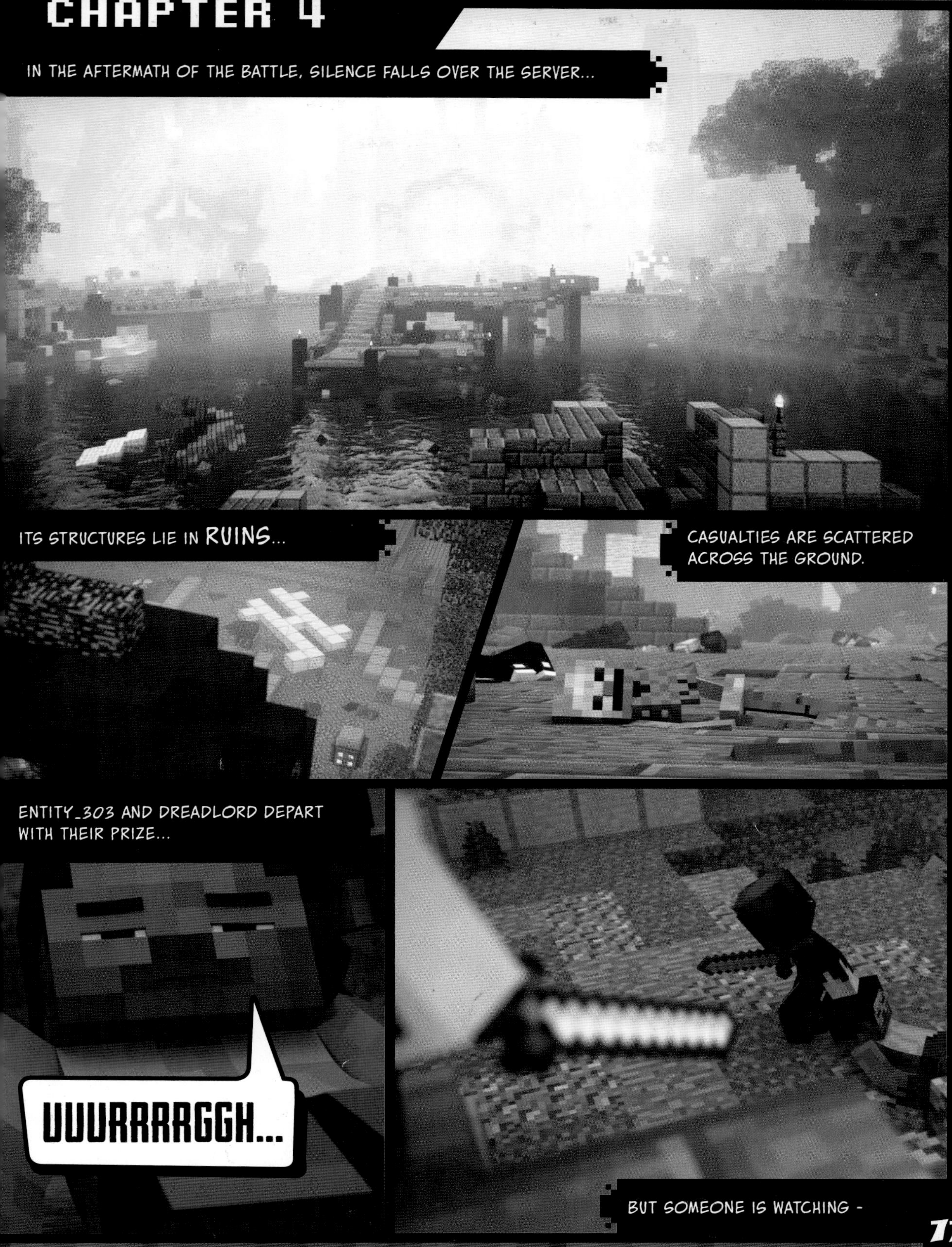
IN THE AFTERMATH OF THE BATTLE, SILENCE FALLS OVER THE SERVER...
ITS STRUCTURES LIE IN RUINS...
CASUALTIES ARE SCATTERED ACROSS THE GROUND.
ENTITY_303 AND DREADLORD DEPART WITH THEIR PRIZE...
UUURRRRGGH...
BUT SOMEONE IS WATCHING -

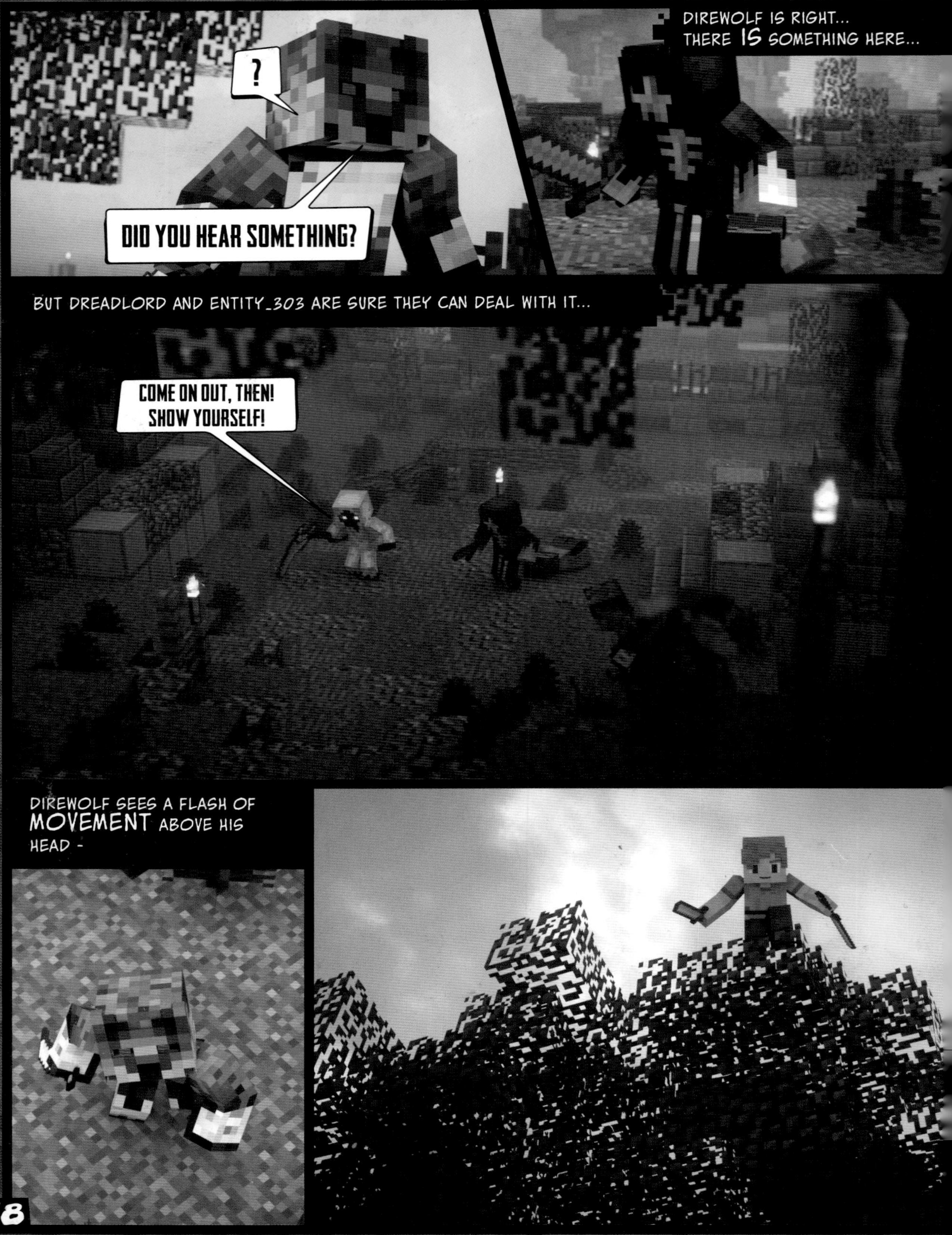
?
DID YOU HEAR SOMETHING?
DIREWOLF IS RIGHT...
THERE IS SOMETHING HERE...
BUT DREADLORD AND ENTITY_303 ARE SURE THEY CAN DEAL WITH IT...
COME ON OUT, THEN!
SHOW YOURSELF!
DIREWOLF SEES A FLASH OF MOVEMENT ABOVE HIS HEAD -

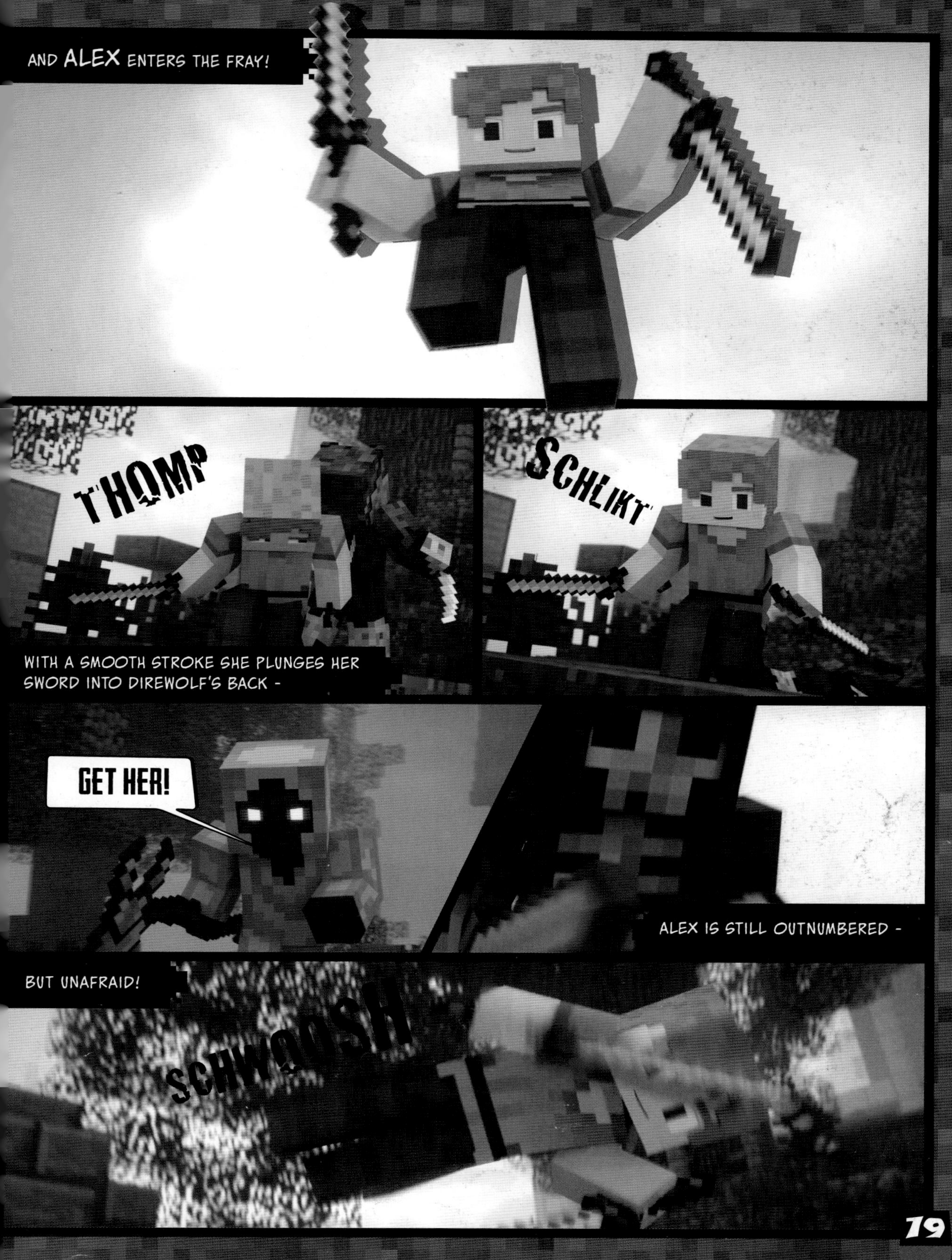

AND ALEX ENTERS THE FRAY!
THOMP
SCHLIKT
WITH A SMOOTH STROKE SHE PLUNGES HER SWORD INTO DIREWOLF'S BACK -
GET HER!
ALEX IS STILL OUTNUMBERED -
BUT UNAFRAID!
SCHWOOSH

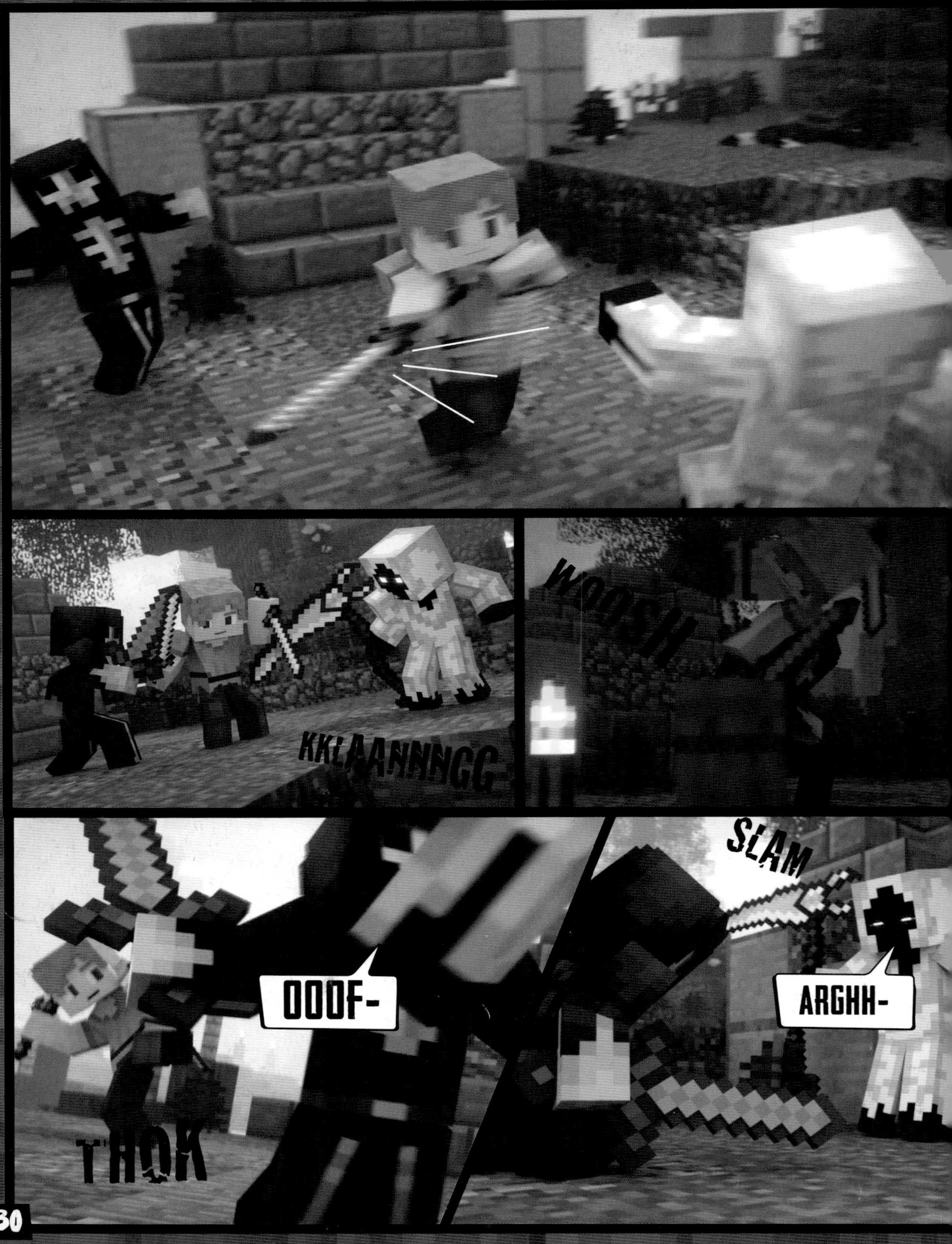
KKLAANNNGG
WOOSH
OOOF-
THOK
SLAM
ARGHH-

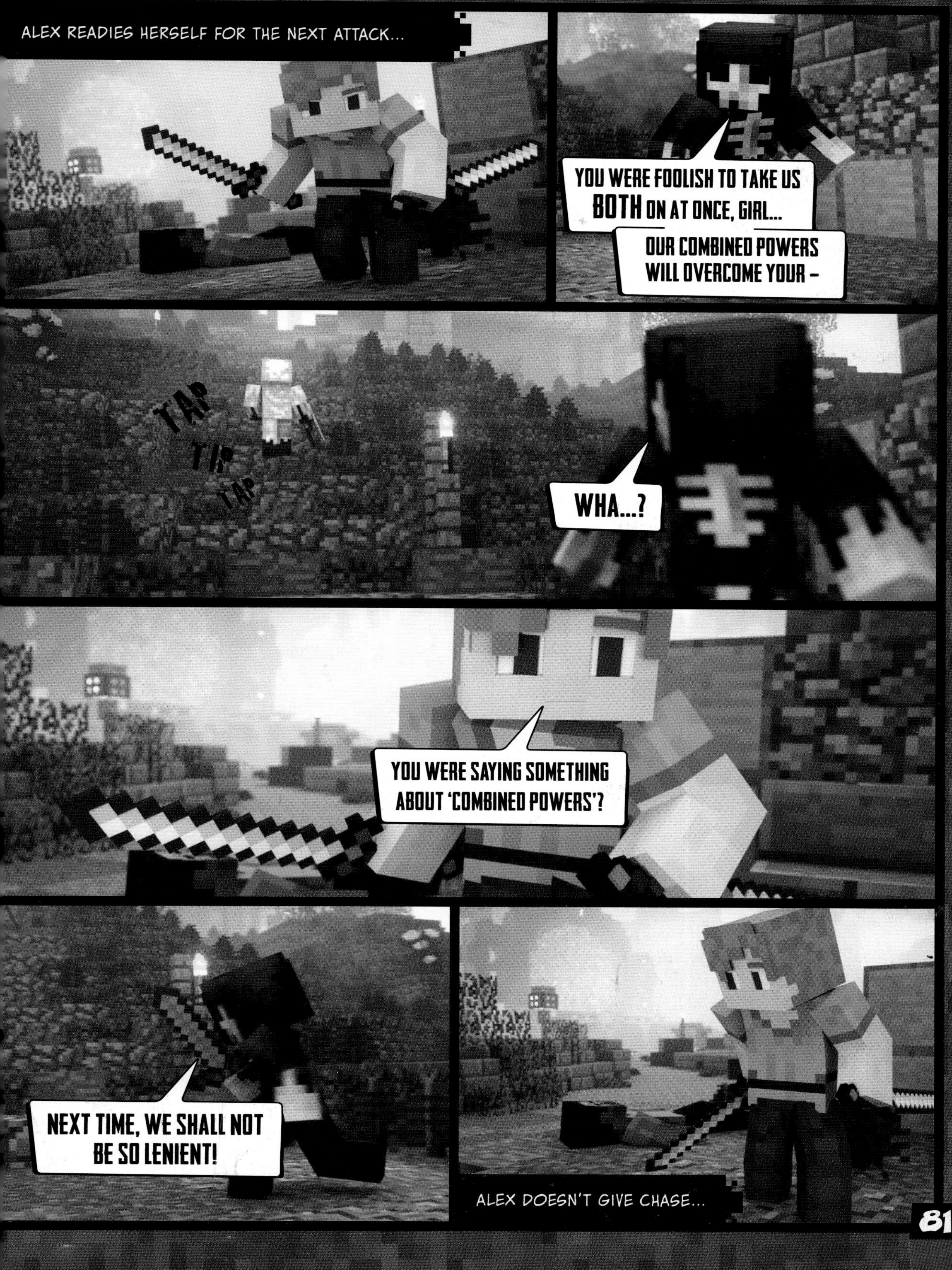
ALEX READIES HERSELF FOR THE NEXT ATTACK...
YOU WERE FOOLISH TO TAKE US BOTH ON AT ONCE, GIRL...
OUR COMBINED POWERS WILL OVERCOME YOUR –
TAP
TIP
TAP
WHA...?
YOU WERE SAYING SOMETHING ABOUT 'COMBINED POWERS'?
NEXT TIME, WE SHALL NOT BE SO LENIENT!
ALEX DOESN'T GIVE CHASE...

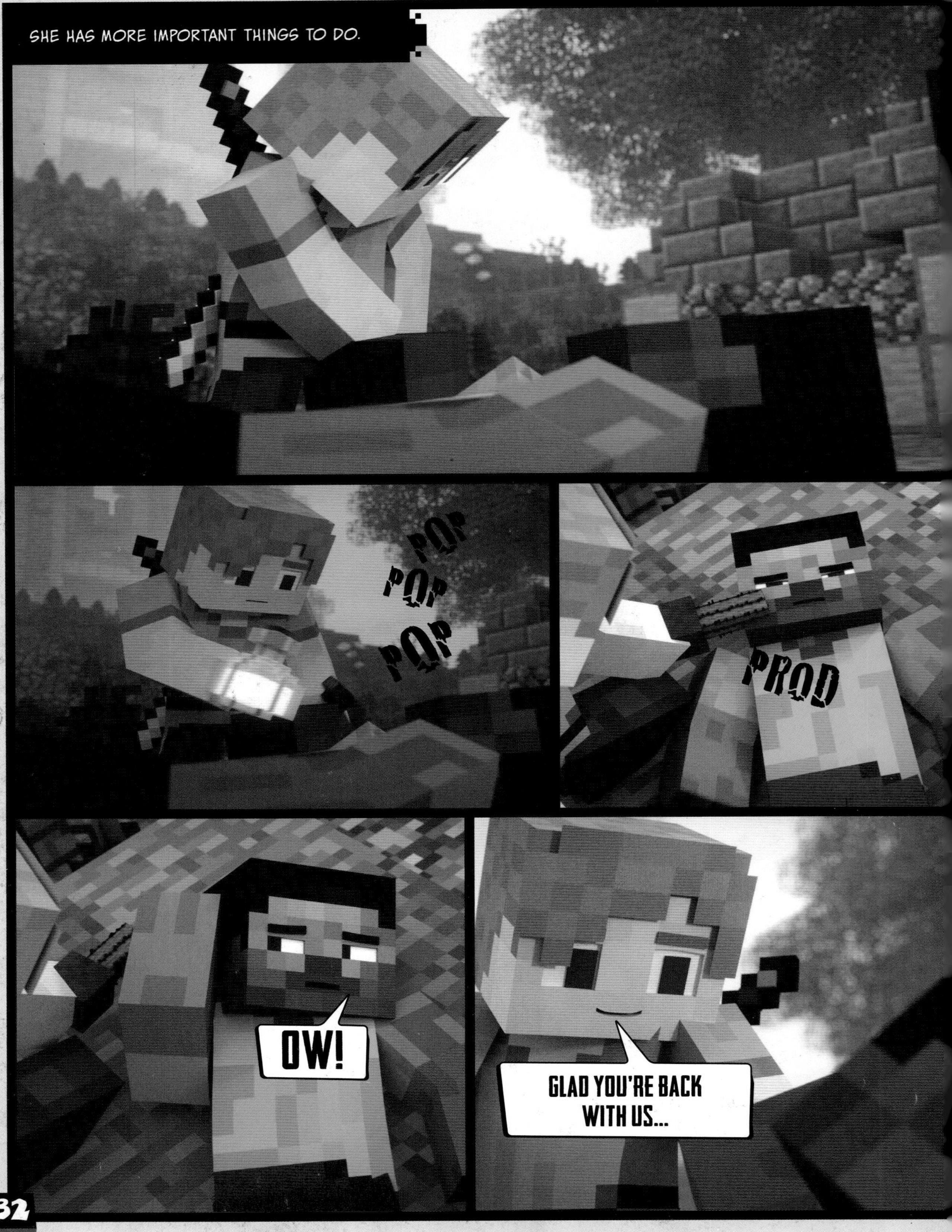
SHE HAS MORE IMPORTANT THINGS TO DO.
POP
POP
POP
PROD
OW!
GLAD YOU'RE BACK WITH US...

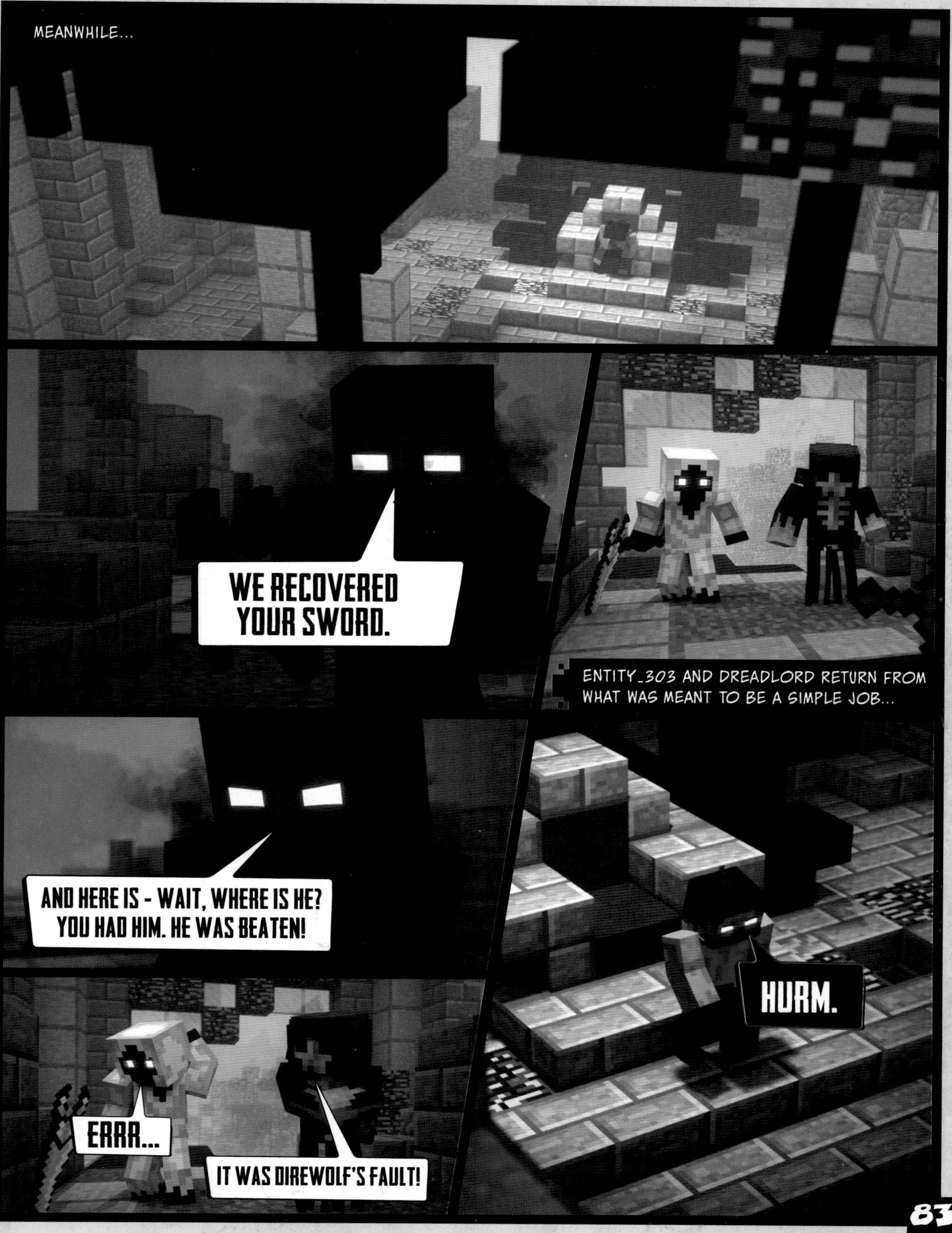
MEANWHILE...
WE RECOVERED YOUR SWORD.
ENTITY_303 AND DREADLORD RETURN FROM WHAT WAS MEANT TO BE A SIMPLE JOB...
AND HERE IS - WAIT, WHERE IS HE? YOU HAD HIM. HE WAS BEATEN!
HURM.
ERRR...
IT WAS DIREWOLF'S FAULT!

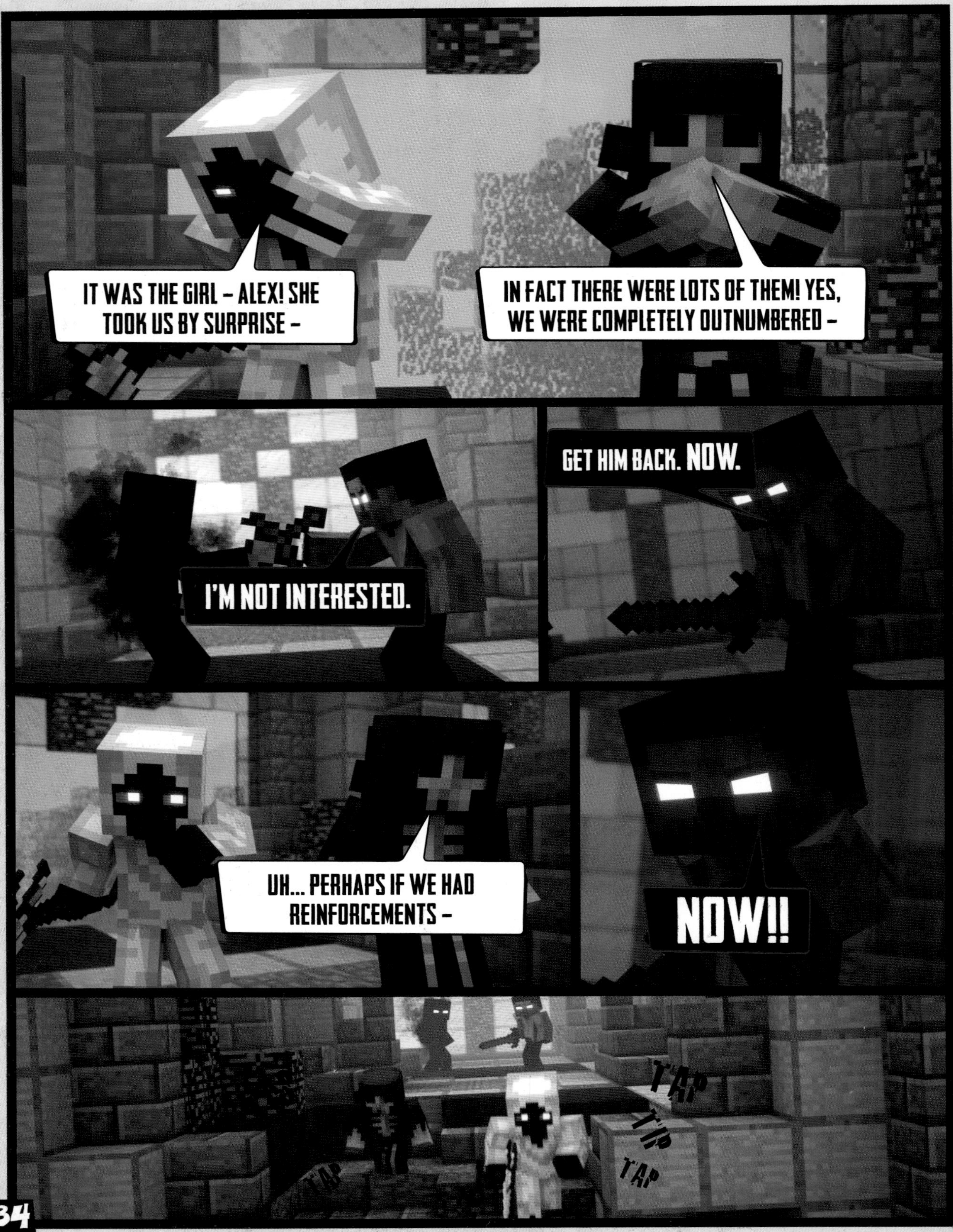
IT WAS THE GIRL – ALEX! SHE TOOK US BY SURPRISE –
IN FACT THERE WERE LOTS OF THEM! YES, WE WERE COMPLETELY OUTNUMBERED –
I'M NOT INTERESTED.
GET HIM BACK. NOW.
UH... PERHAPS IF WE HAD REINFORCEMENTS –
NOW!!
TAP
TAP
TAP
TAP

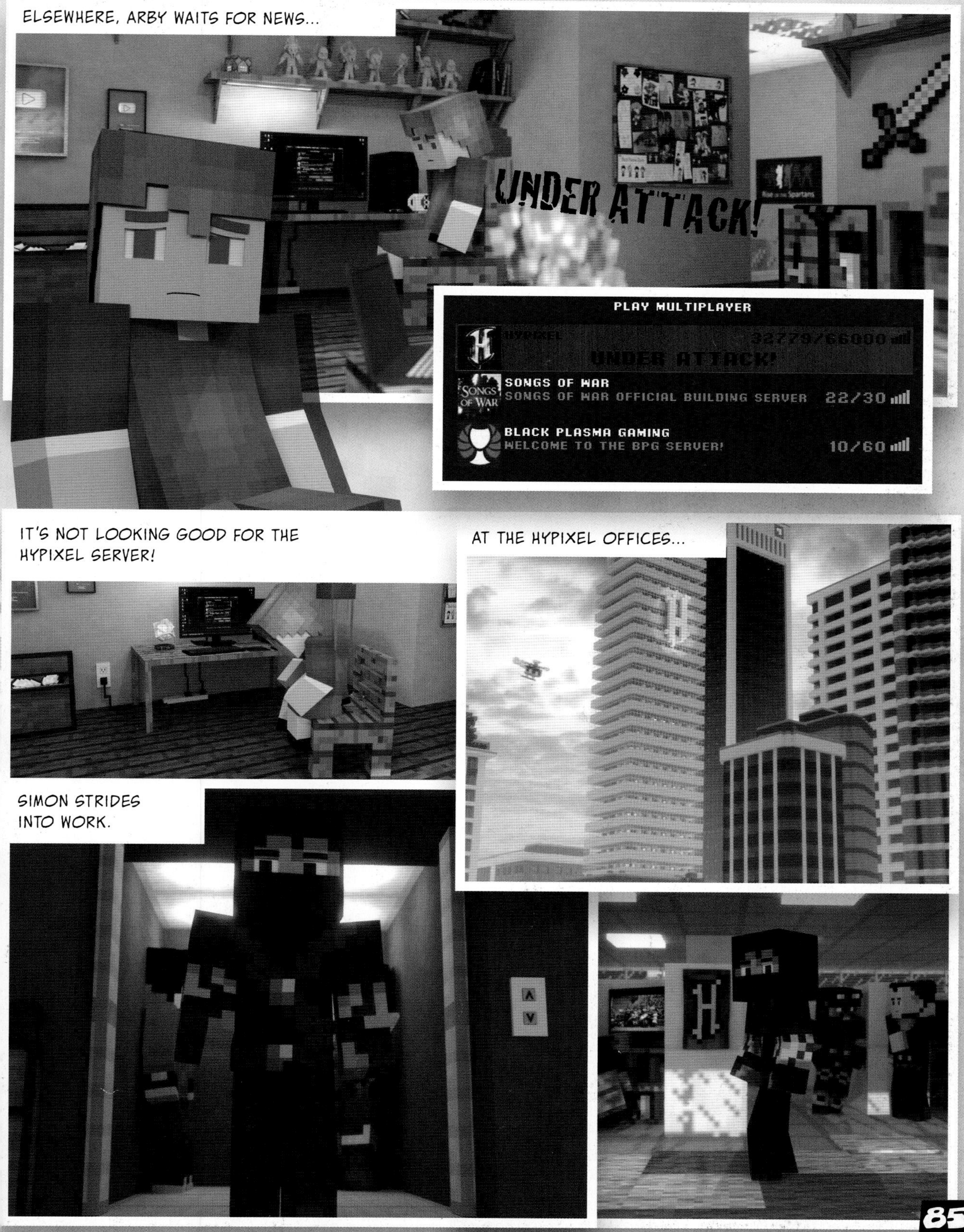
ELSEWHERE, ARBY WAITS FOR NEWS...
UNDER ATTACK!
PLAY MULTIPLAYER
HYPIXEL 32779/66000
UNDER ATTACK!
SONGS OF WAR
SONGS OF WAR OFFICIAL BUILDING SERVER 22/30
BLACK PLASMA GAMING
WELCOME TO THE BPG SERVER! 10/60
IT'S NOT LOOKING GOOD FOR THE HYPIXEL SERVER!
AT THE HYPIXEL OFFICES...
SIMON STRIDES INTO WORK.

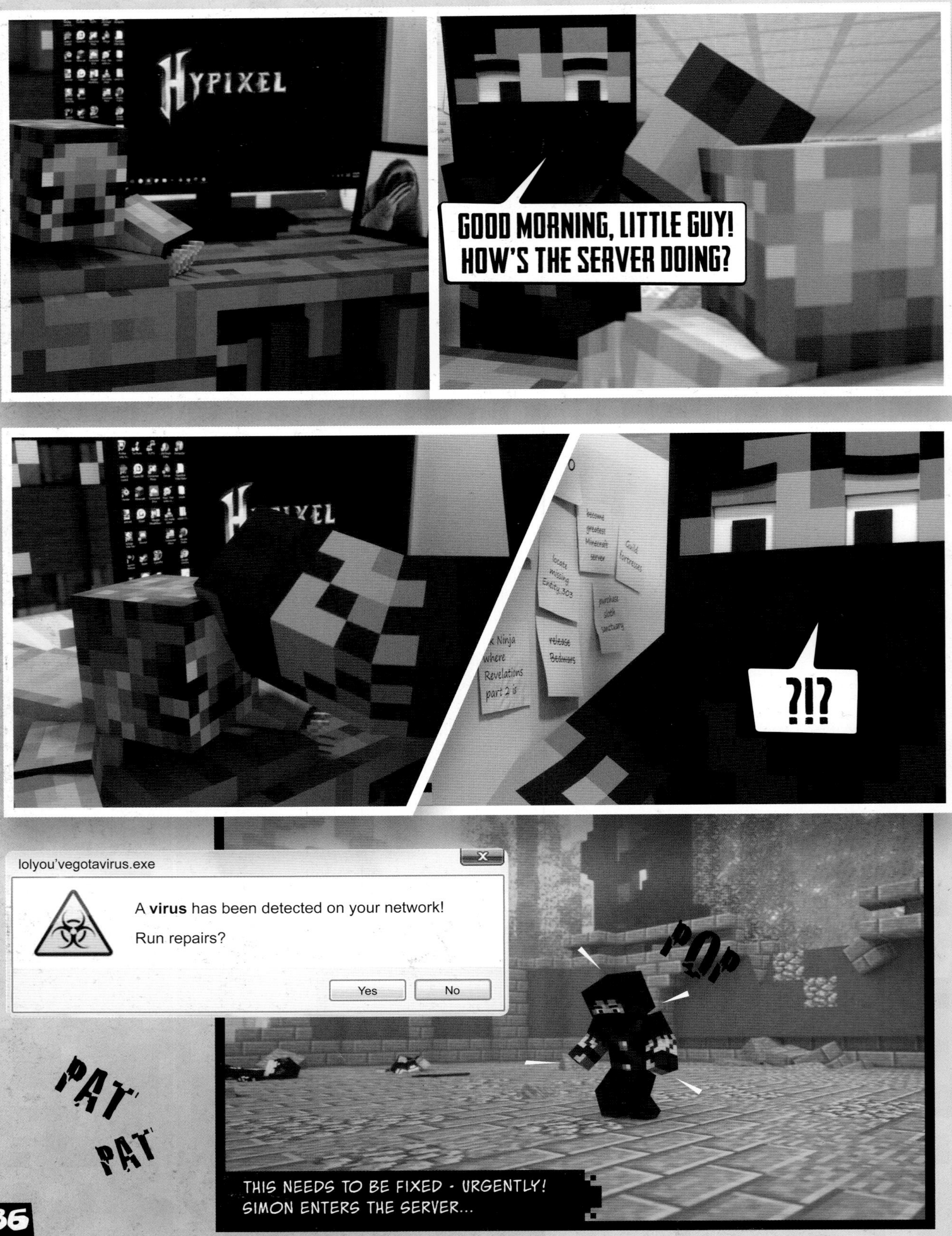
HYPIXEL
GOOD MORNING, LITTLE GUY! HOW'S THE SERVER DOING?
HYPIXEL
become greatest Minecraft server
Guild fortresses
locate missing Entity 303
purchase sloth sanctuary
release Bedwars
Revelations part 2 is
?!?
lolyou'vegotavirus.exe
A **virus** has been detected on your network!
Run repairs?
Yes
No
POP
PAT
PAT
THIS NEEDS TO BE FIXED - URGENTLY! SIMON ENTERS THE SERVER...

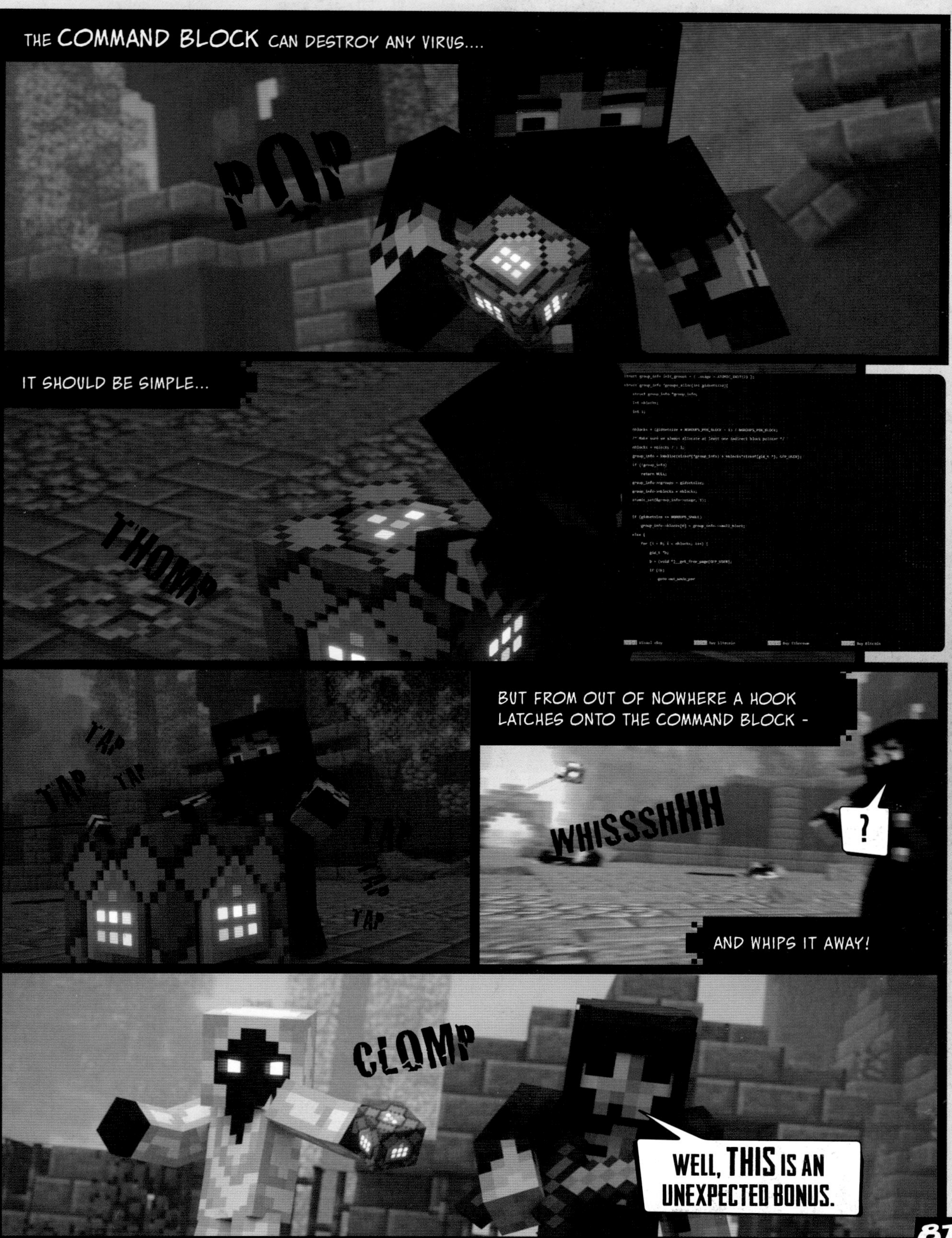
THE COMMAND BLOCK CAN DESTROY ANY VIRUS....
POP
IT SHOULD BE SIMPLE...
THOMP
TAP
TAP
TAP
TAP
BUT FROM OUT OF NOWHERE A HOOK LATCHES ONTO THE COMMAND BLOCK -
WHISSSHHH
?
AND WHIPS IT AWAY!
CLOMP
WELL, THIS IS AN UNEXPECTED BONUS.

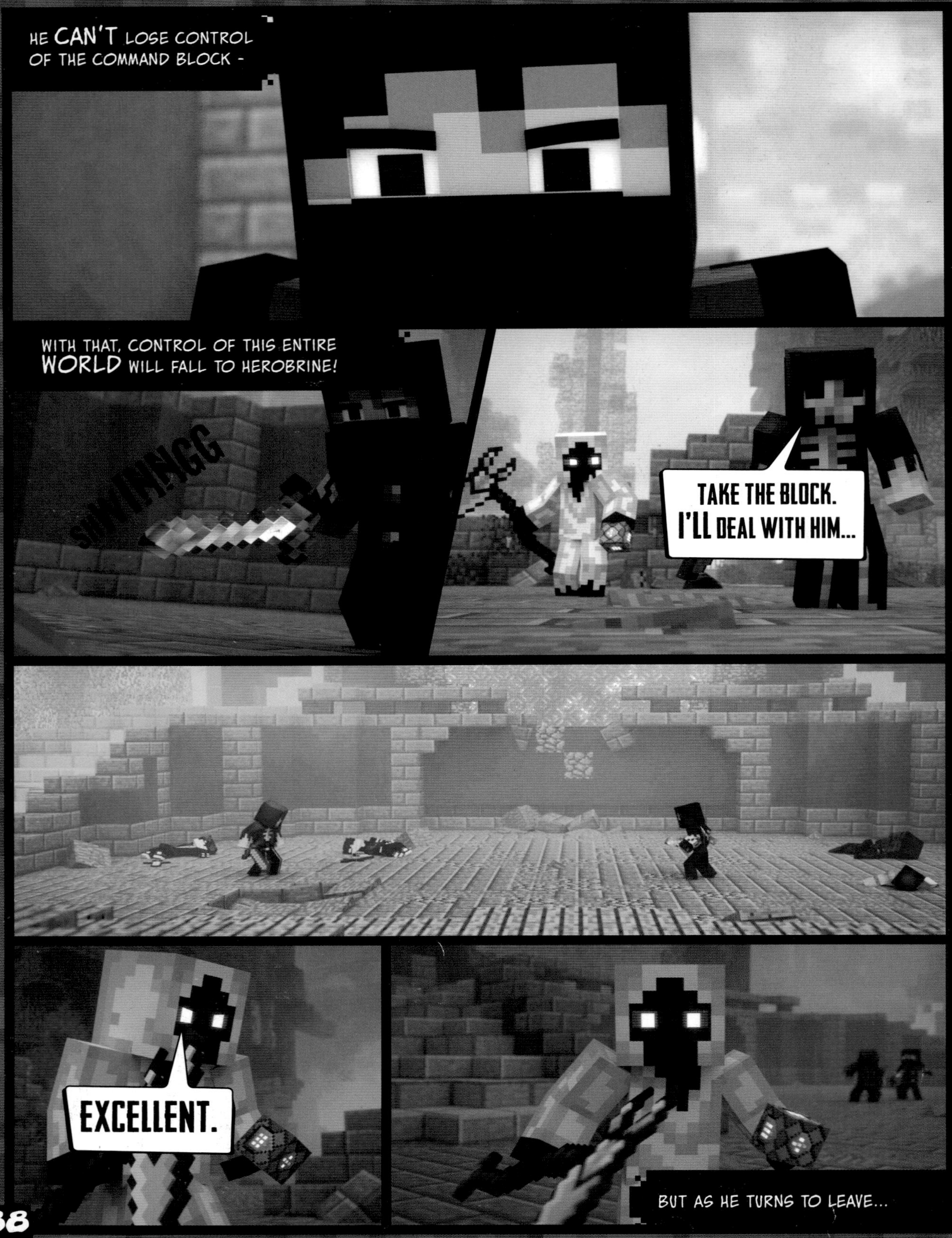
HE CAN'T LOSE CONTROL OF THE COMMAND BLOCK -
WITH THAT, CONTROL OF THIS ENTIRE WORLD WILL FALL TO HEROBRINE!
SHWINNGG
TAKE THE BLOCK. I'LL DEAL WITH HIM...
EXCELLENT.
BUT AS HE TURNS TO LEAVE...

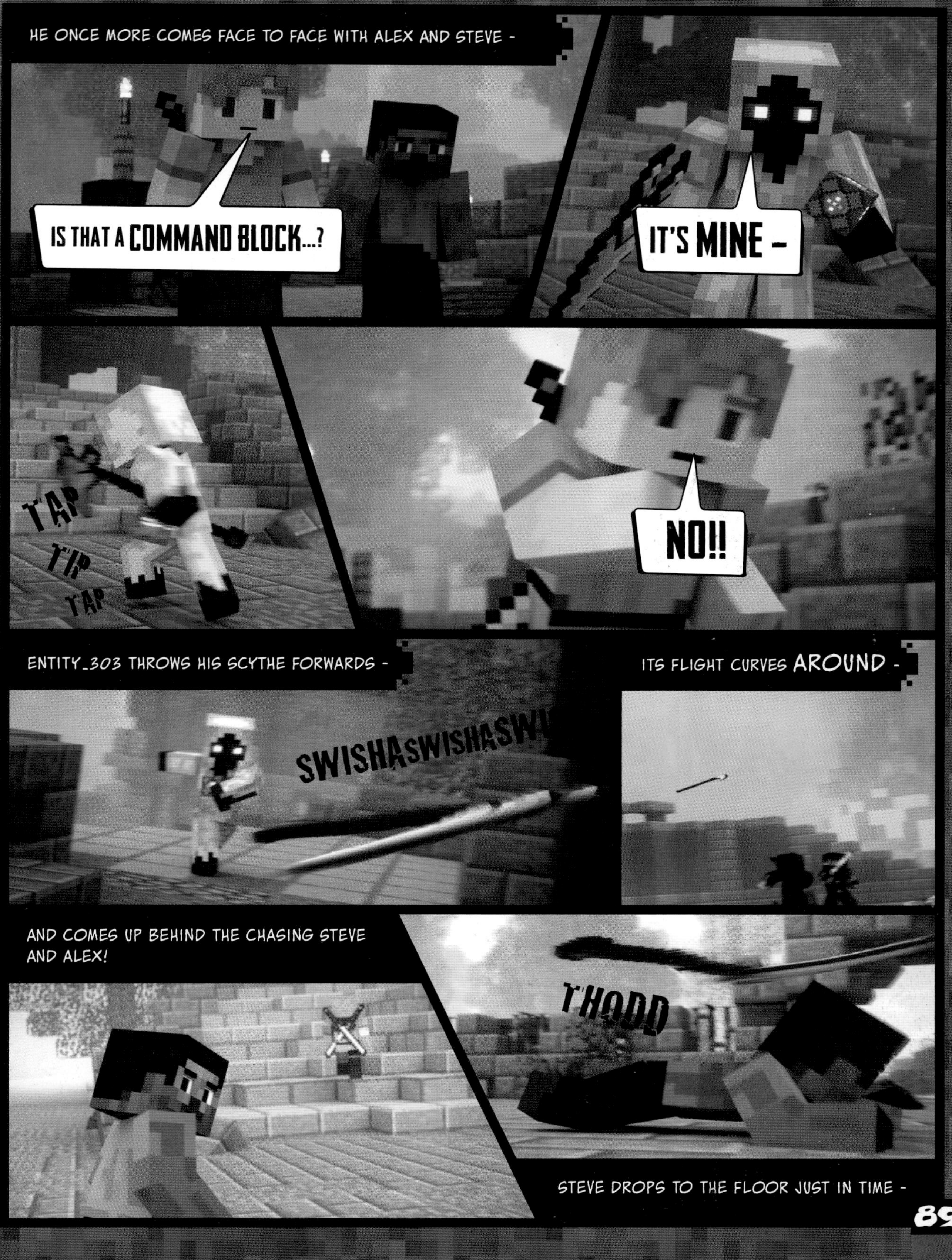
HE ONCE MORE COMES FACE TO FACE WITH ALEX AND STEVE -
IS THAT A COMMAND BLOCK...?
IT'S MINE -
TAP
T'IP
TAP
NO!!
ENTITY_303 THROWS HIS SCYTHE FORWARDS -
SWISHASWISHASW
ITS FLIGHT CURVES AROUND -
AND COMES UP BEHIND THE CHASING STEVE AND ALEX!
THODD
STEVE DROPS TO THE FLOOR JUST IN TIME -

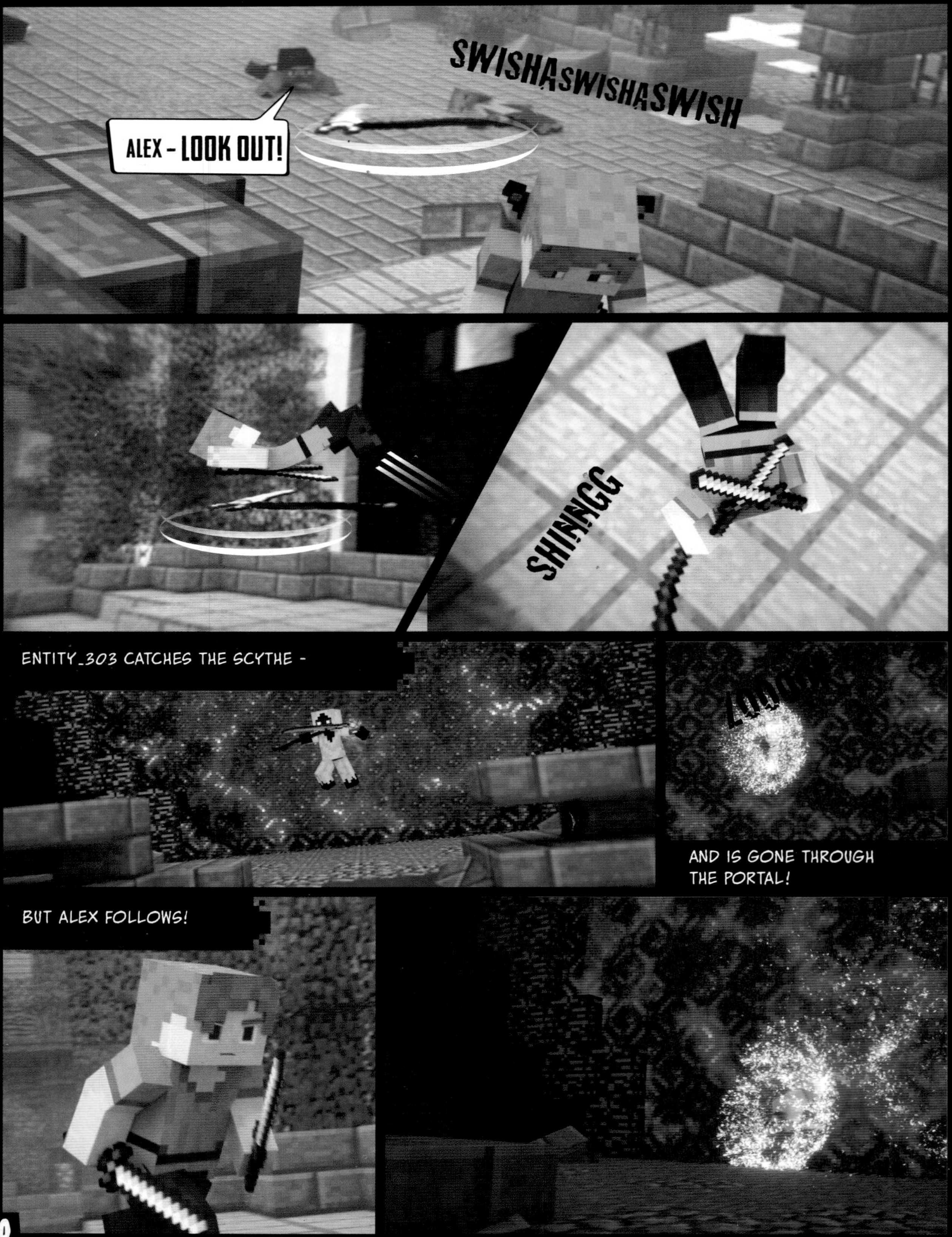
SWISHASWISHASWISH
ALEX – LOOK OUT!
SHINNGG
ENTITY_303 CATCHES THE SCYTHE –
AND IS GONE THROUGH THE PORTAL!
BUT ALEX FOLLOWS!

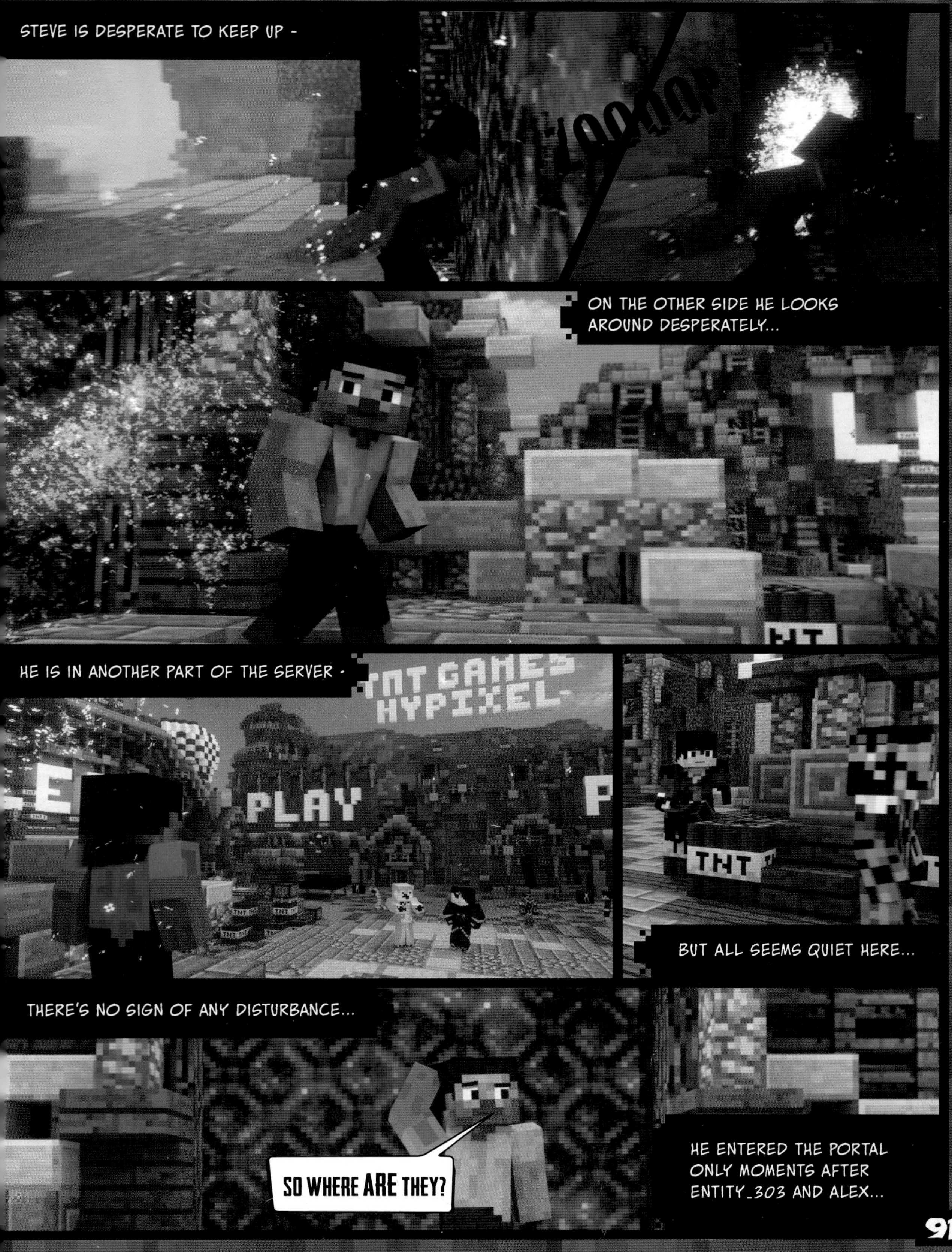
STEVE IS DESPERATE TO KEEP UP -
ON THE OTHER SIDE HE LOOKS AROUND DESPERATELY...
TNT
HE IS IN ANOTHER PART OF THE SERVER -
TNT GAMES
HYPIXEL
PLAY
TNT
BUT ALL SEEMS QUIET HERE...
THERE'S NO SIGN OF ANY DISTURBANCE...
SO WHERE ARE THEY?
HE ENTERED THE PORTAL ONLY MOMENTS AFTER ENTITY_303 AND ALEX...

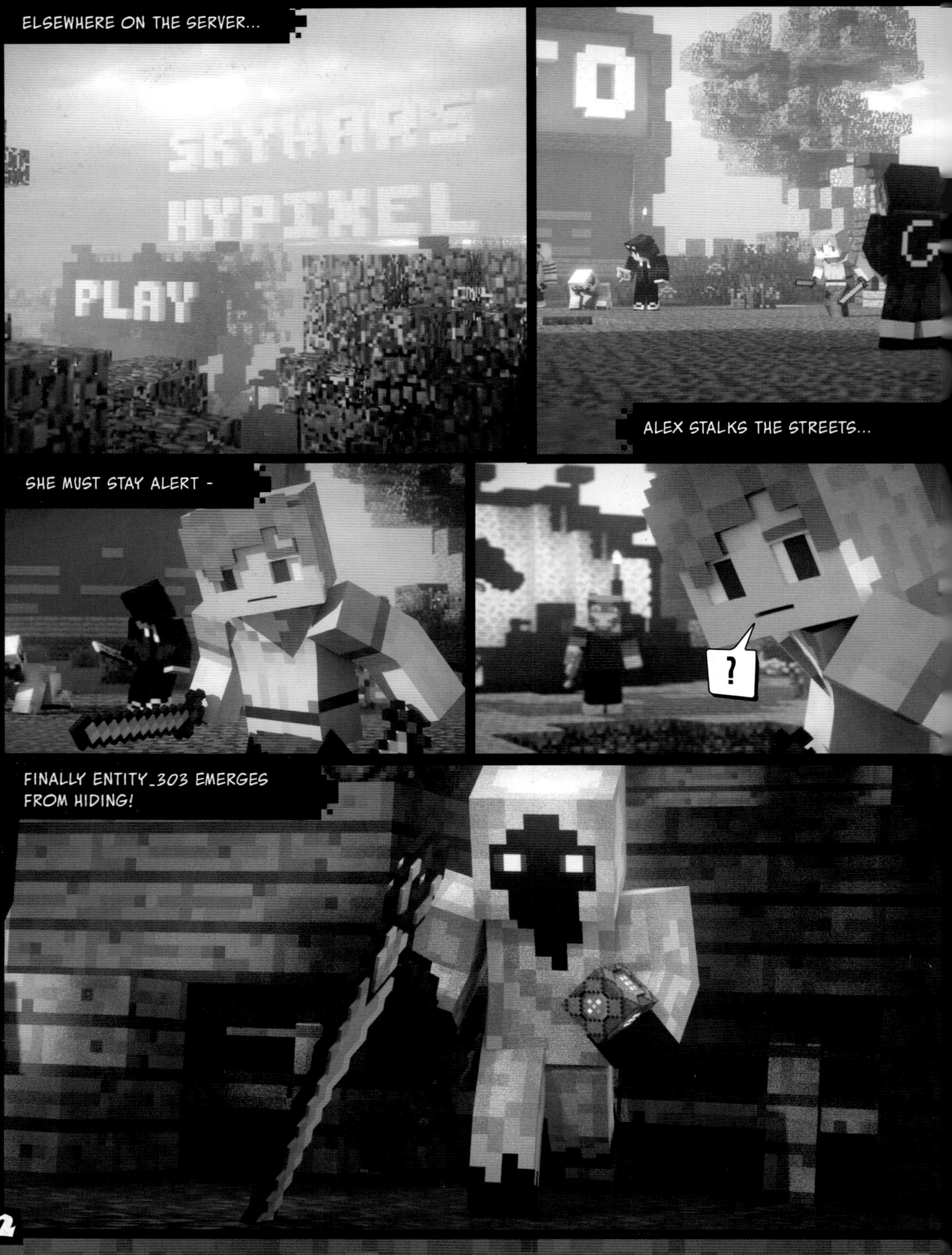
ELSEWHERE ON THE SERVER...
HYPIXEL
PLAY
ALEX STALKS THE STREETS...
SHE MUST STAY ALERT -
?
FINALLY ENTITY_303 EMERGES FROM HIDING!

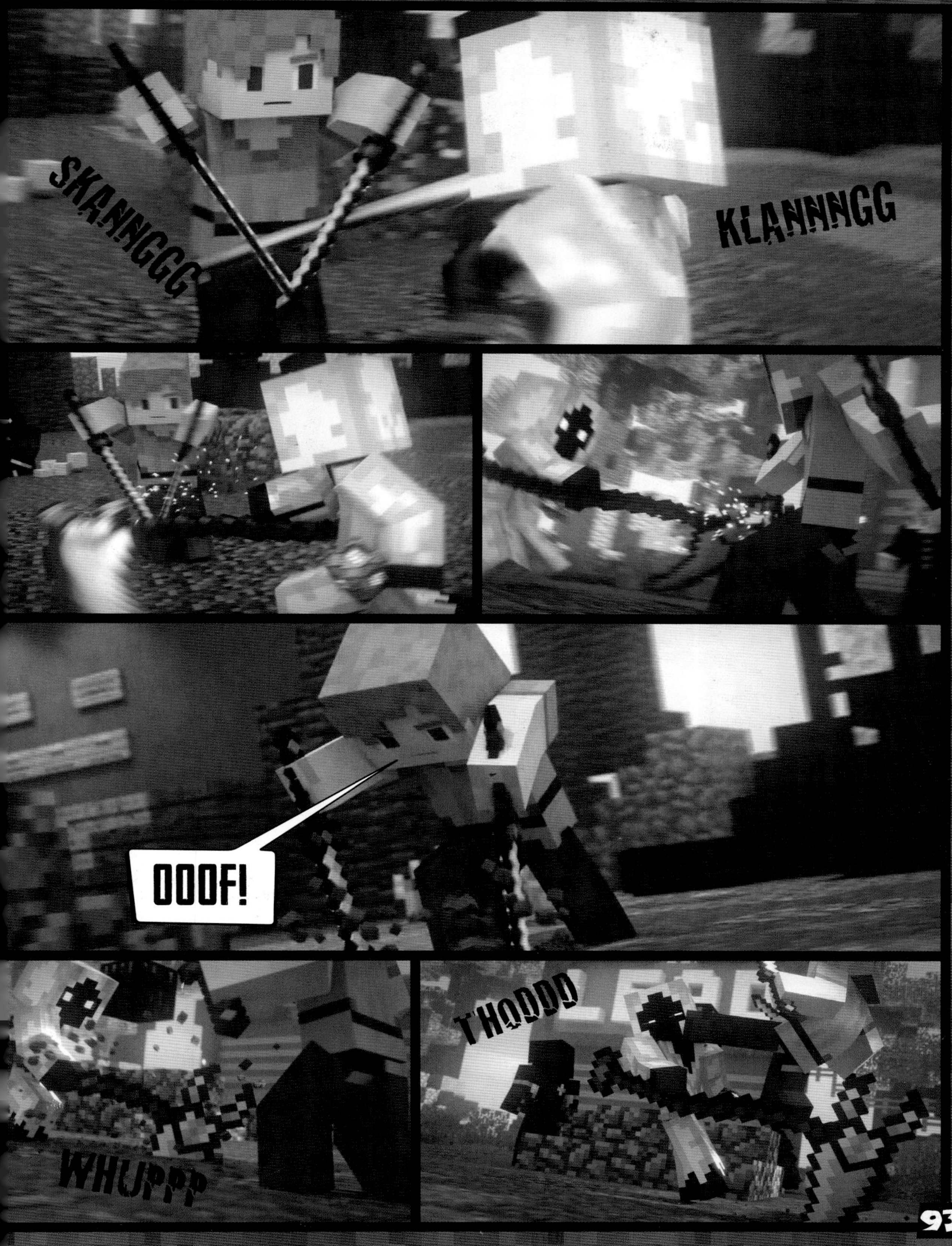
SKANNGGG
KLANNNGG
OOOF!
WHUPPP
THODDD

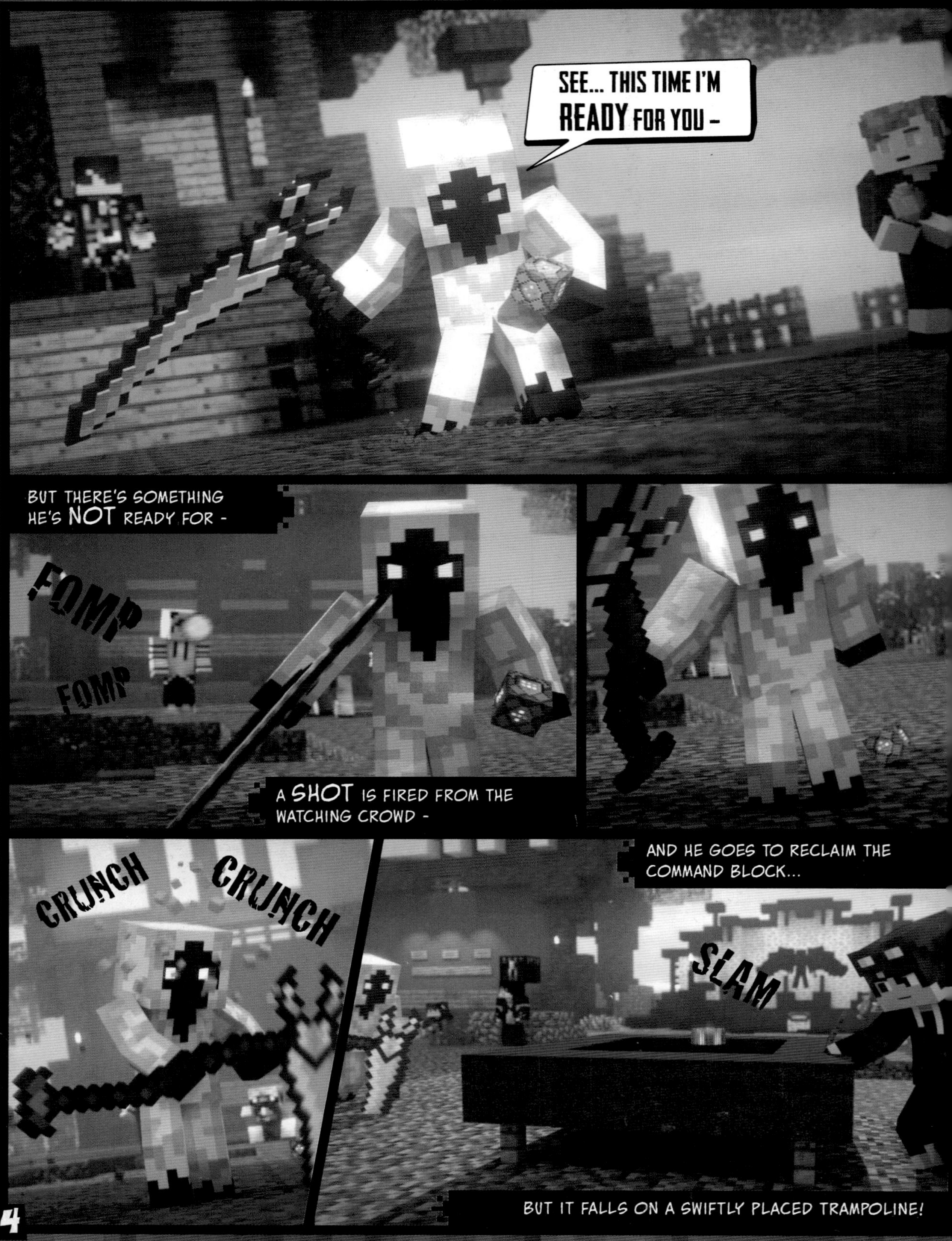

SEE... THIS TIME I'M READY FOR YOU –
BUT THERE'S SOMETHING HE'S NOT READY FOR –
FOMP
FOMP
A SHOT IS FIRED FROM THE WATCHING CROWD –
CRUNCH
CRUNCH
AND HE GOES TO RECLAIM THE COMMAND BLOCK...
SLAM
BUT IT FALLS ON A SWIFTLY PLACED TRAMPOLINE!

BDOOIINNNGGG

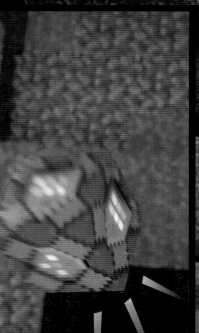

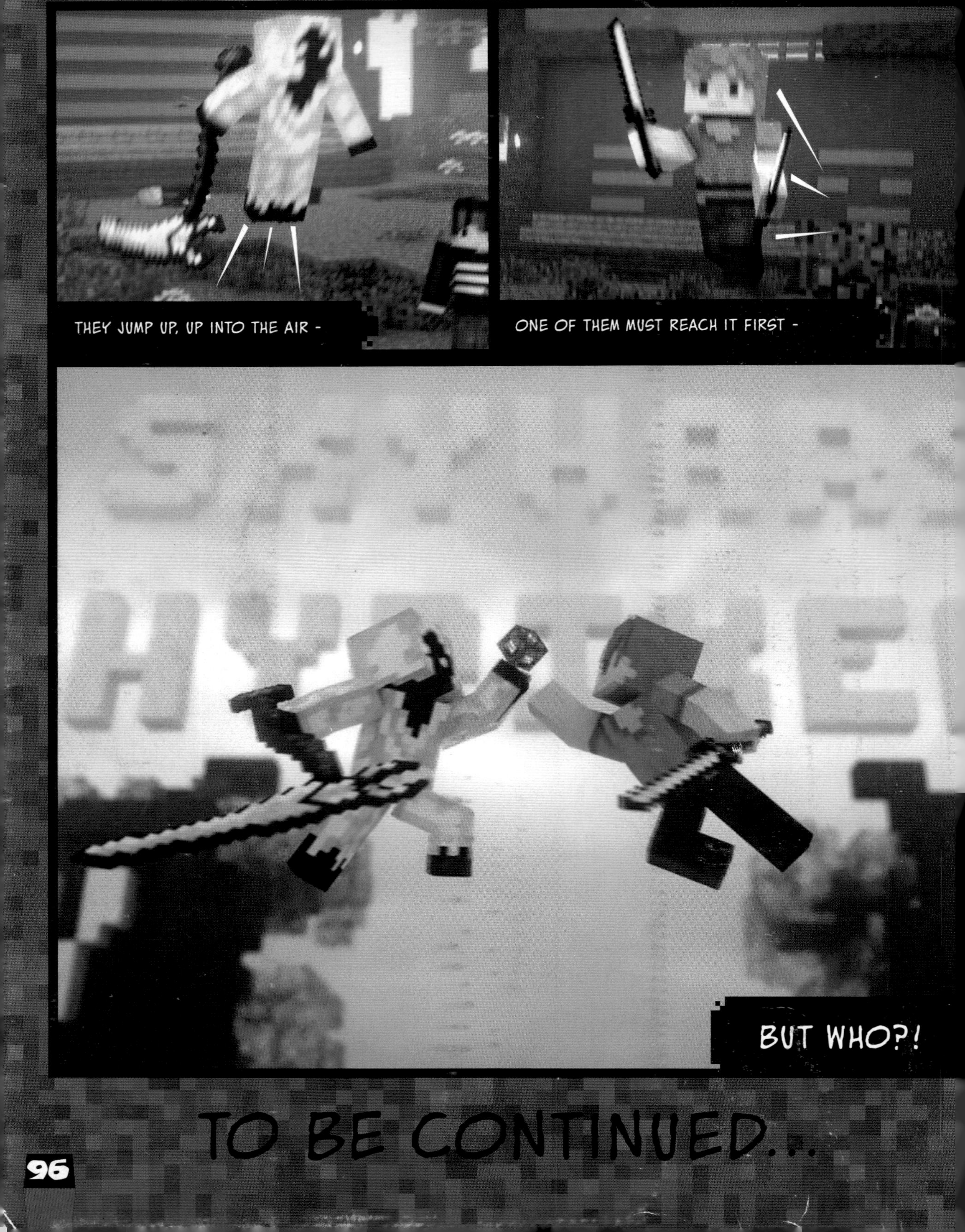
THEY JUMP UP, UP INTO THE AIR -
ONE OF THEM MUST REACH IT FIRST -
BUT WHO?!

TO BE CONTINUED...